STALKED IN PARADISE

A DESTINATION DEATH MYSTERY

CHARLEY MARSH

TIMBERDOODLE PRESS

CHAPTER 1

A great wave of pleasure washed over Harriet Monroe as she first walked into her new office. She set down her meager luggage and looked around the large, airy space. It was everything she had dreamed of and more. Much, much more.

To think she had beat out dozens of older applicants, many with stronger resumés than her own slim one, to land the position of Public Relations Director for the brand new Island Resort.

Harriet had never met Jan Rhymes in person–the woman who had designed the offices for the senior staff of Island Resort–but they had spoken several times over the comm link about Harriet's needs. Harriet couldn't be happier with the result. She made a mental note to send a thank-you to Jan as soon as she got settled in.

Everything had been designed in keeping with the warm, tropical island theme, from the light-colored bamboo flooring to the full wall of large glass doors that opened onto a covered veranda. Lanai, Harriet corrected herself. In this part of the world a porch was called a lanai.

Harriet's dress heels tapped softly on the floor as she crossed the room and opened the glass doors. A gentle, warm breeze entered her office, carrying with it the fresh salty scent of the sea mixed with the rich perfume of exotic flowers. She breathed it in, tingling with happiness.

A broad band of white sand separated the lanai from the turquoise blue water. Palm trees rustled in the breeze and small waves gently lapped at the beach.

Paradise. After years of struggle she had landed in paradise.

Everything about Island Resort was new and different to city girl Harriet. Foreign. She felt as if her life had been divided into two very separate and opposing parts: the dark age before Island Resort and today–her idea of heaven on earth.

She turned back to the office with a wide smile and set about exploring the generous space that had been allocated to her. Scatter rugs in swirls of softly hued turquoise and white anchored the seating area opposite the French doors. Soon Harriet would meet with the other department heads for planning sessions here in her very own office.

She sat in one of the large rattan arm chairs. The pale peach cushions were soft and comfortable.

She breathed a sigh of relief. She had been secretly afraid that corporate would override her ideas and insist on the hard, straight-backed chairs used around board-room tables, chairs guaranteed to have attendees squirming in their seats after a short while.

Harriet had always felt that a comfortable setting made it easier to hash out problems.

She slipped off her high heels and set her bare feet on the edge of the bamboo and glass oval coffee table. Jan had listened to her ideas here as well. The table had been built higher than the current vogue, so that the table top sat at the same height as the chair seats.

Anyone meeting with Harriet would not have to fold themselves in half to pour a cold drink or reach a snack like they did with the current low coffee table design trend, a trend that Harriet personally hated.

She jumped out of the chair and padded barefoot to her desk. Jan had chosen the desk without input from Harriet, saying that she wanted it to be a surprise.

Running one hand over the gleaming rosewood surface, Harriet wondered if she'd ever seen anything so beautiful. The desk was large, much larger than she had envisioned, but the single set of drawers on the left hand side and the elegantly simple, curved legs gave it a light, airy feel that a traditional desk would not have had.

Harriet amended her mental note to send Jan a small gift along with her thank you note. The designer had gauged Harriet's personal style and tastes perfectly.

She pulled out the desk chair and adjusted the height and lumbar support. The chair had been upholstered in a muted blue-gray and green pattern of waves and dolphins, a whimsical touch. Harriet grinned. She was beginning to feel very warm and fuzzy toward the resort's designer.

A loud knock sounded at the door. Before Harriet could call "come in" a head piled high with bright pink curls popped around the door's edge.

"Ms. Monroe? I've brought you some lemonade."

The young woman, dressed in cargo shorts and a bright peach polo shirt with the Island Resort logo stitched over one breast, carried in a tray with a frosted pitcher and a single tall glass.

Harriet blinked. The combo of bright pink hair with the peach shirt made the woman look like a piece of walking candy.

The woman frowned at Harriet's desk, then carried the tray over to the coffee table and set it in the center before turning and smiling at Harriet.

"I'm Lana. I'm liaising between the kitchen and the offices until the resort gets up to full manpower, so when you want anything to eat or drink just punch five on your comm link, place your order, and I'll deliver."

Before Harriet could respond Lana crossed the room to a wall of bookshelves and opened a waist high panel.

"This is your chiller. We'll keep it stocked with cold drinks for you once you tell me what you like. Over here is the coffee maker and this gadget makes tea. Just choose your flavor. Cups and mugs are here. Napkins, that sort of thing. No paper napkins here, laundry will supply you with fresh ones daily. Just leave your dirty ones on the tray in the hall and someone will gather it all at the end of the day. Or sooner if you want. Just tell us."

Lana smiled brightly and kept moving as she talked, rapidly opening and closing various panels and explaining the appliances as she went. When she reached the end she turned and smiled again at Harriet.

"Can I do anything else for you?" she asked.

Amused, Harriet looked at the curvaceous woman with her wide smile and warm brown eyes. The bright pink curls were a little garish and unexpected and she wondered briefly if they complied with the resort's employee regulations.

They must, or Lana wouldn't be wearing them, she decided. Good to know that the resort owner allowed personal expression among the employees. She smiled back at Lana.

"Yes, there is one thing you can do. You can call me Harry. Ms. Monroe feels awfully formal, wouldn't you agree?"

Lana's smile widened even more. "Oh, good. You're going to fit right in, Harry. We were all a little worried since we didn't get a chance to meet you before you started."

She lowered her voice to a conspiratorial whisper and waggled her dark eyebrows at Harriet. "To tell you the truth, I came over to scout you out. I'll report back that there's nothing to worry about. Everyone will be relieved. So far the staff that Mr. Wade has hired is aces."

"That's good to know. I look forward to meeting everyone." Harriet walked over to the coffee table and poured herself some lemonade. It tasted fresh and tart, with just the right amount of sweetener and felt cool and refreshing in her mouth.

"Yum. My compliments to whoever made the lemonade. It's excellent. Do you know if anyone has been assigned to show me around the resort and introduce me to the rest of the staff? I came straight from the airlift to my office," she confessed. "Mr. Wade sent me a map so I'd know where to find it but I only arrived an hour ago and haven't had a chance to see the place."

Lana looked surprised. "This is your first trip here?"

"Yes. I . . . had things to tie up in Portland and couldn't get away."

"Well, that explains why nobody had a chance to meet you. Most of us took up Mr. Wade's offer to visit the resort before we signed on. How did you know you'd like it here if you didn't check the place out?"

Harriet gave a grim smile. "Trust me, I knew I'd be very happy here. About that guide . . . ?"

Lana frowned a moment, then her face lit up. "I know. I'll send Albion. He doesn't have much to do until the guests start arriving. You just enjoy getting to know your office and he'll be along shortly."

Harriet found herself alone again a moment later. She opened her smaller bag and pulled an old cherrywood-framed hologram from it. She turned the box-like frame gently in her hands.

"Well, Mom, Dad, I'm here. Wish me luck." She looked around the room, chose a spot on the shelves where she would be able to see her parents from her desk, and carefully placed it. Her beautiful mother, dressed in a long pale green robe, stood smiling, wrapped in the arms of a tall, handsome man with silver-blue eyes and a strong chin. Both looked happy and in love.

Harry stood back with a rueful sigh. Her parents had died in an accident when she was eight. Eighteen years had passed since then and she still mourned their passing. All she had of them was the holo.

A knock on the door interrupted her thoughts and she shook off the sadness.

"Come in," she called.

A dark-haired, dark-skinned, wiry man stood in the doorway. Harriet guessed him to be in his mid-fifties.

"I'm Albion. You Ms. Monroe?"

"Yes. But please call me Harry, Albion."

Albion frowned at Harriet. "Not very pretty name for pretty lady."

Harriet simply stared and said nothing. He shrugged.

"Right-o. Harry it is. No skin on me. Lana says you need grand tour. You ready?"

"I think it's 'no skin *off* me,'" Harriet said. Albion gave her a blank look.

"Never mind. I'm ready." She bent to pick up her luggage.

"Get those later. Tour first."

"Will the grand tour include my room?" Harriet asked.

Albion scowled at her. "Yes. If you want."

"I want. In fact, you can show me to my room first and I'll just drop my bags off at the same time." Harriet smiled sweetly at Albion. To her relief he didn't argue with her.

He also didn't offer to help with her luggage. He took off down the corridor, leaving Harriet to grab her bags and close her office door. She took several steps before remembering she was still barefoot.

"Albion, wait," she called. She dropped the bags and retrieved her heels, then picked the bags back up and hurried after Albion's rapidly retreating figure.

"Welcome to Island Resort," she said under her breath.

If Lana and Albion were any indication, Harriet had a feeling she was going to have some interesting co-workers.

CHAPTER 2

By the time Harriet caught up with him, Albion sat waiting in a turquoise blue, chrome-trimmed golf cart with the Island Resort logo on the side.

"Easiest way," he answered when she asked him why they weren't walking.

Harriet placed her bags in the back of the cart and climbed in the passenger seat. They drove beyond the office complex, following a pale pink, crushed-shell single lane road that followed the beach until they reached a row of four cottages set on the ocean side of the road.

Albion pulled up to the third cottage and stopped. "This yours. I wait."

"Thanks." Harriet managed to keep the sarcasm from her voice. She couldn't help but wonder why Mr. Wade had hired the unfriendly Albion. So far her guide hadn't impressed her with either his personality or his helpfulness. He hadn't even cracked a smiled at her. Did he even have all his teeth?

Harriet pulled her bags from the cart and entered the cottage, dropping her luggage just inside the door. She was halfway out the door before she decided to turn back and take a quick look around her new home.

She stepped inside again and stopped cold, mouth agape. This was no employee's cottage. Albion had surely made a mistake. This had to be one of the luxury cottages for paying guests.

The entire room, even the ceiling, was paneled in a dark wood. She poked her face close to the wall next to the door and sniffed. Yep, real wood. Mahogany, if she had to make a guess. Harriet had a small collection of tiny hippos carved from a variety of woods, the only real wood she could afford.

Between wars, deforestation, and strict environmental laws, real wood in the late twenty-first century was priced for the exclusive use of the very rich.

There was no way Mr. Wade would waste his fortune putting real wood in an employee's cottage. Albion had definitely made a mistake.

Opposite her, floor-to-ceiling sliding glass doors similar to the ones in her office faced the sea. A large rectangular woven grass mat sat under a cozy arrangement of a couch and two chairs, and another desk, this one of cherry and smaller than her office one, sat to one side of the room.

Definitely a guest cottage, Harriet decided. She turned to leave again but then thought, what the heck. She was here and she was curious to see how the resort's guests would live while they visited the resort. Besides, as the resort's new PR Director she *needed* to see where the guests would stay.

She would just take a quick tour. The dour Albion could wait.

The single bedroom off to her left also had a wall of floor-to-ceiling glass doors facing the sea. A massive, king-size bed surrounded by cream-colored gauze insect curtains dominated the large room. Floor, wall, and ceiling were paneled in the same dark red mahogany.

Harriet wondered why the resort's designer had chosen a dark wood for the cottage interior and then realized that they were on a tropical island with a hot sun. The dark wood would make the cottage interior feel cool and soothing to the guests after a day's outside activities.

She wandered through the bedroom to the bathroom and gasped. Never had she seen such a beautiful bathroom. Here the mahogany had been used only as an accent. The floor and walls were a pale, creamy marble, the curved ceiling a mosaic of colorful one inch tiles depicting a mermaid sitting on a rock surrounded by the sea.

A large tile and glass-walled shower sat in one corner and a free-standing slipper tub stood in front of a pair of carved wooden doors. Harriet opened them to the ocean breezes and a stunning view of the beach.

"Wow." Harriet knew that Mr. Wade had planned to build the ultimate resort, but somehow, even with the photos and videos he had sent her, she hadn't been able to quite envision what that meant.

Now she *felt* the atmosphere of luxury that Mr. Wade and his designer had captured and it inspired her. Her new position would be a snap if this was any sample of what she would have to work with.

Harriet closed the doors and poked around for a few more minutes, then remembered Albion–probably waiting impatiently–and hurried into the kitchen/dining area, noting the high-end appliances and rose-granite counters as she walked through.

She had thought that the guest's meals were all catered, but maybe Mr. Wade felt they should have the option of cooking if they were so inclined.

The cottage could grace the pages of the high-end architectural e-mags she liked to read.

She grabbed her bags and hurried back out to the golf cart. "You've made a mistake, Albion," she said as she lifted her bags into the back of the cart again. "This is a guest cottage."

Albion smirked at her, letting Harriet know she was too ignorant for words. "No mistake. This your cottage. Mermaid Cottage. Guest cottages north of resort hotel. This south."

"But-" Harriet turned to look at the cottage, then turned back to Albion. "Are you sure?"

"Yes. This your cottage. Mermaid." He scowled at her. "Grand tour now?"

"Yes. No. Wait a minute. I want to take my bags back in." Harriet barely knew what she was saying. This incredible cottage was where she was going to live?

It was beyond anything she had ever imagined. Beyond her most daring dreams.

She set the bags down by the door, then picked them up again and carried them into the bedroom and set them on the bed. Albion and Lana were dressed casually. Surely she could put on something more comfortable than heels and the slim wool skirt suit she wore.

She quickly changed into a pair of lightweight linen capris, a silk tee and sneakers, then rejoined Albion.

"Okay, I'm ready now. Show me the rest of the resort."

As Albion continued down the palm tree lined shell road, Harriet slowly began to relax. Her spirits were lifted by the gentle breeze carrying the scent of tropical perfumed flowers and salt air, and the sun glinting off the aqua blue sea to her right. For the first time since her parent's death Harriet dared to hope that she could truly feel happy again.

Albion pointed out the building that housed the laundry, and a very long garage that held the motor and sail boats, jet skis, kayaks, and other water toys for the guests. A mechanic's garage sat next to it.

The buildings were all one story and built of stone with thatched roofs–camouflaged to look like they belonged to the island. Behind the garage sat a series of narrow greenhouses.

"Stop here, please," Harriet said, when it became clear that Albion planned to drive past.

"No stop. Just plants. More to see."

"I would like to let Solomon know I arrived safely. Stop here," Harriet repeated firmly.

Albion heaved a dramatic sigh and stopped the cart in front of the center greenhouse. Harriet hopped out. "I might be a few minutes. Would you like to come in with me?"

"I wait." Albion reached under his seat and pulled out a crushed straw hat. He slouched down in his seat and placed the hat over his face.

Harriet shrugged and entered the greenhouse. "Sol? Solly, are you in here?"

An incredibly good-looking man popped his head out of a glass-walled office on her right and smiled. Tall and slim with brown hair, warm brown eyes, and the classic features of a Greek god, Solomon Ayers turned heads everywhere he went, even with his limp.

He also happened to be Harriet's best friend. They had met up on the streets of Portland, Maine eleven years ago. Both were teenaged runaways struggling to survive without getting sucked down into the drug scene that seemed to catch every street person, or forced into prostituting for money so they could eat.

They had buddied up, watched each other's backs and shared what food they could scrounge or steal. They earned money here and there doing odd jobs and eventually were able to rent a small one room apartment together.

They had remained roommates as their situation continued to improve, renting nicer and larger apartments until Harriet had moved out two years before. Solomon had recommended Harriet to Mr. Wade after he had been hired on as the resort's head gardener. As far as she was concerned she pretty much owed her existence to her friend.

Solomon opened his arms and gathered Harriet into a warm hug. "There you are, Harry. I was beginning to wonder if you'd chickened out."

Harriet pulled away and scowled at her friend. "Chickened out? Why would I do that?"

Solomon shrugged. "You know. I thought maybe Bradley applied some pressure and talked you into staying."

"Not a chance." Harriet didn't want to talk about Bradley Higgins. He was the past. Over and done with. She was all about her future. "So, this is your new domain, huh?"

Solomon grinned, exposing white, even teeth. He spread his arms. "Seven greenhouses. We grow the flowers for the guest cottage bouquets and the arrangements for the public areas like the dining rooms and check-in, and anywhere else flowers are needed. We also provide the kitchen with fresh veggies and some fruits. Do you have time for a tour?"

Harriet thought of Albion waiting in the golf cart and almost said no, but then thought that her guide was probably sleeping under his hat. "Sure. I'd love a tour."

She hooked her arm through his. "You can tell me about the staff you've met while you show me around."

They spent the next forty minutes touring Solomon's domain and catching up. Harriet loved the greenhouses. They smelled of rich, moist earth, fresh greenery, and heady perfume. The variety of flower shapes and colors were a feast for her eyes.

Solomon introduced her to his crew. He had three men and five women to help him plant, weed, trim, harvest, create arrangements, and keep the greenhouses clean. They were all pleasant and seemed content with the work. He told her that he also managed a crew of groundskeepers who were all out working at the moment.

"It looks like you picked yourself a good crew, Solly. I'm happy for you," Harriet said as she followed him into the last greenhouse. "Any new men in your life?"

Harriet's friend had been upfront with her about his homosexuality the first day they met. She loved Solly for the warm and loving friend he had become, but still struggled to accept how loose and easy about sexual partners he could be.

She was a little old-fashioned that way, she admitted to herself. While easy birth control and disease protection made casual sex commonplace, it had never been easy for her. Unlike Solly, who picked up and dropped partners based on how attractive he found them, she had to feel a connection with her partner, no matter how attractive he was.

"I've been too busy," Solomon answered with a rueful grin. "Once the guests start arriving and we get settled into a daily routine I might have time to look around."

They walked down the greenhouse's center aisle in a companionable silence, stopping now and then to examine a special plant he wanted to point out.

Harriet studied her friend. She had never seen him look so happy, even without a current lover.

Solomon had a true affinity for plants and his love and understanding of them showed in each greenhouse and the way he had trained his workers. The plants were handled with respect and care and were obviously thriving under his attention.

They had almost reached the back wall of the last greenhouse when Solomon stopped and swore.

"What is it?" Harriet looked at the tables on either side of the aisle but couldn't see anything out of place.

Solomon strode toward the end wall which was covered with a thick flowering vine.

"Oh, that vine is beautiful. What is–" Harriet stopped, dumbfounded. A man's body hung from the center of the thick vine, surrounded by drooping clusters of heavily scented purple flowers.

"Is-is that a mannequin?" she asked. The stiff form hung with its back to them. "Is someone playing a joke?"

Solomon reached the body. He lifted one hand and touched it briefly. It felt cold and stiff and real. He snatched his hand back.

"No. I'm afraid it's a real man." He turned back to Harriet. "And he's very dead."

CHAPTER 3

It took a minute for Solomon's words to register in Harriet's brain.

"A dead man? What-what is a dead man doing in your greenhouse?"

Harriet felt a little faint. She steadied herself against the plant table closest to her and waved one hand at the body without looking at it again. "And why is he hanging from that vine?"

"That's a very good question." Solomon looked grim. "I'd better call Alex." He activated his wrist comm and spoke briefly to someone.

"The security director will be here shortly," Solomon told her when he finished the call. He frowned at the dead man, then moved to stand between Harriet and the body, trying to block her view.

"Wait until you get a look at this guy, Harry. Hubba-hubba. I'd definitely have a go at him if I thought he'd respond." He wagged his eyebrows and leered at her, trying to distract her from the body in the vines.

"You're incorrigible, Sol."

Harriet's stomach rolled and she wondered if she was going to be sick. The last time she'd seen a dead person was at her parents' funeral. Although come to think of it, they'd had closed caskets. Why did she think she had seen them?

The familiar dull throb of a migraine began to beat in Harriet's skull. She pushed against it, willing it away. Recognizing Solly's transparent attempt to distract her she played along.

"How can you think about sex when there's a dead man hanging right next to us?"

"I admit it's a bit of a challenge, but I can always think about sex, sweetie, you know that. It is my learn-ed o-pinion that sex makes the world go round."

Harriet shook her head at her friend. Solly's brain seemed to run on only two tracks—gardening and sex. Fortunately he also had a big heart.

They heard the rumble of an engine outside the green-house. It cut off and a moment later Harriet felt the slight change in air pressure as the greenhouse door was opened and closed.

"Solomon? You in here?"

The voice sounded deep and slightly rough. For some reason it reminded Harriet of the power of ocean waves pounding on the rocks after a storm. A slight shiver ran through her body.

She looked at Solomon out of the corner of her eye and saw that he was watching her closely. She scowled at him and he grinned.

"Hubba-hubba," he mouthed silently. She deepened her scowl to keep from smiling back at her friend. Smiling while standing next to a dead body definitely hit the inap-propriate column in her mental account book.

"Solomon?" The deep voice sounded closer.

"Back here, Alex," Solomon called out. He bent down to whisper in Harriet's ear. "The best is yet to come."

She stuck her tongue out at him, then quickly collected herself and pulled it in when the security director popped around a large red-flowered hibiscus and joined them.

Solomon wasted no time making the introductions. "Alex, this is Harry Monroe. Harry is the resort's new PR person. Harry, this is Alex Hayes, our security director."

He turned and pointed at the dead man. "And *that* is the reason I called."

Harriet studied the security director as he stepped over to the body and stood with his back to them examining it without touching.

He was tall, as tall as Solly, which meant about six two. Where Solly was slim, Alex's close-fitting polo shirt revealed well-muscled arms and broad shoulders that tapered to a narrow waist. His olive green khakis skimmed well-defined buttocks and strong thighs.

Harriet realized she was ogling Alex's body and blushed. She turned away, but not before Solomon saw her. He fanned his hand in front of his face and grinned, but hastily lost the grin when Alex turned back to them.

"What's his name?" asked the security director.

Solomon shrugged. "I have no idea. We didn't turn him so I haven't seen his face. I assume it's one of the workers from the resort. Harry only arrived on the island a couple of hours ago so I'm sure she's never seen him before."

Alex turned piercing, dark blue eyes on Harriet. His eyes were fringed with thick, dark lashes, better than any vanity transplants currently on offer.

Science had progressed to the point that a person could get just about any body enhancement they wanted in the name of beauty–if they had enough money. Harriet knew ordinary working women who practically bankrupted themselves keeping up with the latest beauty trends.

Unlike the current fad of ultra-short hair for men, the security director wore his black hair tied back in a short queue. His nose had been broken at one time and was no longer quite straight.

She wondered why he hadn't had it straightened. Only the ultra-poor and street people would keep that nose. She had to admit though, it gave the man a certain attractive bad-boy look.

The crooked nose and the thin white scar that topped his right eyebrow also gave Harriet the impression that the man standing before her did not back down from a fight.

She couldn't decide if she liked his eyes or his beautiful sensual mouth better. She realized she was staring at it and lifted her gaze to find him still watching her. His eyes were amused.

"What's so funny?" she asked. Damn the man. Women probably fell all over him and here she was acting like a young girl who'd never stood so close to this much walking testosterone before.

"Alex asked you if you'd ever seen the dead man." Solomon sounded amused as well.

Harriet flushed and made herself as tall and imposing as possible–an easy task since she stood nearly hit six feet in flats.

"No. How could I know him? I haven't even seen his face. Besides, I just got here, as Solly already told you."

The amusement left Alex's eyes and he became all business. "Did either of you touch him?"

"I did," Solomon answered. "Just his right ankle to see if he was real. I thought he might be a joke mannequin that one of my workers had left for me."

"All right. I don't want anyone inside this greenhouse

until I can execute a thorough search. I'll let you know when you can get back in. Might be a week or more."

"That won't work," Solomon said, shaking his head. "That won't work at all. I need to water and check on these plants daily. There's a lot of money invested in the stock in this greenhouse. I can't let everything in here die while I wait for you to investigate. You'll have to work your investigation around my work."

Harriet watched the two men try to stare each other down and wondered who would win. Normally she would put her money on Solly, who could charm anyone, but she had a feeling Alex could best her friend in a stare-down.

Alex pursed his lips, then sighed. "You're right, it would be a huge waste to let all these plants die. I didn't realize they needed daily tending. I assumed the work was automated. Don't you use bots?"

Solomon nodded. "We do for some things, but a bot can't touch a delicate leaf without damaging it, so most of the work with the specialty plants is done by humans. A bot can't look for insect damage, or fungus, for example, although once identified I use the micro-bots to deal with the problem."

"All right. In that case, you, and you alone, Solomon, may enter this greenhouse. But–" he held up a finger–"I want you to keep track of when you enter and leave. And I'll need to know who was last in here."

Solomon smiled and held out his hand for a shake. "Deal. And the last person in here was me. A lot of these plants are our more rare and difficult plants to grow so I personally take care of this greenhouse. I was in here yesterday afternoon, and then just now when I brought Harry in for a tour. I hadn't tended the plants in here yet today."

Alex's expression grew sharp. Harriet had the feeling

that Alex Hayes missed very little. "And you didn't notice the body yesterday?" he asked.

Solomon shook his head. "Nope."

The security director gave Solomon a considering look. "That would point to you as the killer," he pointed out mildly.

Solomon's eyes widened, then he grinned. "Not me. I don't have the killer instinct. I'm strictly a lover. Ask anyone."

"You can be sure I will. And I'll need to ask you a few more questions later as well," Alex replied, "but first I need to deal with this body. My team will move it into a cooler after they're done their initial examination. I'd like you both to leave now. Do you keep this greenhouse locked?"

"Yes, at night when no one is here working. It's open during the day. I'm the one who opens."

"How many keys?"

"I keep one with me at all times and a spare locked in my office."

Alex held out his hand. "Give me your key. Don't touch anything in your office or let anyone else into your office until I get a chance to dust for prints. Gather your crew and wait for me outside your office. I'll lock up the greenhouse after we remove the body and check for anything the killer might have left behind. Then I'll want to interview you all."

He checked his wrist comm. "It's eleven hundred hours now. Let's meet in, say, one hour. That will give me time to get my team going. We'll figure out the keys then. In the meantime, please say nothing to your crew about the dead man."

He escorted Harriet and Solomon out of the greenhouse and began making calls. Harriet saw that he had arrived on a sleek black motorcycle.

She knew nothing about motorbikes, but thought that this one looked powerful and expensive. Unlike the golf carts, the motorbike ran on fossil fuel.

She wondered why Alex hadn't used a golf cart, then realized there might be times when the security director would need to cover ground fast. The golf carts had a top speed of twenty miles an hour.

"You okay?" Solomon squeezed Harriet's hand.

She nodded. "A little weirded out. It's not every day I see a dead body hanging from a vine."

"I'll come by your cottage later."

"You know which one it is?" she asked. With the shock of finding the dead man she had forgotten all about her beautiful new home.

"Yep. I'm next door in Venus." He placed a quick kiss on Harriet's mouth and hurried off to round up his crew.

Harriet climbed into the golf cart and nudged Albion who, unbelievably, had slept through Alex's noisy arrival. "Let's go," she said. "I'm suddenly tired. Please take me back to my cottage."

"No tour?"

"I want to go back to my cottage," Harriet repeated firmly.

Albion turned the golf cart around, but before they could take off, Alex held out a hand to stop them.

He ended his call and stepped to the cart. "I'll want to talk with you later as well, Harry."

Harriet gave the practiced smile she used with clients she didn't particularly care for.

"It's Harriet," she said coolly. "My name is Harriet. Only my friends call me Harry. You'll find me in my cottage when you're ready. Do you know which one it is?"

Alex stepped back. His cool tone matched her own. "Of course. I'll be by later."

As they drove off Harriet tried to take some pleasure in putting Alex in his place but it was negated by the little thrill that coursed through her at the thought of seeing him again.

Was she becoming as much of a tart as her friend Solly?

She shook her head, pushing away the thought. She was absolutely *not* attracted to the resort's security director. Hadn't she just made it clear to him that they were to keep their dealings on a distant, professional level only?

She sighed. The only reason she had behaved so poorly toward Alex was because she had been embarrassed by the amused expression in his eyes when he had caught her practically drooling over him.

She had only recently extricated herself from an emotionally abusive relationship with her ex, Bradley Higgins. She certainly wasn't ready to become involved with a man who most likely had every woman on the resort lusting after him.

Not that Alex had given even the slightest indication that he was interested in her.

Harriet settled into her seat with a grumbled harrumph. It dawned on her that she had only been on the island for less than two hours and she already had a public relations nightmare to deal with.

How could she put a positive spin on a dead body?

CHAPTER 4

Fortunately the ride back to Mermaid Cottage didn't take long. Harriet thanked Albion for the lift and waved him off.

This time she noticed the small plaque over the door identifying the cottage–an exact replica of the tile mural in the bathroom etched into the bronze with *Mermaid* in Greek-style type over the top.

She let herself into the cool, soothing space and walked straight through to the large glass doors and stared out at the white sand and blue water beyond. The beauty of the scene felt surreal after the harsh reality of finding a dead man hanging in Solomon's greenhouse.

A dead man! She shuddered. Who was he? And why did the killer leave him in the greenhouse? Was he trying to pin the murder on her friend?

She felt too agitated to sit and wait for Solomon–there were too many emotions whirling around inside her. She needed to think, and she did her best thinking while moving.

She quickly slipped off her sneakers and stepped

through the door, closing the screen behind her. The soft warm ocean breeze in her face and the palm trees flanking her narrow lanai brought home the fact that she was not in cold New England any more. She now lived on a tropical island at the most luxurious resort in the world.

Even a dead body couldn't change the fact that she had landed her dream job.

She stood for a moment and listened to the palm fronds rattling overhead in the breeze, and took several deep, calming breaths. Feeling slightly less jittery, Harriet headed down to the beach and turned in the opposite direction from the main resort.

Tomorrow she would tour the remainder of the resort: the kitchens and dining areas, the guest cottages, the amusement park, the circus, the spas, the marinas, and the theatre.

Mr. Wade had set out to create the ultimate vacation resort with something for every taste. Children were as welcome as adults, but not everyone liked being around them, so Harriet knew that a separate area for those who wanted nothing to do with the young crowd had been constructed away from the main resort.

It was a large island and Mr. Wade owned it all. She couldn't wait to see more of it.

The smooth white sand felt warm on Harriet's bare soles. She felt as if she was walking through fine sugar crystals. She ground and twisted her feet into the soft sand as she walked, reaching for the cooler, damp sand underneath, and soon felt her calf muscles burning from the effort.

Seagulls cried overhead and plopped onto the water next to her, gently bobbing on the shallow waves. Some sat for a few moments, watching her curiously before lifting off with a cry to join the others.

The occasional pink, white, or brown shell caught her eye and she stooped to pick them up, examining them before setting them back on the beach.

By the time all the tension left her body and her mind had emptied, she had reached the end of the beach and faced an impenetrable mangrove swamp. She sat on an exposed mangrove root and lazily dipped her feet in the warm water.

She felt bad that she had acted like a bitch toward Alex Hayes. She had actually told him to call her Harriet. She *hated* the name Harriet and always went by Harry.

What had come over her? She even told strangers to call her Harry.

She brooded as she watched a school of small, bright orange fish dart around her feet. A tiny green crab scuttled out from beneath a root and disappeared under another, and a large brown and white striped periwinkle made its slow way across the sandy bottom.

She knew exactly why she had behaved badly toward the security director. She just hated to admit it to herself.

Solly had been right, the man was a hubba-hubba of walking testosterone and she had felt a strong attraction to him.

Well, she wasn't going there. She'd already made that particular mistake and paid dearly for it. She had no desire to repeat the experience.

Her ex Bradley was a very handsome and macho man and she had fallen for him hook, line, and sinker. When he asked her to live with him and move into his beautiful home on Portland's Eastern Promenade, she had foolishly leaped at the chance, moving out of the large apartment she shared at the time with Solly.

In the beginning living with Bradley had been wonderful. Then the manipulation had started, so subtle at first that Harriet hadn't even picked up on it.

Bradley wanted her to cancel a dinner date with Solly and be with him, so she had.

Or he'd ask her to cancel her yoga class to accompany him to the movies.

She had felt flattered that he wanted to spend time with her and cancelled her class. And she didn't even like slasher films.

A year and a half passed before Harriet realized that her friends had stopped asking her to join them because she always had to do something with Bradley. She had even been dropped from her yoga class because she didn't attend often enough to keep up her practice.

When she tried to talk with Bradley about needing to do more things on her own he accused her of having an affair and kept an even closer eye on her.

That's when she knew she had made a terrible mistake.

She had examined her feelings and found that she no longer felt any love for Bradley. She had been seduced by the idea of having someone like him actually want a nobody like her, tall and gawky, runaway Harriet Monroe.

She realized then that she needed to move out and get her life back.

She also realized that a move to anywhere in the Portland area wouldn't do it. Bradley was obsessed with her and would never leave her alone.

She began to feel afraid. Her work and her health had suffered.

Fortunately Solly had come through with an amazing job offer, and after a tense week of negotiating with Mr. Wade, here she was, thousands of miles away from her controlling ex.

She had packed only minimal summer clothing and her

two treasures—her carved hippo collection and the holo of her parents—and caught a shuttle flight while Bradley was at work.

Afraid that Bradley might follow her, she had flown to several destinations before finally buying a ticket under an assumed name and flying to the island resort.

That was another thing she owed Solly for; he had found a way to provide her with a fake i.d. for the last shuttle flight.

A plop in the mangrove swamp brought Harriet out of her reverie. Solly was coming by to see her, and so was Alex Hayes. She needed to get back to her cottage.

She stood abruptly, sending a couple of small crabs and the fish darting away from her feet.

She had walked less than halfway back to the cottages when she saw Solly coming along the beach toward her. Despite his slight limp his long legs covered the ground at a good pace. He had ditched his shirt and put on a pair of ragged jean shorts. He looked tan and fit and handsome as hell.

She sighed. It really was a shame her best friend was gay. He could have been her perfect mate.

"Hi, doll." Solly turned to join her and slung an arm around Harriet's shoulder. "How's my best girl doing? I hope the dead body hasn't soured you on your new job. This is a great place to work, I promise."

Harriet realized that Solly hadn't heard her tell Alex Hayes to call her Harriet. That was a good thing, otherwise Solly would know she had been attracted to the security director and tease her. Sometimes she thought Solly knew her better than she knew herself.

"I admit finding a dead body rattled me," she said, placing her arm around Solly's waist and matching her step to his, "but this place is so beautiful I couldn't give up my job without at least giving it a solid shot."

Solly squeezed her. "Good girl. Soooo, tell me, what did you think of Alex McDreamy? Is he worth several hubbas or what?" He grinned at her and Harriet laughed.

"Hubbas" were the way she and Solly rated the sex appeal of anyone they found attractive. It had started as a joke when they were teens, then stuck.

"Yeah, maybe," she admitted. "I'll give him one and a half hubbas, although his personality might negate them. He must have all the women on the resort panting after him the way he shoots out all that male T."

"Ahhh, noticed that steamy testosterone, did you? I can tell you that many of the hired help, young and old, male and female, have all tried to catch our security director's attention but so far none have succeeded."

Harriet frowned. "I wonder why not. He seems normal. Maybe he has a wife stashed somewhere."

"Or maybe he was injured in some war and no longer has the use of his . . . equipment."

"Sol! That's an awful thought."

"I agree. It would be a real shame for that hunk of man flesh to be impotent."

They had reached Harriet's cottage and stepped up to the lanai.

"Leave a towel out here when you take walks on the beach," Solomon advised. He showed her an outside faucet with a short hose attached. "You can rinse your feet here. That way you won't track sand inside."

Harriet poked her friend. "Leave it to you to think of that, Mr. Neat and Tidy. I promise I will leave a towel when I take a walk and not track sand inside my new home."

Solomon acted offended. "I'm just thinking of the help. Rebecca and her daughter Amy clean our cottages once a week, on Thursdays. Their salary is covered by the resort but I always leave a little extra for them on the kitchen counter."

"Good to know. I can't believe that I'll actually be living in this cottage. When Albion brought me here to unload my bags I thought he'd made a mistake and taken me to a guest cottage."

They rinsed their feet and went inside. Solomon sat on the couch and stretched his arms along the back. "Mr. Wade is using psychology on us," he said as he put his bare feet on the bamboo coffee table.

Harriet sat in one of the chairs opposite and tucked her legs up under her. The chair cushions were roomy and soft and comfortable. It felt good to be sitting like this with Solly again. Over the years they had spent many an hour simply sitting and talking when they lived together.

"What do you mean?" she asked him.

She had missed having Solly in her life. Missed his unwavering friendship, his irreverent view of anything that wasn't related to plants. She had especially missed his keen insight into people.

Unfortunately she hadn't listened when Solly had tried to warn her early on about Bradley Higgins.

"Wade wants to hire and keep good help," Solomon answered. "One way to do that is to pay us well, which he does. Another way is to provide us with beautiful accommodations so we never want to leave."

""He sure nailed the accommodations. My office is beautiful too. Have you met our employer yet?" Harriet asked. "We talked several times before he hired me but he always blocked the vid screen. I'm curious about him."

"Nope. He did the same thing with me. I tried to find a photo of the man but there's nothing. Plenty of stories about his businesses and charitable donations but apparently he keeps his personal life well under the radar. He even sends representatives to charity functions rather than attend himself. No one here that I've asked has met him in person either."

"Hmmm. I wonder if Alex Hayes has met him. You'd think Mr. Wade would want to get the measure of the resort's security director personally before hiring him."

Solly shook his head. "I have no idea. Why don't you ask him when he comes to question you?"

"I'll do that."

A soft chime sounded. "What's that?"

"Your doorbell." Solomon rose from the couch. "That'll be Alex. I'll catch up with you later. Come to my place around seven for dinner. I'm right next door in Venus."

Solomon slipped out the back door and was gone.

CHAPTER 5

Alex stood outside Harriet's door waiting for her to answer. He had observed her walking down the beach with Solomon, their arms wrapped around each other.

Were they an item? He could have sworn Solomon was interested in men, not women. Maybe the head gardener swung both ways.

He found the thought irritating.

The door opened and Harriet stood there looking windblown and flushed. He noticed that her bare feet were fine-boned, nicely shaped, and she had painted her toenails a soft shell pink.

She had the strangest colored silver-blue eyes he'd ever seen. Not quite silver-gray, not quite blue. They seemed to change, like liquid silver reflecting the sky. Changing eye color was a popular fashion choice these days but something told him Harriet Monroe had been born with hers.

"Are you coming in or did you want to interrogate me on the stoop?" she asked him.

Alex gave her his best ex-cop stare, eyes hooded. "I think inside would be best."

"Very well." She stood back and ushered him inside. "I suppose you'd like something to drink. I'm not sure what, if anything, has been stocked in my chiller. I haven't been on the island long enough to find out where to get supplies."

"That's easy," Alex said, following her into the kitchen. "Room and board is part of your salary. You place your grocery order by end of day Monday with Lana and the kitchen will add it to their own order. You'll have to eat in the employee dining room until then."

He pulled out a padded stool at the pale rose granite counter and sat. "You should find an order form in the drawer beside the chiller," he continued. "A member of the kitchen staff will deliver your order on Wednesdays and stock your Redi-Meal unit if you request made-up meals. Of course you can cook your own meals or as I said, you always have the option of dining in the employee dining room."

Surprised, Harriet stopped and looked at Alex. She hadn't expected such a long, helpful answer from him.

She opened the chiller and peered inside. "I have lemonade, water, some kind of red fruit juice, and white wine."

She pulled out one of the white wines. "Sauvignon Blanc. I'm going to have a glass. It's been a long day. Do you want one?"

"I'm working, so no, thanks. Lemonade would be good." He didn't really want anything to drink, but he sensed that Harriet was nervous and figured having something to do would help her relax.

"So," he said, taking the tall, frosty glass she handed him, "what do you think of our island so far? You haven't been here long, have you?"

He watched her closely over the glass as he took a sip of

the cold, tart drink. The island's kitchen staff made the best lemonade Alex had ever tasted. He set the glass on the counter and waited for Harriet to pour her wine.

He knew the precise time Harriet's shuttle flight had landed. He even knew she had traveled under an assumed name and he definitely intended to find out why.

Harriet returned the wine to the chiller and took a sip from her glass. It tasted crisp and cold with just the right balance of tart and fruity. She felt some of her tension over being interrogated ease away.

And why did she feel tense? she wondered. She didn't have anything to do with the dead man. She should look on this as an interesting life experience. She gave a small shrug.

"I've only been here a few hours, Mr. Hayes. My office is lovely. This cottage is lovely. I love the beach and the warm sun and I'm thrilled to hook up with my friend Solomon.

"Let's sit in the living room," she suggested, moving out from behind the granite island. "I just took a walk on the beach and between travel and the flight and the fresh air and sun I suddenly feel exhausted. I want to put my feet up."

She led the way to the living room where she plopped down into a chair and stacked her bare feet on the coffee table. Taking another sip of her wine she stifled a sigh. It was true, she did suddenly feel exhausted. She looked at the security director and waited.

Alex sat on the couch across from Harriet so he could watch her. Her skin had paled beneath the slight sunburn she had picked up and he noticed a sprinkling of small freckles across the bump on the bridge of her somewhat prominent nose. Her intelligent eyes–those odd, mesmerizing silver-blue eyes–were steady on him.

She pushed her thick honey-blond hair off her face and sighed. "Was it suicide?" she asked, when he didn't speak right away. "The way he was just . . . hanging there." She shuddered. "So sad. Was he one of the resort's employees?"

Alex ignored her questions. He set his drink on a coaster shaped like a scallop shell. "So, you arrived on the island today?" he asked instead.

"Yes. I took the nine o'clock shuttle flight from the mainland."

"And you went straight to the greenhouse?" He had spoken with both Lana and Albion so he knew that wasn't true.

"No. I had the driver who met the shuttle take me to my office where I met Lana from the kitchen. She sent Albion to me to give me a tour of the resort. He brought me here first."

Harriet yawned and covered her mouth. "Sorry."

She shook her head to try to clear it. She hoped the security director didn't have too many questions, the day had caught up with her and what little wine she'd drunk had put her over the edge. She wanted to crawl into her bed and take a nap.

"Have you ever seen the dead man before today?"

She shook her head. "I don't know, I didn't see his face, but you already knew that because we didn't turn his body around."

"We've identified the body. He flew here from Portland, Maine yesterday. You and Solomon are both from the Portland area, aren't you?"

Harriet nodded. "Yep. Maybe we know him. What's his name?"

"His name was Bradley Higgins."

Harriet's hand jerked and wine slopped over the rim of

her glass and splashed onto her lap. She hastily set the glass down.

Alex watched her for a minute. Her eyes were wide with shock and even her lips had paled.

"Did-did you just say that Bradley Higgins is dead?"

"Yes. Do you know him?" Obviously she did, but he wanted to hear her say it.

Harriet jumped to her feet. "I'll be right back. I need to change out of these wet pants." She ran out of the room.

She stood in the bedroom and stared unseeing out the door to the beach. Bradley was dead? How? And why? And what on earth was he doing at the Island Resort? Had he followed her?

She shook her head. No, Bradley couldn't have followed her. Solly had told her that the body was cold. And hadn't Alex just told her that he had arrived on the island yesterday? But how had he known that she was coming here?

Harriet took several deep breaths, trying to clear the confusion from her thoughts. Change. She needed to get out of her wet capris. She dug a pair of soft sweatpants from her suitcase and quickly pulled them on.

Bradley was dead. How? Had he committed suicide because she had left him?

What a horrible thought.

No, it was impossible. Alex Hayes must have made a mistake. She headed to the bathroom to splash water on her face and give herself a few extra minutes to pull herself together.

Alex slowly sipped his lemonade and mulled over Harriet's reaction as he waited for her to return. The new PR Director certainly hadn't expected to hear the name Bradley Higgins.

She had obviously known the man. And if Harriet had

known him there was a good chance that Solomon Ayers had as well.

Several minutes passed before Harriet reappeared wearing a pair of faded blue sweatpants that hung low on her curvy hips. She had washed off any makeup and tied her hair up into a high ponytail that made her look ten years younger.

Alex blinked. Had he ever met a more attractive woman? The thought startled him.

It wasn't her face–her nose kept her from being beautiful, but paired with those eyes it also made her face interesting. He usually liked his women petite and voluptuous. Harriet stood just under six foot, and while she definitely had breasts they weren't very large, although she did have a nice ass and very shapely legs.

It was the whole package, he decided. There was an air about Harriet–an innocent honesty that appealed to his jaded ex-cop soul.

He reminded himself that he was interrogating her in a murder investigation.

Ignoring her wine, Harriet perched on the edge of her chair and clasped her hands on her knees to hide their trembling.

Alex waited.

Harriet couldn't stand not knowing. She cleared her throat. "Did he . . . did he commit suicide?" she whispered.

"No. Bradley Higgins was murdered."

"Murdered?" Harriet blinked. "I don't understand. Why would anyone want to murder Bradley?"

"I don't know–yet, but I *will* find out. Could you answer my question, please?"

Harriet shook her head. "I'm sorry, I've forgotten it. What did you ask me?"

"I asked if you knew the dead man, Bradley Higgins."

Alex watched her carefully as she picked up her wine and took a small sip. Her hand shook only slightly.

Tough cookie, Alex thought. She's pulled herself together. Tough enough to murder a man? The timing didn't work, but she could have hired someone to do the deed. Someone like her friend Solomon Ayers.

"Yes." Harriet took a deep breath and let it out. "Yes I knew him," she answered, setting down her wine glass. "Quite well, in fact."

Alex waited for more. When Harriet remained silent he prompted her. "How did you know Mr. Higgins and do you know why he came to the island?"

Harriet took another deep breath to steady herself. She could see no point in hiding the truth from Alex.

"Bradley and I lived together for the last two years. I left him two days ago. As for why he's on the island, I can only assume he came to find me, which is a surprise because I never told him I was coming here. The truth is, I did everything I could to hide that fact from him."

Alex studied her for a moment. That was not the answer he had been expecting. He had guessed that Mr. Higgins was Solomon's lover and that was why the body was displayed in the greenhouse.

Don't assume anything, Alex, he reminded himself ruefully. It always makes an ass out of you.

"Care to explain that further, Miss Monroe? Why would he come looking for you if you had split up?"

Harriet looked at the security director, her eyes steady. "Bradley was–" she hesitated and groped for the right words. ". . . he was possessive and a control freak," she finished. "He controlled everything in his life with a firm hand, including me."

She shrugged one shoulder and picked up her glass again. "I finally got fed up and left him."

"Why did you travel to the resort under a false name today?" He watched Harriet's knuckles whiten on the wine glass stem.

"I knew Bradley wouldn't let me go without an ugly scene, and that he would follow me if he knew where I was going. I didn't tell him about this job. I wanted to make a clean break and just disappear."

She sighed and set the wine glass back on the table. Her next words came rushing out.

"You have to understand, I couldn't live with him any longer. I wasn't me anymore. Bradley went to his office and I packed two small bags and I left. I took a transport and flew to three different cities and then this morning I took the shuttle flight here under an assumed name so he wouldn't be able to track me."

Alex gave her a considering look. "You can't buy a ticket, even with cash, without identification."

"Right." Harriet fidgeted and looked away.

"Where did you get the fake i.d?"

"I-I can't tell you that. I don't want to get anyone else into trouble. They were only trying to help me. Are you going to have me arrested?"

"Did you have anything to do with Bradley Higgins's murder?"

"What? No! Of course not."

"Do you do drugs of any type? Bear in mind that I'm authorized by Mr. Wade to administer a drug test on any resort employee whenever I feel it necessary."

"No! No. I've never done drugs. Not even—well, never mind. I've never been tempted to touch drugs."

Alex frowned at her. What had she been about to say? It was obvious the woman was hiding something from him. He drummed his fingers on his thigh for a minute, watching her carefully.

"Are you in the habit of skirting or breaking the law?"

"No!"

Harriet saw no reason to tell the resort's security director of her time living on the streets. In the early days she had shoplifted and broken into vehicles and stolen petty change and small things to sell so she could buy food to stay alive. Only Solly knew how low she had sunk during those desperate times.

"Didn't you do a background check on me for Mr. Wade before I was hired?"

"No. Mr. Wade employed an agency to do the background checks for the resort's key personnel, including me, before I was hired."

And that was something Alex planned to redo as soon as possible. He mentally moved background checks to the top of his to-do list.

Alex stood. "That's all I have for the moment, Ms. Monroe. As the old cop shows used to say, 'Don't leave the country.' In this case, don't leave the island. I will definitely have more questions for you about your boyfriend."

He looked at the tired woman with the long blonde ponytail and fascinating eyes. He found her face arresting. She had a mouth that made him want to taste it and a strong chin that he somehow knew could be stubbornly set when the mood suited her.

"I'll be back," he said.

"Great. I can hardly wait," Harriet replied sourly.

He grinned suddenly, absurdly pleased to find that she possessed some backbone. To his disgust he found himself hoping she wasn't involved in Bradley Higgins's death.

He gave himself a mental shake. Never in his career as a murder detective had he let himself become involved with a witness or a suspect—and he damn sure wasn't about to start now.

"Don't get up. I'll let myself out," he said gruffly, and left.

CHAPTER 6

Harriet barely registered the sound of the cottage's front door shutting. She stayed seated, too shocked by the news that Bradley Higgins had been murdered to move.

Who would want to kill Bradley? she wondered. She couldn't think of anyone. Oh, there were plenty of people who disliked him, some intensely, but enough to follow Bradley to the island and kill him? She didn't think so.

She picked up the wineglass and carried it to the lanai, plopping into a low-slung deck chair. She sipped her wine and watched the setting sun turn the aqua water gold, then a deep blood-red before it slipped suddenly below the horizon and the ink black sky overhead filled with a billion stars.

What a day.

Just when she was sure that Alex Hayes was an unfeeling, officious prick, he had smiled at her.

He had a dimple in his right cheek.

That smile had changed the dour security director's whole face and character.

In truth, that brief smile had lifted Alex from Harriet's

one and a half reluctant hubbas to a *HUBBA-HUBBA*. All capital letters.

Wait until she told Solly.

She felt a stab of guilt. What kind of woman lusted after a man she had just met when her recent fiancé had been found murdered only hours before?

That brought her back to wondering who had murdered Bradley. What had brought her ex to the island? He had to have come here for her. She'd place a bet on it and she never gambled.

Bradley Higgins was dead. Murdered, no less.

She set the wine glass down on the lanai deck and waited for the tears to flow but only a few came. Her love for Bradley had burned out months earlier.

The following morning Harriet woke to birdsong. She stretched luxuriously in the king-sized bed and sighed happily. The filmy insect curtains, light as spider silk, floated gently around her, wafted by the lightly perfumed breeze coming through the doors she had left open last night so she could hear the waves lapping the beach and the night insects doing their thing.

She lazed for several more minutes before she crawled from the bed and padded to the lanai doors. The sun, rising behind her on the opposite side of the island, sent shafts of light dancing across the crests of the waves.

A pod of dolphins or porpoises–she'd have to ask someone what they were–surfaced near the shore, their sleek blue-gray bodies glistening in the sun. They curved back into the water as one and were gone.

While dinner with Solly last night had almost been like old times–relaxed, with lots of talk and some laughter–

they had both been subdued by the shock of Bradley's murder.

They had figured out that since moving in with Bradley Harriet had only dined with Solly twice in the previous two years, and both meals had been rushed and stressed because Harriet knew that Bradley was waiting impatiently for her to return to his house.

They had finally agreed to chalk those two years of her life up to temporary insanity and drank a toast of margaritas to their renewed friendship.

The toast didn't mean that Harriet was glad that Bradley was dead. No, that wasn't it at all. She would never wish murder on anyone. She was simply happy to be free of Bradley's emotional shackles and to have her best friend back in her life again.

Her love for Bradley had died long before a few months ago, she realized, looking back. The few tears she had produced the previous evening had not been shed over the death of a man she once loved. They had been shed for the death of a dream. The dream that one day a man would love her above all other women. That she would be special to one person who was special to her.

She wondered then if Bradley had somehow suspected that her feelings for him had changed. Was that why he had become even more possessive and controlling over the past year?

Harriet pushed the thoughts away. She didn't want to spend any more time dwelling on the wreck that had been her relationship with Bradley. There was no point now that he was dead. He had possessed good points too. True, they were few and all work related, but he hadn't been all bad.

She hoped Alex would find the murderer quickly so she could finally put Bradley Higgins behind her.

Coming to the island yesterday, she had felt lighter and more carefree than she had since Bradley had come into her life. She felt ready for the challenges of her new job and had made a silent promise to herself that she would show Mr. Wade that he had made the right choice in hiring her as the resort's PR Director.

She couldn't let Bradley's murder interfere with that. Her entire future was riding on her new job.

She turned away from the beautiful view and decided it was time to get ready for the day. Stripping off the cotton boxers and tank top she wore as pajamas, she stepped into the shower and programmed the jets at ninety-nine degrees.

She groaned with pleasure as streams of hot water hit her from two sides and overhead. Harriet fumbled with the marble tiles until she found the one hiding the soap and shampoo and soon the scent of sandalwood filled the shower stall. She felt as pampered as any guest.

Thirty minutes later she was back in the blue golf cart with Albion, who had shown up at her door unexpectedly. "Time for tour," was all he said.

While she would have preferred to explore the resort without Albion at her side, Harriet decided she wasn't going to let his lack of friendliness get to her and spoil the day.

She felt excited to finally get to see the resort in person. The pictures Mr. Wade and the designer had sent could only tell her so much. She needed to feel the place to really do it justice in her ad campaigns.

Albion headed off in the opposite direction from the one he'd taken the previous day, driving past the complex which held Harriet's office.

"Kitchens," he pointed out, as they passed a long, single story stone building with several smoke stacks.

"I'd like to see the kitchens and meet the staff," Harriet said when she realized Albion intended to drive by.

"Later."

"Albion, I want to see the kitchens. Turn around."

Albion scowled, but to her relief he made a big u-turn and stopped in front of the kitchen's central entrance. "I'll wait." He pulled out his battered straw hat and placed it over his face.

Harriet thought briefly of insisting that he accompany her into the kitchens and introduce her to the staff but decided it wasn't worth the effort. Again she wondered why Mr. Wade would hire such an obviously lazy and unfriendly worker.

She climbed out of the golf cart and pulled open the wide wooden door. Instead of the foyer or entryway she expected to find, she found herself in a small courtyard open to the sky.

A round dark stone fountain with three bronze dolphins cast to mimic the very action she had witnessed earlier that morning dominated the center of the court-yard. Water spouted from the creatures' mouths, cascading down several tiered catch-basins.

Large, perfumed tropical flowers in brilliant reds, pinks, and yellows grew around the courtyard's edges and three palm trees grew far above the roof edge. There were several seating areas with cane chairs and small round tables.

"It's lovely, isn't it?" Lana approached from the left of the fountain. She had lost the pink curls from the previous day and fashioned her hair into an emerald green ponytail on top of her head. Her eyes matched.

Harriet experienced a quick stab of jealousy over Lana's petite, curvaceous body. Experience had taught her that men preferred short, curvy women to tall Amazons like herself. At five-eleven, Harriet towered over most men. She bet the petite Lana never had a problem getting dates.

"I see you found us," Lana said, joining Harriet with a smile. "Is Albion treating you right?"

Harriet hesitated, then decided to say nothing. She didn't want to appear to be critical of the staff, especially as it was only her second day here.

"We really didn't get to see much yesterday," she said instead. "This is my first stop today. I was hoping to see the kitchens and meet some of the staff if that's possible."

"Absolutely. Follow me." Lana headed to a door opposite the one she had appeared from. She turned to Harriet with a sympathetic expression on her face.

"It must have been awful finding that dead man in the greenhouse. I heard that you and Solomon knew him."

Harriet didn't want to talk about Bradley Higgins, and for all she knew, Alex wouldn't want her to say anything, so she gave a noncommittal answer. To her relief, Lana dropped the subject.

The door opened onto a short, functional corridor painted white that ended in an expansive, brightly lit kitchen.

Harriet looked around the space with admiration. The white tiled floor and walls were bright and spotless. She counted a dozen workers, all dressed in resort blue double-breasted chef coats and toques, working at one of the three long rows of stainless tables that dominated the center of the kitchen.

Six of the chefs chopped fresh vegetables on large wooden cutting boards, two were butchering chickens, two were kneading dough, and one was running dough through a pasta machine. The remaining chef was ferrying large trays and platters of prepped ingredients to the head chefs.

"I thought there were no guests yet," Harriet said. "Why are they so busy?"

"They're testing recipes and training. Plus we have a couple of early bird guests that Mr. Wade allowed on the island before the official opening."

Harriet followed Lana deeper into the kitchen, taking care to keep out of everyone's way. A row of industrial dishwashers and several sinks big and deep enough to hold the extra-large pots and pans sat against one outside wall. Two walls held eight-burner gas stoves, stacked built-in ovens, and several charcoal grills.

Harriet was excited to see that the kitchen even sported an old-fashioned wood-fired oven in one corner. Wood-fired ovens were rare, found only in exclusive restaurants that could charge enough to cover the cost of the wood fuel. She should have guessed there'd be one at the resort.

Bradley had taken her to one of those restaurants during a business trip to New York City early on when they were still only dating. She had been suitably impressed and loved the pizza.

She spotted two pair of huge stainless doors on the fourth wall that she guessed must lead to the industrial chillers. Several chefs dressed in head chef whites stood before the stoves or barked out orders to the staff working at the prep tables.

A huge assortment of gleaming pots and pans in stainless and copper hung overhead. Wooden racks held knives and stainless holders were filled with more utensils than she even knew existed.

Harriet breathed in the scent of garlicky red sauce and the heady aroma of baking yeast breads. "They all look so busy," she remarked.

"This is nothing. Wait until the resort officially opens

and the guests arrive in full force. I hear we're already booked solid for the next six months."

Lana waved a dainty hand at the mostly empty stainless tables. "We'll have triple the staff working in here by next week and it will be a madhouse with everyone yelling and pots clanging."

Harriet looked at Lana and saw that she was smiling. "You love the intensity of a busy kitchen, don't you?" she asked, understanding.

Lana's smile grew and the green ponytail bobbed as she nodded enthusiastically. "I do. I really do. There's something about all the activity and skill that appeals to me. The head chefs are like conductors leading an orchestra–everyone has their part to play and everything has to be timed and performed perfectly or it will fail and people will be disappointed."

"What do you do here?"

"I order everything for the kitchens: food, equipment, the staples, the extras, even the uniforms. And I do the hiring of the kitchen staff. I'm also responsible for making sure the guest cottage Redi-Meals are stocked. The guests are sent a questionnaire when they book their visit so I'll have their preferences before they arrive."

"Wow. They do all that in this kitchen as well? That sounds like a logistical nightmare."

Lana laughed. "The Redi-Meals are prepped in a separate, dedicated kitchen. Separating the Redi-Meals from the restaurant food prep makes it far easier to manage. We also have a third kitchen with its own staff and dining room for the resort's employees. That reminds me, I'll need your grocery-slash-meal requests by end of day Monday so I can add it to the other orders. Any later and your meal orders won't get put into the system."

"I'll be sure to place my order before Monday so I don't

mess with your system," Harriet said with a smile.

She narrowed her eyes at Lana as something occurred to her. "So, when you showed up at my office yesterday–you weren't actually "sent" to check me out, were you? You came of your own accord. And you told me you were the liaison. You're actually the kitchen manager."

"Caught me." Lana didn't look the least bothered that Harriet had caught her lies.

"I really need to get back to my office," she said with a smile. "The first guests are arriving in three days and I still have a lot to do. I'll walk you out."

"Was it hard for you to leave your family behind to take this job?" Harriet asked as they returned the way they had come.

The decision to commit two years of her life to working on a secluded tropical island had been an easy one for Harriet, but she suspected others were sacrificing their personal lives in order to work at the high-end resort.

Lana hesitated. "No," she answered. "My siblings are scattered all over the planet and my parents are happily settled in the south of France. What about you? Did you leave family behind?"

Harriet shook her head. "Nope. It was an easy choice for me too."

Back at the fountain, Harriet thanked Lana for the tour. She reached for the door but Lana stopped her.

"I heard Alex Hayes paid you a visit last night."

Harriet blinked at the unexpected comment. Who was talking about her and why did anyone care what she did or who she spent time with? She hated, absolutely hated, being the subject of gossip.

"He came to question me about the dead man."

Lana pursed her lips. "So what do think of our security director?"

Harriet shrugged. She did not want to discuss Alex Hayes with Lana any more than she wanted to talk with her about Bradley.

"He seems competent enough, I guess. I've had very little interaction with him. Why?"

Lana's expression turned steely-eyed. With the green hair and eyes she reminded Harriet of an angry elf.

"Alex and I are an item. I thought you should know so you don't get any ideas about going after him yourself. Keep in mind, when you live on an island everyone knows what you're up to."

Harriet looked more closely at the kitchen manager. "That sounded like a threat."

"No." Lana smiled again. "Not a threat. Consider it a friendly warning. Keep away from Alex."

Harriet decided it was time to change the subject. "I think I'd like to do some ad campaigns featuring the kitchens. I'll let you know when I have the details worked out so we can set it up. The food here will certainly be a draw for a certain type of resort client. Maybe we can even plan some special food-oriented weekend get-aways."

"What a fun idea. I'll talk to the head chefs and ask them for some themes. Now I really must get back to work. I'll see you around."

Harriet let herself out. Albion was still snoozing. She climbed into the golf cart and snatched the hat off his face.

"Let's go." She tossed the hat onto Albion's skinny lap. What had Lana meant, she didn't want Harriet to "get any ideas" about Alex? Did she *look* like a woman who went around trying to steal away other women's lovers?

Somehow Harriet had assumed that such a beautiful place would not harbor the petty squabbling and jealousies that she saw elsewhere.

She felt sorely disappointed to learn otherwise.

CHAPTER 7

"What's eating you?" Instead of starting the cart, Albion stared at Harriet. He stuffed his hat under his seat, scratched at one dark wrinkled cheek and let his hand fall in his lap.

Apparently her unfriendly tour guide had no intention of doing as she asked.

Harriet glared at him. She'd only met three people on the island so far and two of them had turned out to be disappointing. The jury was still out on Alex Hayes.

"Nothing's eating me," she snapped. "I'm just ready to see more of the resort. Let's go."

Harriet knew her irritation was with Lana, not Albion. Ordinarily it would have bothered her that she was lashing out at Albion unfairly, but Albion hadn't shown himself to be a friendly co-worker.

Two could play the unfriendly game. "*Let's go,*" she said again.

Her two year contract was going to feel like a lifetime if Solly turned out to be the only friend she made on the resort.

But Albion still didn't move. He continued to stare at her for another minute. Then he smiled, the first smile she'd seen from him, exposing strong white teeth. The smile lit his whole face and made him look like a different man altogether.

"Queen Lana show her claws? Ignore her. She power-hungry."

He started the golf cart but didn't put it in gear.

Harriet suddenly found herself smiling, her irritation gone. "*Queen* Lana?" she repeated.

"Oh yes. Lana just like tyrant queen. Need to know everybody's business. Very bossy. Ignore her."

Harriet's smile widened. "All right, I will. Thank you, Albion." She settled back into her seat. "So, where to next?"

"Your choice. Spa or guest cottages. We'll hit a fork in the road in a minute."

Harriet realized that Albion's grammar had suddenly improved. She pointed a finger at him. "You've been putting me on," she accused.

Albion's smile lit up his face again. "I have to take my fun and giggles where I can find them. For all I knew, you were another Lana. I did you no harm."

"No," Harriet grumbled, "you did me no harm, although I have to admit I wondered how you ever got hired as a baggage clerk with all the personality you showed me."

Albion chuckled and shot Harriet a sideways look. "*Head* baggage clerk. Mr. Wade hired me away from the Singapore Palace."

Harriet looked at the small man beside her in amazement. The Singapore Palace was the most expensive hotel in the world. They boasted of—and delivered—only the best of everything, including hotel staff.

Harriet would have assumed that the Singapore was in

Wade's stable of hotels, but if he had to hire Albion away then obviously he didn't own it.

"The Palace. I'm impressed. Is Albion your real name?"

"Yes." He placed his right hand over his chest and turned toward Harriet, bowing his head slightly, his voice suddenly deep and sonorous. "Allow me to introduce myself, mademoiselle, I am Albion Aloysius Carter."

Harriet laughed. "I'm pleased to meet you, Mr. Carter."

"Call me Albie, please," he said in his normal voice. "All my friends do."

Harriet's day brightened again. Maybe the resort would work out after all. "All right, Albie, what do you suggest I see next?"

"I suggest we start with the nearest guest cottages, miss."

"Nearest cottages? Are there more somewhere else?"

"Oh yes. There are four different groups of cottages on the west side of the island and another twelve cottages on the east side of the mountains. Those are for the guests who aren't interested in the regular attractions and simply want to enjoy the island's natural attractions like hiking in the mountains.

"We would need one of the resort's all wheel-drive vehicles to get to the far cottages. The road is quite rough–purposely so, as it's meant to be part of the experience for the guests–and it discourages the more regular guests from intruding on the east side guests."

"Okay, then. Take me to see the nearest guest cottages." Harriet settled back in the comfortable golf cart, prepared to enjoy her tour with the new Albie.

Queen Lana. The nickname made her giggle.

They had barely passed the kitchens when Alex roared up on his motorcycle and stopped them. He was dressed in another snug, resort blue polo shirt and tan khakis but instead of being tied back, his black hair curled loosely over his shirt collar.

In the sunshine Harriet could see that the blue shirt made the blue of the security director's eyes seem even more intense as his gaze locked on her. She felt her pulse flutter in response.

"Good morning Albie. I wonder if I could have a quick word with you, Miss Monroe?"

Lana's warning echoed clearly in Harriet's brain. "Hands off, bitch, this man belongs to me" had been her not-so-subtle message, but Solly had told her that Alex wasn't dating anyone, and she trusted Solly to know. Her friend always managed to pick up any gossip, no matter the situation.

"Of course." Harriet smiled. "What can I do for you?"

"I have the names of everyone who was on the island when Bradley Higgins was murdered. I'd like you to take a look at the list since you knew the deceased and see if any of the names look familiar."

Harriet frowned. "Do you think he was meeting someone here?"

"Possibly. Now that I know you were living together I'm operating on the theory that he came to the resort looking for you. But he came over in the shuttle before yours—I checked the passenger list. Unlike you he traveled here under his own name."

Harriet blushed. The only reason she had used a false name had been to fool Bradley. Obviously that hadn't worked and now she felt a bit foolish over the amateur cloak and dagger act.

"But if he came here to find me that would mean he knew I was coming here before I left him." If Bradley had known about her new job that meant that he had gained access to her personal computer.

How long had he been invading her privacy and checking up on her? She felt a surge of anger–at Bradley and at herself for being so stupid. Why had she waited so long to leave the control freak?

"Yes, it does." Alex's gaze was steady

"Yes, what does?" Harriet couldn't remember what she had last asked. Her mind was reeling from just how far Bradley had gone to keep control over her. What an idiot she'd been.

"Yes, he must have known you were coming to the island," Alex said patiently. "He either planned to confront you here or he was meeting someone else here. That's why I want you to look at the list of names."

"Fine. Tell me when and where and I'll meet you."

"Come to my office in an hour. Albie will show you where it is."

Albie patted Harriet's knee. "Don't worry, Harry. We'll check out the guest cottages and then I'll deliver you to Alex's office. We can see the attractions another time."

"Thanks, Albie. Is that all, Mr. Hayes?"

"For now." Alex roared off.

Harriet turned in her seat to look after him and saw Lana's figure standing outside the kitchens staring at her. Great, just what she needed. Lana must have heard the motorcycle and stepped out to catch Alex, but he had driven right past her.

Lana had no way of knowing that Alex had only stopped Harriet because he had a question about the murder.

Harriet sighed. She hoped she hadn't made an enemy of the possessive Lana. She seemed to wield a lot of power on the resort.

She almost asked Albie to turn around so she could explain to Lana why Alex had stopped to speak with her but decided against it. There wasn't a damn thing she could do about the jealous queen.

She turned forward and pointed.

"Let's go see the guest cottages."

"As you wish." Albie glanced back to see what had upset his passenger just as Lana stalked back into the kitchens with her hands fisted at her sides.

Despite a feeling of unease, Albion kept his expression smooth and pleasant. He had decades of practice schooling his features. In his business it was important not to give away how he really felt about the obnoxious guests he often had to deal with.

Over his career he had learned to be a good judge of character—anybody who wanted to be successful working with hotel guests had to be if they wanted to survive—and his gut told him that Harriet Monroe was a sincere, warm and caring person. It would be a real shame if Lana drove her off.

He made a silent vow to do what he could to make sure that didn't happen.

CHAPTER 8

Harriet gave herself up to the island's beauty as Albion followed the crushed shell road. The day was too perfect to let Lana's unfounded jealousy ruin it, she decided. She had her dream job and a beautiful cottage on a tropical island. She would find a way to deal with Lana.

Albion veered along the first left-hand fork to a wide cove and stopped the jeep.

"Kidd's Cove," he informed her as he parked the cart.

Harriet climbed out of the cart and sighed with pleasure. The island's three mountains, covered with green and lush forests of tropical plants, provided a soothing backdrop for the guest cottages strung out along the white sand beach that lined the wide cove.

Green mountains. White sand. Turquoise blue water. Harriet had never seen anything so beautiful in her life. The dark rocks of the Maine coast offered few beaches and the North Atlantic was often either a cold, steely gray or a cold deep, deep blue. While it had its own beauty, it lacked the inviting aura of the island.

The cottages ranged in size from the smallest–the same

size and configuration as her own—to the largest ones offering four bedrooms.

Albie explained that the larger cottages were limited to eight guests at the most. If a big family group needed more beds they had to rent more cottages.

Jan Rhymes, the resort's designer, had spoken with Harriet about Mr. Ward's desire to limit the number and size of the guest cottages to make them fit in with the landscape and not be intrusive. It was one of the selling points Harriet intended to play up in her ads for the resort.

Seeing the cottages in person, she thought Jan had succeeded admirably. The single-story cottages were well spaced and their surrounding areas planted to create real privacy for the guests.

A soft warm breeze freshened off the water and kept the bugs away as they walked the beach path and explored each empty cottage. No two cottages were exactly alike. Each one had its own personality and decorating focus, with a name plaque over the door, similar to her own Mermaid.

Small waves lapped gently at their feet as they walked the beach, disappearing into the sand with a soft sizzle. Bird song came from the vegetation around the cottages and Harriet caught an occasional glimpse of the brightly plumed singers as they searched the foliage for insects to eat.

When they reached the farthest cottage in the cove she took a deep breath of the salt air. "Mmmm, what's that scent? I didn't smell it at the other cottages."

"Must be those." Albie pointed to a profusion of pink trumpet-shaped flowers climbing over the side of the last cottage.

This cottage had a slightly different look to it from the others. Harriet studied it for a few moments before realizing that it looked settled into the spot, not new like the ones they'd just toured. It was also set farther apart from the other cottages.

"I need a closer look." Harriet walked up to the vine-covered wall and stuck her face in the blossoms. "They're so pretty. It's these all right, Albie, and they smell divine. You should see all the pollinators in them. There's even an iridescent green bee that reminds me of Lana's hair."

"The flowers are nice, aren't they?" The masculine voice came from around the corner.

"Oh! I'm so sorry, I didn't mean to intrude. I thought the cottages were all empty." Dismayed, Harriet took a quick step back.

Bothering the resort guests was a big no-no, written right into the employment contract and grounds for being fired.

A handsome white-haired man appeared on the edge of the lanai. He managed to exude elegance even in neatly pressed khaki shorts and a dark green polo shirt. Despite the pair of sandals he wore on his tanned bare feet, Harriet could easily picture him in a boardroom dressed in a custom suit and tie.

"No need to apologize," the man replied, holding out his hand. "I'm Payson Douglas. And you are?" His pale blue eyes were sharp with intelligence.

Harriet reluctantly stepped closer and held out her own hand. He clasped it and gave a brief shake. His grip felt pleasantly firm and dry.

"I'm Harry Monroe," she said. "I work for the resort and am not allowed to bother the guests. I'm so, so sorry I invaded your privacy. I never would have approached the cottage if I'd known it was occupied."

A twinkle appeared in Mr. Douglas's eyes. "It's not

every day an attractive young woman appears from nowhere. I'm not going to complain to the management."

Harriet blushed. "That's very kind of you, Mr. Douglas." She turned and pointed to Albion standing a short distance away on the beach path.

"This is my friend, Albion Aloysius Carter. I just arrived yesterday and Albie was showing me the guest cottages while they were empty," she explained. "But they aren't all empty are they?"

Before Mr. Douglas could say anything she began to back away. "I really didn't mean to bother you, sir. Please enjoy your stay on the island and if you need anything at all don't hesitate to look me up. Harriet Monroe. I'm the resort's PR director."

She turned and quick-stepped back to the beach, not waiting for the guest to answer.

"Let's get out of here, Albie, and leave Mr. Douglas alone," she said under her breath. "I'm so embarrassed."

Albion grinned. "I don't think you need to feel embarrassed, Harry. You were only enjoying the flowers and Mr. Douglas didn't seem bothered." He waved at the guest who was still watching them from the lanai with a bemused expression on his face.

Mr. Douglas lifted his hand in response and disappeared from sight.

"It's time for your meeting with Alex," Albion reminded her. "Would you like to meet me for lunch afterward? We could see some of the attractions after we eat."

"I think I'd better spend the afternoon in my office, Albie, but thank you. I don't officially start work until the day after tomorrow but I want to get my thinking organized."

"Seems there shouldn't be too much for you to do with

the resort already booked for the next six months," Albion remarked as they headed back for the cart.

"You wouldn't think so," Harriet agreed, "but I need to familiarize myself with all of the island as well as the resort's attractions. That will take time. And I'll be photographing the first group of guests for my ads and the articles I'll place in travel and vacation magazines.

"The first guests have already signed release forms agreeing to let the resort use their images in future ad campaigns so I don't want to drop the ball on that or I'll have to recruit another group of visitors."

"It might not hurt to photograph different groups," Albion said as they climbed into the cart and headed toward the security office. "It's been my experience that people like to see themselves in print or on the screen. It could become a "thing"–guests vying to see if they can get their photo published."

"Mmmm. I don't know. Some people can be quite competitive. What if the guests began to harass me to use their pictures? That could become rather unpleasant. No, I think I'll do one big photo shoot a year and maybe discreetly sneak in a few shots at other times, like when we have special packages or events."

She turned to Albion suddenly with a wide grin. "I know! I can create a revolving display of guests' photos in the resort's admission lobby and maybe one of the dining areas. They'll get a kick out of that. And the resort can gift the framed print to the guest when we change the display."

Albie smiled at Harriet's enthusiasm. "You like what you do."

"I love it. I couldn't imagine a better job than enticing people to come enjoy a piece of paradise."

"That sounds like an ad right there."

"Oh! You're right. I need to record that." Harriet dug

through the leather backpack she carried instead of a pocketbook and dug out a small pc. She keyed in the phrase and replaced the pc with a contented sigh.

"You only have tomorrow to tour the attractions if you start work the day after," Albion pointed out. "Why don't I pick you up early, say seven, and I'll take you around. I'll get a picnic lunch from the kitchen so we don't have to come back until we're ready. Tomorrow's my last free day as well. Then I have to get my crew together and prep for the guests."

Harriet touched Albion's arm. "Are you sure? I hate to use up your last free day. You're going to be swamped when the guests arrive."

"I would like nothing better than to escort you around the island tomorrow," Albion assured her. "You're pleasant company and I have nothing else planned. I was only going to sit around my rooms. I would have been bored silly."

"It's a date," Harriet agreed happily. She found that she liked the now friendly Albion's company and would enjoy having him guide her around the island.

Albion pulled up in front of a compact, two-story building tucked behind the kitchens. "Security offices," he said. "Turn to the right after you enter. You'll find Alex in the first office on your left."

Harriet grabbed her backpack and climbed out of the golf cart. "Thanks for everything, Albie. I'll see you tomorrow."

"Early," he reminded her and drove off.

Harriet turned to inspect the security building. Like the other resort offices, it was built of thick, pale stone walls and had a thatched roof. She pulled open the heavy wooden door and stepped into a wide, shallow room.

Blue and green striped upholstered chairs lined the wall on either side of the door. No hard plastic seating for the resort guests, noted Harriet. The pale wood floor gleamed. Green plants were scattered around the lobby and a hot and cold drinks fountain sat in one corner.

The space resembled a hotel lobby more than a police station. Only the best for the resort guests, even the troublemakers.

The door snicked shut behind her, closing out the noise and heat.

A woman, dressed in what Harriet now recognized as the security uniform of khakis and the resort-blue polo, stood behind a waist-high counter facing the door.

Harriet turned right. Before she'd taken two steps toward the set of double doors the woman came out from behind the counter and hurried toward her.

"You can't go in there, Miss. May I help you?" she asked sharply.

Harriet turned and inspected her carefully. Not a human. A droid. The droid's black hair was worn in a cropped short style and her body was muscular. She had a pug nose, a square jaw, and her face had been designed with permanent frown lines etched between her eyebrows, perhaps to give her a more serious look. Her name tag read "Mary."

Harriet smiled to show she wasn't a threat. "Yes, thank you, Mary. I'm Harriet Monroe, PR Director. I have an appointment with Mr. Hayes."

"I need to scan your i.d."

Harriet dug out her resort i.d. card and handed it to the droid. The droid's facial expression blanked while a beam from her left eye performed the scan. "Have a seat. I'll let the director know you're here."

Harriet perched on one of the chairs and waited while the droid spoke quietly into her wrist comm. Alex came through the double doors almost immediately.

"Good, you're on time," he said. "Let's get this done." He turned on his heel and held the door for Harriet.

No "hello, how are you," Harriet noted ruefully. The security director was all business. Fine. She could be very businesslike as well.

She followed Alex for ten short steps, noting that the double doors were not wood as she'd thought, but solid metal painted to resemble wood.

Alex placed his hand on a palm security plate beside another door and keyed in a code. "After you."

"Thank you." Harriet entered the office and looked around the space. Her first thought was how impersonal it was. No artwork hung on the off-white walls or sat on the shelves, no photos of family or girlfriends adorned the desk.

The desk itself was large and glossy black and was half covered with neat stacks of paper and a modern, very expensive communications system. The shelves lining the wall next to the door were filled with forensic manuals and international rules and regulations and law books.

What had she expected? The role of security director had to be high-stress and quite varied in its job description. She imagined Alex Hayes had to be a little bit of everything to do the job properly—from hard-core private eye to personal counselor.

She wondered about his background and decided she'd check up on him later.

"Sit." Alex waved at the pair of black chairs in front of the desk.

No upholstery here, Harriet noticed as she chose one of the hard metal chairs. Apparently Alex didn't want anyone to get too comfortable in his office.

She had to give him credit. Making the seating uncomfortable was a smart strategy for a busy man to discourage visitors from stopping by to chat and taking up his valuable time.

She waited in silence for Alex to start. He had tied his hair back again, she noted, accentuating his strong cheekbones and beautiful mouth.

Nope, not going there again. She'd embarrassed herself in front of the man enough already. She raised her eyes to his own.

"Here's the list of everyone who was on the island yesterday." Alex handed her two sheets of paper. "Please look it over carefully." He sat back in his well-padded swivel chair and waited, watching Harriet closely while she read through the list of names.

"Why isn't Payson Douglas's name on the list?" she asked as she set the papers on the desk. "Did he just get here today?" For some reason she had assumed that Mr. Douglas had been in his cottage a while.

"How do you know Mr. Douglas?" Alex had not expected Harriet to notice the omission of Payson Douglas's name. She shouldn't even know the man was on the island.

"I met him earlier. Just before I came here to see you, in fact. Albie took me to see the cottages at Kidd's Cove and he came out and spoke to us. Why?"

Alex frowned. "Did you recognize any of those names?" he asked.

Harriet pursed her mouth. Apparently Alex Hayes was the only one who got to ask questions since he wouldn't answered any of her's.

"No. Yes," she amended. "Solly's name, obviously. And Lana's and Albie's. And Bradley's, of course."

Before she could ask about Payson Douglas again, Alex leaned back in his seat and steepled his fingers. He gave her a hard stare.

"Well, that's a problem, then, isn't it?" he said eventually.

"What do you mean, 'that's a problem?' Is there a name I should know on there?" She picked the papers up again and took a second look at the names.

Nope. She didn't recognize any of them besides the ones she'd already mentioned.

Harriet set the papers down again. "What's the problem?"

"Well, if you don't know anyone on that list then the only murder suspects I have are you and your pal Solomon Ayers."

CHAPTER 9

Harriet froze with shock. Alex thought she and Solly could be murderers? What? How?

For a few moments her mind went blank, then her temper took over. She stood and pressed her hands on the glossy desk top and leaned closer to Alex, glad for once for her height.

"There is no way that Solly or I killed Bradley Higgins," she said, making sure to enunciate slowly and clearly. "I wasn't even on the island when he died, was I?"

She waited for Alex to answer. "Well, was I?"

"No. You were not on the island. But you could have arranged for your new lover to off your former lover while you were traveling in order to give yourself a solid alibi."

Harriet's mouth fell open. "Lover? Do you mean Solly?" She pointed at Alex's chest. "Are you *insane*? What kind of security director are you?"

Throwing her hands up in the air, she scowled down at Alex. "Do you even have a clue as to how to investigate a murder?"

She turned away, then turned back, placed her fists on her hips, and glared at the man watching her closely.

"Solomon Ayers is not, nor has he ever been, my *lover*. And while he *is* my closest friend, he would never, *never ever*, kill for me. It just isn't in his DNA. Solly is a lover, not a killer. But he is not, I repeat, *not—my* lover. I'm afraid you're going to have to look elsewhere for your murderer."

"Sit down, Ms. Monroe," Alex said mildly.

Harriet ignored him. She was too upset to sit. She stalked around the stark office, fuming. "How could you even think that we would resort to murder—*murder*!—just because I needed to get Bradley out of my life? That's the most . . . the most *ludicrous* thing I've ever heard."

She whirled around and pointed her finger at Alex again. "Ludicrous!"

"Sit down, Ms. Monroe."

But Alex could see that Harriet had worked up a full head of steam and wasn't listening to anything he had to say at the moment. As he had suspected the previous evening, her chin was set stubbornly.

He sighed, crossed his arms over his chest, tilted his chair back, and put his feet up on his desk to watch the rant and wait for her to wind down.

The tirade continued on for several more minutes before she began to sputter and run out of steam. "We are *not* your murderers." Harriet stopped mid-stride. She hurried back to the chairs and took a seat.

"Mr. Hayes," she began, more calmly.

"Alex."

"All right . . . Alex, but you must call me Harriet, not Ms. Monroe."

Alex cocked the eyebrow with the scar. "Not Harry?"

Harriet hesitated, then scowled. "No. You just accused

me of murder. I think Harriet is familiar enough under the circumstances."

"I only said that you and your friend Solomon were my only two suspects at the moment. That's a long way from accusing you of murder. Harriet–"

Harriet leaned forward on the chair seat and held up a hand to stop him. "Don't you see? If Solly and I didn't murder Bradley that means someone else on the island is the murderer. We have to find out who it is before the guests start arriving."

"We?" Alex took his feet off the desk and leaned forward. "There is no "we," Harriet. You leave the detecting to me."

He watched Harriet's jaw firm again. She definitely had a stubborn streak, he thought, amused but also a little worried. The last thing he needed was an amateur sleuth mucking about in his murder case.

"You haven't exactly shown yourself to be much of an investigator up to this point," Harriet pointed out. "I think you need all the help you can get."

All amusement left Alex's face. His eyes turned cold.

"I don't need to show you my credentials, Ms. Monroe. But since you seem to have zero faith in my abilities I will tell you that I left the New York City Law Enforcement Department at the top of my game. I was a senior Homicide Detective with one of the highest solve rates on the force."

And you can take that and stuff it in your bra, Alex added silently.

It irked him that Harriet Monroe thought so little of his abilities. It didn't occur to him to wonder why he should care what she thought of him.

Harriet sat back in the chair. She realized that once again she had let her mouth get away from her and she'd said more than she should have. She took a deep breath and blew it out.

"I apologize. I know Mr. Wade must have checked you out thoroughly or he wouldn't have hired you. I really am sorry. I just–you rattled me when you accused me and Solly of murdering Bradley. No one's ever accused me of anything so heinous before."

She waited.

Alex continued with his hard-eyed stare for several long moments, then he blew out a loud breath as well and rubbed his hand over his head. Some hair pulled loose from his queue and he pulled off the thong he used to tie it back.

Harriet watched, fascinated, as the thick, silky black hair curled slightly around his neck. Her fingers twitched involuntarily with the urge to feel that hair.

"All right," he finally said. "Let's start over. I have a murder to solve in less than two days or we'll have to cancel the first set of guests."

Alarm shot through Harriet. "Oh no, we can't do that. That would be bad for the resort's image."

"I can't have strangers tramping all over the island and destroying possible clues or evidence."

"Okay, fine," Harriet conceded. "I can see your point. That just means that you'll need my help so we don't have to cancel anyone's reservations. Where do we start?"

Alex started to argue, then closed his mouth. As Harriet was his best resource on the murdered man, he might as well use her.

"We start with background. Tell me about Bradley Higgins. Is there anything in his personal or professional life that might drive someone to murder him?"

"Well, I'm your best suspect if Bradley was killed for his

personal life," she said with a rueful laugh. "Bradley became obsessed with me after I moved in with him."

"Where did you live before?"

"Solly and I have shared a place since we were . . . young."

She hesitated, then decided to tell Alex the truth. If he was as good a detective as he claimed he would find out anyway.

"You know we both came from Portland, Maine. We were teenage runaways. I was fifteen and Solly was seventeen when we met on the streets and teamed up. We watched each other's backs, shared what food we could scrounge, protected each other, that sort of thing. Then when we both had jobs we shared a small room. The jobs got better, our apartments got better, we helped each other through schooling."

"I can understand why Solomon is your best friend. You were fortunate. Most runaway females end up living a short, hard life."

Harriet nodded.

"So when did Bradley Higgins come into the picture?"

"I met Bradley at a function I organized for a hotel I worked for at the time. That hotel was my first real PR job. Bradley and I started dating. He was an attorney and had inherited a lovely old Victorian on Portland's Eastern Promenade. I was . . . enchanted that someone like Bradley Higgins–successful attorney from one of Portland's wealthiest families–could seemingly fall in love with a nobody like me."

She shrugged. "He asked and I moved in. And he changed. He became possessive and controlling. I lost contact with the few friends I had. I knew I had to get away but it wasn't until Solly told me about the PR position with the Island Resort that I saw a way to make it happen."

"Did you tell Bradley about your plans to leave and come here?"

"No." Harriet shook her head. "I made a point to conduct all communications with Mr. Wade away from the house so Bradley couldn't overhear. I don't know how he found out."

Alex entered a few notes into his desk pc. "I'll find out. I'll need the names of your co-workers."

Harriet supplied them. "What if Bradley's murder doesn't have anything to do with me? Maybe it was because of something else entirely."

"Very doubtful. But we'll explore all avenues until we find the answers–and the killer. Did you bring your personal pc with you to the resort?"

"Yes. It's in my bag." Harriet rummaged through her bag and came up with the sleek handheld unit.

It had been a one year anniversary gift from Bradley. She'd been touched and so proud of it, an item she could never afford to buy herself.

She handed the pc to Alex. "What do you need it for?"

"I want to look and see if it's been hacked. You say you didn't tell Bradley you were leaving, or about taking the PR position here. So how did he know?"

Harriet's eyes widened, then narrowed with anger. "You think Bradley hacked my pc?"

"That, or he planted a bug in it. I'll look at it this afternoon and return it to you this evening if that's all right with you."

Harriet rubbed at the ache that was starting to throb behind her forehead.

"Sure. Whatever you need. I'd offer to feed you but I

haven't placed a food order yet so the cupboards are still bare."

"I'll bring something. Pizza okay with you?"

Harriet remembered the wood-fired oven she had seen in the resort's large kitchen the previous day.

"I love pizza," she admitted.

"Good. I'll see you out and then get to work on your pc. Where are going now?"

"To my office. I need to organize myself so I can start work day after tomorrow."

Alex walked her to the entry. "Follow the alley between here and the kitchens to the left. You'll come out opposite the office complex."

Harriet followed Alex's directions and found herself at her office building in a few short minutes.

She never noticed Lana watching her from the kitchen's back doorway.

CHAPTER 10

Harriet decided to take a few minutes to re-acquaint herself with her office space and shake off her recent meeting with Alex Hayes. How could he believe that she and Solly had anything to do with Bradley's murder?

She opened the glass doors to let in the warm, fragrant breezes and took off her thick-soled sneakers before settling at her desk. She found it ironic that there had been a time when she couldn't afford to buy a pair of sneakers and was forced to roam Portland's streets barefoot. Now she owned shoes and still preferred to be barefoot when possible.

Firing up her comm unit to check for messages as well as to see what, if anything, the news feeds had to say about Bradley's murder, she mulled over the possible repercussions.

With luck, news of Bradley's death wouldn't have reached beyond the island yet. That wouldn't last long, she knew. The Island Resort was news all by itself. To have an unsolved murder only days before the world's poshest resort was scheduled to open would be a worldwide story.

The fallout from the story could go two ways, she mused as she scanned the headlines.

There would be guests who would be afraid to come to the resort and would cancel their reservations, no matter what assurances the resort manager gave them.

And then there would be the opposites–the ghouls and freaks who would want to come to the resort *because* of the murder.

The second group were not the class of visitor that Island Resort wanted to encourage. They needed to try to prevent the rush of cancellations that Harriet expected to see so there would be no openings for the ghouls to take advantage of.

She stood and went to the hidden chiller and pulled out a bottle of water. Sipping the cold water as she walked in circles around her office, Harriet tried to come up with an ad blitz idea to counteract the news stories.

She was interrupted by a soft tap at the door.

Expecting to find either Solly or Albie on the other side, she padded to the door in her bare feet. Instead, a large woman with a worried face stood in the hall.

"Hi. I'm Cassie," she said. Her voice was the warmest contralto Harriet had ever heard. "Are you Harriet Monroe?"

"Sure am. Come on in." Harriet ushered Cassie into the office and led her to the comfortable seating area. Taking one of the upholstered chairs and tucking her bare feet under her, she waved Cassie into another.

"What can I do for you?" she asked, after Cassie declined her offer of something to drink.

"I'm the resort manager."

"Oh! Of course. You're Cassandra Montgomery. I should have realized. I meant to look you up today. We need to talk."

Harriet inspected the woman who was responsible for most of the day-to-day decisions at the resort. She was an older woman–Harriet guessed her to be around fifty-five or sixty–with intelligent brown eyes set in a round, pretty face covered with a mass of dark brown curls.

A floor-length caftan printed with brightly colored flowers flowed around her ample body and she wore several rings and bracelets on both hands and wrists.

Cassie looked like a woman who knew who she was and was comfortable with it. Harriet liked her immediately.

"I wish we could have met under different circumstances," Cassie said, "but the murder is already causing problems."

Harriet furrowed her eyebrows. "I was just checking the news feed. I didn't see anything about it yet. What kind of problems?"

"Apparently someone on the island called the *World News* and told them about the murder. I just got off the comm with one of their reporters. Their headline should go live immediately."

Harriet sighed. "I was just now thinking about how to counter the story, but I'd hoped to have more time. Do you think people will cancel their reservations?"

Cassie gave a humorless laugh and shook her head. "Oh, yes. Are you kidding? The Nervous Nellies will be calling any minute now. I've already programmed an auto-response into my comm system stating that we are confident the murderer has left the island and there is no danger to our guests."

"Smart. Unfortunately no one has left the island since Bradley was killed, according to Alex."

"Bradley?"

"Bradley Higgins. The dead man. Solomon and I knew

him, although neither of us knew he was on the island. Are you sure I can't get you something to drink?"

Cassie's eyes widened. "You knew the victim? Maybe I'd better take a glass of lemonade after all."

Harriet set down her water and walked to the chiller. She found a fresh pitcher of lemonade and after a few false starts, a cupboard containing glasses. She carried the drink back to Cassie and sat again.

"We need to do something," she said, picking up her water again. "I was thinking about a new ad campaign but people will be focused on the murder and ads won't change that."

"Nope, once this breaks that's all people will be talking about," Cassie agreed. "The timing couldn't be worse. Days before we open? Sheesh. How did you know–Bradley was it?–and what was he doing here?"

"He was my ex. I'm not sure why but it looks like he followed me here. Only he didn't follow me, he arrived before I did. If that makes any sense."

"He was stalking you?"

Harriet thought about Alex's theory that Bradley had somehow bugged her personal pc and frowned. "I hadn't really considered it in those terms but yes, I suppose he was."

"Exes can be bad news. I sympathize. I'm about to have one of my own. Unfortunately he works for the resort too so I can't get very far away from him." She set down her lemonade. "What are we going to do? I'd like to take care of this ourselves before it gets dumped in Mr. Wade's lap."

"I agree. I don't officially start my job until the day after tomorrow. I'd hate to start with this cloud hanging over the resort."

They sat in silence for several more minutes, mulling over the problem and sipping their drinks.

Harriet set her water down and got up to pace around the office.

"What if . . . ," she began.

Cassie raised finely arched eyebrows. "Yes?"

Harriet hurried back to her seat and sat on the edge. "Well, first off the murder needs to be solved in the next day or two and the killer removed from the island. The security director is working on that. But what if we turn the murder into an attraction?" She waited expectantly for Cassie's reaction.

Cassie stopped with the lemonade glass halfway to her mouth and frowned at Harriet.

"I don't understand," she said, lowering the glass to the table. "You want to make the murder . . . an attraction? Isn't that rather macabre? In bad taste?"

"Yes and no. Not if we do it right. A century ago dinner theatre was a popular form of entertainment, and one of the most popular types was what they called Murder Mystery Dinner Theatre."

Harriet grew more excited as the idea began to gel. She stood and began to pace again. "Basically the actors would choose some of the diners to play various roles, including suspects and the actual killer, and the other diners would follow the clues and figure out the killer's identity by the end of the meal."

She saw that Cassie looked doubtful and was shaking her head. She hurried on, eager to overcome the resort manager's quick dismissal of her idea.

"Don't you see, Cassie? If we can solve the murder quickly and quietly we can use it as the set-up for the resort's own murder mystery dinner theatre. People will roll them together in their minds and forget there was an actual murder."

"I don't know, Harriet–"

"Harry, please."

"Right. I don't know, Harry. It seems a little tasteless. What will Bradley Higgins' family think?"

"He doesn't have family so no one will complain. And yes, it might seem somewhat tasteless as you say, but we have to do something. Otherwise there will always be a black cloud hanging over the resort. Whenever the Island Resort is mentioned people will invariably say something like, 'Too bad, didn't they have a murder there?' or, 'Isn't that the place where the guy was found hanging in the greenhouse? I wouldn't want to vacation there.'"

Harriet stopped beside Cassie's chair. "If we try to brush it under the rug it will never go away. It will *never go away*," she repeated with more conviction. "A permanent cloud before we get a chance to really make something of this place. We need to embrace the murder and try to capitalize on it. The Murder Mystery Dinner Theatre could become trendy again and we'll be at the forefront."

"Fine." Cassie shrugged a shoulder. "We'll try it. I don't have any better ideas. I'll need a list of everything we'll need for the dinner theatre, plus a detailed description of how it works so I'll know how the hell to set it up. We'll have to bring Lana in on this. The dining areas are her bailiwick."

Harriet did a mental head slap. She had not thought of Lana. Would she go along with the idea or let her jealousy get in the way? She had a sinking feeling that Lana could prove to be difficult.

Cassie heaved her bulk out of the chair. "Your brain moves in strange ways, Harry. I hope your idea works. Get me that info asap so I can get started on it right away. I assume you'll come up with some type of ad campaign for the dinner theatre?"

"Yes. I'll get you what you need first, then I'll write something up for everywhere we advertise. It will work, I can feel it."

Cassie walked over to the door and opened it. Before she could leave, her wrist comm buzzed.

"Cassie." The resort manager listened for a minute. Her expression turned grim.

She turned back to Harriet. "That was my assistant. News of the murder has hit. Cancellations are already coming in. We'd better pray that Alex finds the murderer soon and your idea works or we'll both be looking for new jobs." She swept out the door.

After closing the door behind the resort manager Harriet sat at her desk to think about the situation.

Losing her dream job was not an option.

She began to compile lists. How complex could it be? She printed out a couple of old reviews on murder mystery theatre and a synopsis of how to conduct one as well as a guesstimate of how many extra staff Lana would require.

She was pleased to see that if the current waitstaff was willing and able, they could pull the dinner theatre off without hiring any more bodies. That would make it easier to convince Lana to give it a try. And if she presented it in the right light the wait staff should be excited to try it.

She shot everything off to Cassie's office before pulling up the latest headlines to see what the news feeds were saying about Bradley's murder. To her horror, her own name was mentioned several times.

As she read the stories it became obvious that someone had leaked the murder to the press, and also that that same someone had not seen the body and had made up "facts" surrounding the murder.

Why would anyone do that?

There was little she could do at the moment, Harriet decided. It didn't help that Bradley was connected to her, that she was the reason he had come to the island and people would naturally assume that she was involved.

A horrible thought struck her. Mr. Wade would also assume that she was involved. He would blame her for the bad publicity and the cancellations. Even the dinner theatre idea might not be enough to save her job.

Feeling shaky and fighting tears, Harriet decided to go back to Mermaid Cottage and take a walk on the beach to clear her head. She found her sneakers and put them back on, then grabbed her pack and locked the office door behind her.

Payson Douglas was parking one of the resort's carts in front of the office building when she exited. He looked sporty yet elegant in lightweight white pants and a blue chambray shirt with the sleeves rolled to his elbows.

"Hi, Mr. Douglas. Can I help you find someone?" Harriet hoped he couldn't hear the tears in her voice. She tried to smile but felt it wobble and gave up the attempt.

"Actually, my dear, I was looking for you. Can I give you a lift somewhere?"

Harriet's already low spirits plummeted. The only reason Mr. Douglas would be looking for her was because he'd seen the news feeds about her connection to Bradley's murder.

"Sure," she answered, resigned. "I was just headed to my cottage and a walk on the beach." She climbed into the passenger seat and pointed the way.

Although she waited in silence for Mr. Douglas to begin questioning her, he chatted instead about the beauty of the island as they headed down the shell road toward Mermaid Cottage.

Harriet felt herself relax just the tiniest bit. Perhaps the resort's early guest hadn't watched or listened to any news feeds yet that day.

Mr. Douglas pulled up beside her cottage and placed a hand on her arm before she could climb out of the cart. "I know you're worried," he said quietly. "Don't be. Alex Hayes will find the murderer and this will soon all blow over."

Hot tears sprang to Harriet's eyes. Whatever she'd been expecting from Payson Douglas, it wasn't this calm understanding and support.

"Thank you." She dashed away the tears with the backs of her hands and wiped them on her pants. "I . . . thank you."

She blew out her breath, sucked in another. "I'm afraid I'm going to lose my job. Mr. Wade is going to blame me for all the trouble–the murder, the cancellations, the bad publicity. And I love it here. I don't want to leave."

She turned to look at the slim, distinguished man beside her. "I really love it here," she said again. "I know I can do a great job for the resort, but now I won't get the chance to show Mr. Wade what I can do. And I feel terrible about everything. The bad publicity. The cancellations. Bradley. I mean, who would kill him and why? It makes no sense."

Mr. Douglas patted her knee. His pale blue eyes were kind. "Don't go borrowing trouble, my mother always used to tell me. Have you heard from Mr. Wade?"

"No. Not yet."

"Then knock that worry off your list. If, and when, you hear from him then you can deal with it. Focus on the things you can do something about in the meanwhile."

Harriet managed a half-smile. "Thanks. Your mother

gives good advice." She climbed out of the cart, took two steps, and turned back to him. "What did you want to see me about?" she asked.

"I think we covered it," Payson Douglas replied, and drove off.

CHAPTER 11

At seven o'clock precisely, Alex stood on Mermaid Cottage's front stoop with two pizza carriers, frowning at the doorbell. He shifted his feet, stepped back, stepped forward, and silently cursed himself.

He had no business being there. Eating pizza with Harriet while he learned more about the victim had seemed like a good idea earlier. Now not so much. And that was because he'd learned something that put her right back in the line-up of potential killers.

But no matter how much he had argued with himself, he'd been unable to bring himself to contact her and cancel dinner.

And here he was, holding two rapidly cooling pizzas. Time to man up.

"You're a fool, Alex," he muttered, then jabbed his finger on the bell. A soft chime sounded inside the cottage and a minute later Harriet opened the door.

He took one look at her face and knew she'd been crying. Her eyes were red and puffy and delicate blue shadows had developed underneath them since he'd seen her earlier. Her honey-colored hair looked windblown and her skin had paled, highlighting the sprinkle of freckles on her nose.

Whatever he'd been expecting, it wasn't the woman standing before him.

"What's wrong?" he asked as he pushed past her and headed for the kitchen. She didn't answer, but he knew she followed him as he set the pizza carriers on the counter.

"What's wrong?" he demanded, turning around to face her.

Harriet just shook her head and pulled a bottle of white wine from the chiller. She poured two glasses without asking and headed him one.

He would rather have had a brew with the pizza but he took the wine without comment.

"I'm not sure I can eat," she said finally, looking down at the pizza carriers.

Alex rubbed his forehead. The sight of Harriet so obviously distressed hit him in the gut and he didn't like that one little bit. He needed to remain remote, unaffected. He needed distance from this woman who happened to be his prime suspect.

"If you don't tell me what's wrong I can't help you." And there was the root of his problem, he realized. He *wanted* to help Harriet Monroe, not nail her for conspiracy to murder.

The pizza could wait.

"Let's go sit on the deck and you can tell me what's troubling you." He grabbed the wineglass from her hand along with his own and headed through the living room and out to the lanai where he set them on a small table cut from a log.

"Sit." Alex took the second chair and pulled it closer to

the one Harriet took. "Now tell me what happened," he ordered.

Harriet shook her head. She had tried to shake the sense of impending doom during her beach walk but it kept returning like the waves on the beach, eroding her confidence until she had convinced herself that she'd failed as PR Director before she'd even begun.

She closed her eyes and lifted her face to the cooler evening breeze. The palm fronds made their now familiar rattle. A night blooming flower perfumed the air.

Memories. She needed to cement these pleasant memories in her mind so she could take them out when she was stuck shivering in Maine's cold and snowy winters.

"Harriet, talk to me." Alex's voice sounded soft and low yet demanding.

"Cassie came to talk to me today after I met with you," Harriet began. She took a sip of wine to loosen the tightness in her throat.

"She warned me that if word of the murder got out people would cancel their reservations. I came up with an idea that I thought might lessen the impact of the murder– I thought we could bring back the murder mystery dinner theatre that was so popular in the late twentieth and early twenty-first centuries.

"I thought that–maybe–people would roll the real murder together with the dinner theatre murders and Bradley's death would fade away from the public's memory."

"I've never heard of dinner theatre. Can you explain it to me?" Alex relaxed a little when he saw some animation come back into Harriet's expression as she described her idea.

"That sounds brilliant," he told her when she had finished. "Are you going to do it?"

Harriet shook her head. "No, I'm afraid not." She didn't tell him that she'd called Lana with the idea and had been shut down flat. Lana had told her that it would be too much extra work for the waitstaff and hung up on her.

"Besides," she continued, "I'm afraid that it's already too late. The fallout began this afternoon. Cassie's assistant called as she was leaving my office to let her know the cancellations are starting to roll in. I'm sure Mr. Wade will be giving me my walking papers soon. After all, if it wasn't for me Bradley wouldn't have been murdered here."

She picked up her wine and took a big gulp. It tasted tart and cold. A second gulp eased a little of the tightness in her chest. She took a third gulp and felt even better. Maybe she should get drunk tonight. Deal with her problems tomorrow.

"So, how did you get on with solving Bradley's murder?" she asked when she realized Alex was watching her. He probably wondered if she was a lush.

"Why don't we talk while we eat? I'm famished." Alex stood and took Harriet's hand. He pulled her to her feet, waited for her to grab her glass, and led her back to the kitchen.

In the soft glow of the under-cabinet lights he could see that some color had returned to Harriet's face. He opened cabinets and drawers until he found plates and utensils and placed them on the counter.

"I brought a veggie pizza with olives, onions, and mushrooms and a meat pizza with ham and pineapple. Which do you want? Or you can have both."

Harriet didn't care for the doctored soy protein that was sold as meat. "Veggie please." She sat at the counter next to Alex, suddenly hungry.

"So tell me, how did Bradley die? Was he . . . was he hung? God, I hope not. I hope it was painless." Not sure she could eat without choking, Harriet set down the slice of pizza she had been about to bite into. "Was he hung?"

"No. He was already dead when he was left in the greenhouse. Someone strangled him."

Harriet frowned. "Strangled? Poor Bradley. Was he hung in the vine to make it look like a suicide then?"

Alex waited to answer until he'd eaten a whole slice of the ham and pineapple. One benefit of taking the position of security director for the resort was that Mr. Wade made real meat available to staff as well as guests.

"They might have. It's hard to say." He grabbed another slice, put it on his plate. "If the killer was trying to make it look like a suicide it was an amateur job. There are distinct finger mark bruises on the victim's neck."

He saw the color wash from Harriet's face again and cursed himself. He was used to dealing with the ugly details of death. Harriet was not.

"There's no sign that he struggled, Harriet, and Bradley Higgins was in good physical condition. I'm guessing he was drugged first and would've been unaware of what was happening, but I'm waiting for the bloodwork results to confirm that theory."

He waited until she picked up her pizza and took a small bite before continuing. "I found a program hidden on your pc that forwarded copies of all your emails, both incoming and outgoing, to another computer. I'm guessing they went to Bradley's and that's how he knew you took the job here."

He saw the shock in her eyes and sympathized. "I'm sorry," he said simply.

Harriet gave her head a shake and looked blindly down at her plate. "It's nothing to do with you so you have no reason to be sorry."

"I'm sorry because I can see that Bradley neither treated

you right nor trusted you. That has to hurt when it's someone you love."

Harriet looked at him then, her silver-blue eyes sad. "He had good reason not to trust me. I was leaving him wasn't I?"

"That still didn't give him the right to audit your correspondence," Alex replied mildly. "Everyone is entitled to their privacy."

He finished the second slice, wiped his fingers, and debated trying the veggie pizza. Nah, he decided, stick with the meat, and grabbed another slice.

"The most likely reason for Bradley to come to the Island Resort was to confront you, Harriet. I can find no connection with anyone else on the island. He arrived the day before you did. I can track him as far as the island's shuttle-port. After that no one claims to have seen him."

The news about Bradley monitoring her emails both angered and saddened Harriet. She wished her ex was still alive so she could fling the pc he'd gifted her in his face and tell him what she thought of him and his invasion of her privacy.

She now saw how lame her attempts to mask her destination had been. If he hadn't been murdered she never would've gotten away from Bradley, she realized with a jolt. He would have stalked her everywhere she went.

She knew his ways. He had come to the island to harass her, to lay a guilt trip on her and make her miserable until she agreed to give up her job and return to Portland with him.

"Bastard." She didn't realize she had spoken aloud until Alex gave her a startled look.

"Me?"

"No. My ex. He was a controlling bastard, and I was a fool not to see it sooner. Solly tried to warn me early on, but I was swept off my feet by Bradley. My first real boyfriend and boy, did I fall for a doozy."

No longer hungry, she pushed the pizza away and finished off her wine. She went to the chiller and refilled her glass.

"Bradley was an only child of only children," she continued. "Both his parents were professionals. Mother was a surgeon and his father a lawyer. Bradley took his father's place when Bradley senior retired. He died less than a year later, left the firm to his son."

Alex listened with half an ear, still stuck on the fact that Bradley Higgins was Harriet's first boyfriend. He found that interesting and wondered why she had waited until almost her mid-twenties to get involved with someone.

"Tell me about Solomon."

"What's to tell? We were both runaways and hooked up on the street. I told you that already. Being part of a couple kept the men away from me."

And why had she needed someone to keep the men away? Alex wondered. The reason had to be lodged in Harriet's past. He'd bet that it had to do with whatever had made her run away in the first place.

Harriet found that the wine had loosened her tongue. She twirled her wine glass on the counter, watching the way the pale gold liquid trapped the light. "Solly likes to have sex with men. You know that, right? He'd be happy to have sex with you if you're interested."

Alex chewed the food in his mouth thoughtfully and swallowed. "What about you?" he asked, his expression suddenly keen.

"Me and Solly? No. We tried it once, but we couldn't get past one kiss."

The memory made her smile. They had been so rational about it at the time. If they went to bed together it would solve a lot of their problems. Only there was no spark there and they became best friends instead.

"No, not you and Solly." Alex waited for Harriet to understand, caring more than he wanted to admit about her reaction to what he was suggesting. The outrageous step that he was suggesting.

"Not me and Solly." Her brow furrowed as she tried to understand his meaning, then suddenly cleared and her eyes widened. "Would I like to have sex with you?"

Her body fairly quivered with the thought and she had trouble getting a full breath. She had never felt so attracted to a man as she did to Alex and wondered if every woman felt this way around him. Fortunately she got a handle on her emotions and realized Alex was just making conversation. Testing her. She could play along with him.

"Are you saying you want *me*?" she asked, pointing to her chest with a finger. "Little ol' me? I don't believe you. Why would you?"

"Yes, I want you." Alex scowled at her, wishing he'd never said anything. He hadn't hooked up with anyone since nearly a year before taking his new position so why start now?

That was easy, he answered himself. Until Harriet came into his life nobody had attracted him in a long, long while.

"Is it so hard to believe that I find you attractive?" he asked her.

Harriet nodded emphatically. "Well, yes, yes it is. Because Solly told me you were a strictly hands off kind of guy and . . . " she hesitated . . . "well, to be honest, men don't usually go for me. I'm too tall–not small and petite and curvy the way men like women to be. And I'm not at all pretty."

"Solomon is wrong. I'm not a 'hands off kind of guy'.

It's more that no one's interested me in a while. Until you showed up. Oh the hell with it."

Alex tossed down the pizza slice he held. He reached Harriet in two steps, grabbed her by the shoulders and pulled her in for a kiss.

Alex's mouth felt soft and tentative at first. As Harriet sagged against him his arms slid around her and pulled her closer and he deepened the kiss.

Harriet felt herself drawn in, wrapped in the safety of Alex's arms, and found herself wanting to press closer still. She leaned into his hard body, wrapped her hands in his hair and gave herself over to the kiss. His hair felt as smooth and silky as she had imagined. A sharp thrill shot through her body, rocking her with its intensity.

When Alex broke away she swayed on her feet, her eyes still closed.

"I have to go," he said, his voice gruff.

Harriet's eyes popped open. She stood for a moment, not understanding what was happening, before disappointment and embarrassment flooded through her.

Once again she hadn't measured up.

Her old insecurities came roaring back. After two years with Bradley she was still inexperienced. Technically a virgin. Her ex hadn't enjoyed having sex with her and had blamed Harriet's lack of expertise, her lack of sex appeal, for his inability to make love to her.

She had tried. She had snuck in and read books on sex, trying to understand what she was doing wrong, but nothing had worked. Bradley remained impotent and she was at fault.

She had been a virgin before Bradley, hadn't even known how to kiss properly. At first her inexperience had been a selling point for him. It was proof that she belonged to him and no one else. He had wanted to possess her, but he hadn't been interested in teaching her how to make love.

She knew that now. At the time she only felt shame that she wasn't enough for the man she loved.

And now Alex had backed off just like Bradley always did. She had been foolish to respond to Alex's kiss–to expose her lack of knowledge to a man she barely knew.

"I'll see you to the door." The cool evenness of her voice surprised Harriet. If she was this good of an actress maybe she could get a job as a waitress in a dinner theatre restaurant after Mr. Wade fired her from the PR position.

"Harriet." Alex cupped her shoulders gently. "I can't do this. That doesn't mean I don't want to. Until I find Bradley's murderer you remain on the suspect list and I can't get involved with you."

Hope blossomed in Harriet's breast. She ruthlessly beat it back. "I thought I was cleared because I wasn't on the island when Bradley was killed."

"You *were* cleared. Until this afternoon when I received word from Bradley's estate attorney. You are his sole heir."

CHAPTER 12

Harriet forgot about seeing Alex to the door. Forgot about Alex breaking off their kiss.

As Alex walked away, she stood rooted to the kitchen floor, stunned. She heard the cottage door close. Somewhere in the back of her brain it registered that he had let himself out. His motorcycle engine revved and took off and still she couldn't move. She stared down blindly at the open pizza boxes on the counter.

Bradley had made her his sole heir? Why on earth would he do that?

"I need to see Solly."

Harriet hastily grabbed the remainder of the pizzas and let herself out the lanai door. The night was clear, the dark sky strung with the lights of countless stars. The small waves beyond the beach sparkled with phosphorescence as they lapped at the sand.

Harriet padded barefoot to Solly's cottage and rapped on his lanai door. The cottage was dark but she knew he had to be in there. She tried the door–unlocked–and slid it open.

"Solly? Are you in here? Wake up, I need to talk to you."

A light came on and Solly came padding naked out of the bedroom, yawning. "Who can sleep with roaring motorcycles coming and going next door?" he complained. "I'll forgive you if you tell me you and the sexy security expert did the nasty and you're here to give me all the juicy details."

He flopped into one of the cushioned chairs and indicated the pizza boxes in Harriet's hands.

"You brought me a late snack?"

"Yes. Pizza. And it's not that late. Why are you in bed so early?"

Solly yawned again, shook his head to clear the cobwebs. "Extra early start to the morning. Worked all day lugging and placing potted plants around the cottages and dining areas. I'm beat. Didn't even have the energy to eat, just face-planted in bed as soon as I got home. I'm hungry now though."

"Go put something on. I can't talk to you when you're .. . dangling like that."

Solly grinned, unabashed. "For you darling, I'll cover my jewels. Be right back. Pour us some wine, will you, luv?"

Harriet grabbed a bottle of white wine from Solly's chiller, two glasses, plates and napkins. He was back in the chair wearing his faded jean shorts and an equally faded tee when she returned.

"So what's up, sugar," he asked as he accepted a glass of wine and a slice of pizza. "Besides Hubba Alex paying you a visit?"

"Bradley left me everything." She blurted it out, took a deep breath, repeated it. "Bradley left me everything."

Solly stopped with the pizza halfway to his mouth. The look of shock on his face was gratifying.

"Come again?"

"In his will. Alex just told me that Bradley left everything to me. His house, art, business, money–everything."

Solly blinked. "Wow. I never saw that one coming."

"Not wow. *Why?*" Harriet demanded. "Why on earth would he leave me his house and money and everything he owned? It makes no sense."

She took a shaky sip of wine and looked around Solly's living room. He'd moved in more plants since she was last there. A vine with deep red flowers climbed a tall piece of bark and two feathery ferns hung from a long chain attached to the high ceiling. Knowing Solly, the place would look and feel like a jungle soon.

"Why would he leave everything to me, Solly?" she asked, looking at her friend again. "He didn't love me, not really. Actually, I don't think he ever loved me. I was just another possession."

Solly set the pizza slice down and focused on his dearest friend. "Think about it, Harry. Your ex didn't *have* anyone else to leave it all to. Bradley Higgins had no family, no friends, no charities. He didn't even have any hobbies. He had only his job and you in his life. He needed an heir–he was a lawyer and paid attention to things like wills–and you were all he had. And I'm sure he didn't plan to die quite so soon."

No wonder Bradley had held so tight to her, Harriet realized. He had no one else. At least she had Solly. Bradley had truly been alone in the world. "You're right, Sol–he didn't have anyone else. That's kind of sad, isn't it?"

Solly shrugged. "I don't know that it's any sadder than you or me, Harry. We have family but we're better off without them in our lives. Everyone has something they have to deal with. That's life." He picked the pizza back up and took a large bite.

"Just so you won't be surprised when the time comes," he said around a mouthful, "I'm leaving everything to you in my will because there's no one else I want to leave my meager possessions to."

Harriet looked at her friend in horror. "I don't want your money, Sol. Give it–give it to some horticulture society, or a community garden. Start a non-profit: Gardens for Kids."

Solly swallowed the pizza. "That's not a bad idea," he said thoughtfully. "In fact, that's a *great* idea."

"I'm full of them. He could have had it all, Solly." Harriet felt bewildered. She took a deep breath and tried to explain her ex to her friend.

"Bradley had looks, intelligence, money. He could even be charming when he wanted to be. That was the Bradley I fell for. He had prestige in his tiny piece of the world. It took me a while–too long a while–to find out that he lacked the ability to empathize, to make friends, to care about anyone except himself."

"You never told me that," Sol said. "Why did you stay with him for so long?"

"I don't know. I wanted to be normal and I thought that meant I had to be in a normal relationship, I guess. Unfortunately I was nothing more than another one of Bradley's possessions. I just didn't see it until it was too late."

Bradley had cared deeply about having possessions. They were how he kept score, how he measured himself against other men, she realized.

He had only appreciated the lovely old house his parents left him for the envy it produced in others. By the mid twenty-first century, Portland had lost the majority of its single family homes to developers–most residents on Portland's famous Munjoy Hill lived in shoulder-to-shoulder apartment buildings or condo towers. The few single homes that remained were priced out of the average Joe's reach.

Bradley hadn't cared about the home's beautiful woodwork or the stained glass windows in the foyer, the polished oak floors or the marble surrounds on the fireplaces, the deep front porch that looked out over the islands of Casco Bay.

No, Bradley only treasured the *having*, the "I have this and you don't." That's what he cared about. That was all he cared about, and he fiercely protected what he had.

Whatever anger and resentment she'd felt towards Bradley leeched from her, leaving only sadness over the wasted potential of her ex's life. He'd had so much to share, but by keeping it to himself he had ended with nothing.

"You're lucky he's dead."

"What?" startled, Harriet nearly dropped her wine. "Why do you say that? Jeezus, Solly, don't ever let Alex hear you say that. He'll think you had something to do with Bradley's murder."

Solly's usually laughing eyes grew hard. "We both know that Bradley would never have let you go, at least not until it was time to replace you with a new trophy."

Although she'd never call herself a "trophy", since Harry agreed. "He bugged the fancy pc he gave me for our one year anniversary."

"What? You're kidding me." Solly's eyes narrowed. "How'd you find out?"

"Alex took it earlier today to look at it. When he dropped it off tonight he told me that Bradley had been monitoring all of my emails–both incoming and outgoing, for the last year."

"That slime. Good riddance."

"He also had a locator planted on it so he always knew where I was. Apparently he never trusted me."

She hadn't wished him dead, but if she were to be brutally honest with herself, now that he was, Harriet felt relieved that she would never have to deal with Bradley Higgins again.

She shook her head in wonder. Bradley had willed everything to her.

As if reading her mind, Solly asked what she intended to do with the inheritance. "The house alone has to be worth several million dollars in value," he noted. "With everything else you're looking at a tidy sum. Enough so you never have to work again."

"I can't keep it. If Bradley had loved me then it would be appropriate, but having all that dumped in my lap by default–it feels like ill-gotten gains." She picked a piece of pineapple off a slice of pizza while she thought about what to do and popped it in her mouth.

"I'm going to sell the house and furnishings and Bradley's art collection and donate everything to Portland's homeless shelters." The idea felt like a good one. "Maybe fund a shelter for battered women and families. Or one for teenaged runaways. We could have used some help early on."

Solly gave her an approving look. "That's a grand idea, Harry. You and I both know there are plenty of people out there who need help."

Remembering the bad publicity the murder had caused, Harriet made a slight adjustment to her idea. "I might hold back a small amount for myself in case I need to start over again."

"Why would you need to start over again? You have a great job here."

While they ate and drank Harriet explained about meeting Cassie and the guest cancellations and Lana shooting down her idea for the murder mystery dinner theatre. She had forgotten what a good listener Solly could be. He didn't step on her words or try to tell her what to do. He simply listened.

When she finished he merely shook his head. "Don't go looking for trouble," was all he said.

They took the last of the wine out to the lanai to finish and were lying back in the deck chairs watching for shooting stars. Solly had turned out the inside lights and Harriet felt comfortably cocooned in the soft, warm darkness.

"So. Tell me about Alex McDreamy."

"There's nothing to tell." She was careful to keep her voice neutral–Solly could always tell when she was being less than honest with him.

"Mmmm. I doubt that. He was at your place for for a while. It doesn't take more than a couple minutes to drop off your pc. And he brought pizza. You love pizza. That sounds like a date to me. Come on, tell Solly all. Did you talk? Did you learn anything about him?"

Yeah, he's a terrific kisser.

Harriet sipped her wine and kept silent.

"Har-ry, do I have to tickle it out of you?"

Harriet's belly clenched. She knew the threat was real. Solly had learned early in their friendship that Harriet was extremely ticklish and would wet her pants if he went too far. Just as he was threatening to do now.

"All right, all right. He kissed me. But then he stopped and said he couldn't kiss me anymore and he left. Oh, Sol, I was so mortified."

Solly screwed up his face. "Mortified? Because he kissed you?"

"No. I'm mortified because he *stopped.* I suck at . . ." she waved a hand in the air . . . "man/woman stuff," she finished lamely. "That's why Bradley and I never . . . you know–actually did *it*."

Oh shit. She couldn't believe she had just shared her darkest secret. She blamed her loose tongue on the emotional evening and the wine and the false safety of the darkness. She could feel Solly's sudden stillness beside her.

"You and Bradley didn't have sex? Why didn't you tell me about this? I thought we could talk about *anything*."

She knew she'd hurt her best friend's feelings. She could hear it in the stiffness of his voice. Solly spoke again before she could try to explain.

"Why did you stay with him? On top of everything else he did? Why, Harry? You could have moved back in with me."

Harriet squirmed in her chair. She hated talking about sex because she was so blasted ignorant on the subject. "I was too ashamed to tell you, Sol. And I didn't want to admit that I was a failure. We tried, but Bradley couldn't . . . you know."

She felt miserable. She still didn't want to admit to her sexual failings but she found that she needed to confide in someone. She drank more wine and soldiered on.

"He said I was so awful at it that I ruined it for him and that's why he couldn't . . . you know."

"Get a stiffy?" Solly said dryly.

At least he didn't sound hurt anymore. Harriet huffed out a breath of air and plowed on.

"Yes. That. I guess I figured I was better off sticking with Bradley than trying and failing with someone else. I couldn't bear the thought of any more humiliation, of another man knowing how awful I am at . . .sex."

"That asshole. I could strangle him myself if he wasn't already dead. Nobody is born knowing all about sex, Harry. It's something you explore with your partner. That jerk was covering up his own pitiful inadequacy by throwing the blame onto you. Asshole," he repeated.

"But I must suck at it because Alex stopped kissing me."

Solly laughed. "Sugar, if Alex stopped kissing you it wasn't because he thought you weren't any good. Trust me. He's the type of man who would get a great deal of enjoyment teaching you the pleasures of the flesh. What did he say when he stopped?"

"He said, 'I can't do this.' Then he told me I'm still a suspect for Bradley's murder. And *then* he dropped the bomb about Bradley's will and left. And here I am."

"Feeling frustrated, no doubt." Solly reached over and patted Harriet's knee. "Poor baby. Is he a good kisser? Do tell."

"Oh, yeah." Harriet recalled the way she had pressed her body to Alex and felt warm again. "I wanted to melt right into him."

She gave Solly a worried look. "Is that normal?"

"It's better than normal, sweetheart. You're a very lucky girl. My guess is that once Alex finds Bradley's killer you'll be seeing him again and doing a lot more than kissing."

Harriet flushed, grateful that Solly couldn't see her face in the dark. Solly was right–she did feel frustrated, and desperately wanted to find out what followed Alex's kisses.

She wanted him to teach her the whole shebang. But first they had to find a killer.

CHAPTER 13

After Alex roared away from Harriet's cottage he drove down to the southern tip of the island until he hit the mangrove swamp and was forced to stop. He shut down the bike and simply straddled it, letting the darkness settle around him.

The stars felt so much closer here than they did in New York City. When he could see them at all in the city they were faint, tiny pricks of light billions of miles away. He knew it was impossible, but here on the island he could almost imagine some of them falling from the sky they seemed to hang so low.

He breathed in the perfume of a night blooming flower. Sometime he'd have to remember to ask Solomon what it was. The resort's head gardener seemed to know every-thing there was to know about plants.

He had behaved like a weak fool at Harriet's–grab-bing her and kissing her like a randy young school boy who couldn't control his hormones. Jeezus. He was thirty-two, not seventeen. She must think him a real buffoon.

Alex scowled and drummed his fingers on the bike's handlebars.

It had been a lousy idea to take pizza to Harriet when he knew he was attracted to her–especially now that she had landed back on top of his suspect list. Still, the terms of Bradley's will had truly shocked her–Alex was sure she'd had no idea that she was sole heir to Bradley Higgins's sizable estate.

"Dammit."

Harriet Monroe was not a killer–he felt it in his gut. She had nothing to do with the murder. The one thing he'd learned to trust during his years as a city murder cop was his gut.

But knowing and proving were two very different things. He still had to clear her and the only way to do that was to find the real killer.

An animal's cry pierced the night and was abruptly cut off. There were predators in the mangrove swamp, stealthy night hunters who kept the wildlife population in check.

Alex could feel sympathy for the prey while accepting that everything had to eat. It was one of Earth's immutable laws. You were either the predator or you were the prey, and even the top predators became prey when they died and their bodies were consumed by microbes. The synergy had always fascinated him.

He reluctantly turned his attention back to his problem. He thought he had left murder behind when he left the NYC force and took up the position as the resort's security director, but apparently murder happened anywhere. Even on the world's most luxurious resort.

He had been desperate for a change when he came to the island. After eight years of processing up to half a dozen bodies a day he had been about to lose touch with his humanity.

No, Alex amended, he *had* lost touch with his humanity. The corpses had ceased to be people for him. They had become just numbers, merely puzzles to solve. He had hoped that the new job would help him care again, that it would help him tear down the invisible barrier he had erected between himself and others so he wouldn't feel their pain.

"Well, your brilliant plan is working, Alex. You certainly care about Harriet Monroe." A small animal scuttled away at the sound of his voice.

Alex thought about kissing Harriet again and this time he smiled at the memory. He hadn't lost his iron self-control in so long he'd forgotten what it was like to be swept up in desire. He definitely wanted to explore that feeling more with Harriet.

All right then, if he wanted to see more of Harriet on a personal level–and he definitely did–then he needed to discover who killed Bradley Higgins. With his expertise it shouldn't be too difficult–there was a limited pool of suspects after all.

Earlier that day he had sent the Worldwide Crime Database a list of everyone on the island when Bradley was killed. The WCD kept records of every person who had ever been arrested over the past seventy-five years no matter how petty the crime. If anyone on the island had brushed against the law he would know about it.

Suddenly anxious to get to the hunt, Alex started the bike and headed back to his office.

The kitchen building was dark when Alex rolled into the narrow lane that ran between it and the security building.

The security office remained open twenty-four seven, made possible because of the droids Alex used to man the front desk.

When the guests arrived the kitchen would also keep a skeleton crew–a mix of droid and human–working during the night in case a guest became hungry and wanted more than his cottage kitchen or hotel suite could provide.

"Everything quiet, Mary?" Alex asked as he entered. He did a quick scan of the room. Nothing out of order. No one sitting and waiting to confess to murder.

One of two identical droids, both named Mary, Mary stood at attention behind the counter, her uniform clean and pressed. "Yes sir. You had one visitor, Miss Lana, at nineteen thirty hours and no phone calls. Miss Lana left when I told her you had gone to question Miss Monroe."

Mary hesitated a moment. "Miss Lana seemed in a bit of a huff but she left immediately, sir."

Alex dismissed Lana's visit. The kitchen head had a habit of stopping by his office at all hours, always for personal reasons. He made a note to program the droids not to give out information about his whereabouts.

"I'm expecting a reply from the WCD," he told Mary, "send it through to my comm as soon as it arrives, please."

"Already done, sir. The information you requested came through at twenty hundred hours and is waiting for you."

"Excellent. Thank you, Mary. I'll be in my office if you need me."

"Yes sir."

Not for the first time, Alex wondered how people had managed without droids. Other than regular maintenance and yearly power boosts, they were almost zero care and were available to work twenty-four seven. The top models could be programmed to perform complicated tasks and even make decisions for a wide variety of situations. And if you didn't examine them closely, they were as close to human as a mechanical being could get. Almost to the point of spooky.

Mr. Wade had offered Alex the choice of humans or droids to man the front desk of the security office. Alex had chosen the droids because they couldn't suffer from fatigue or become overwhelmed if there was a disaster.

He intended to partner his human employees with droids for the remainder of the security force. The droids would back up the humans without question, fear, or failure.

That reminded him, his human personnel would be showing up in the next day or so along with the first guests. He had already set up assigned duties and rotation rosters and instructed the droid half of the teams, but he'd need to help the new arrivals settle in and get started.

One more thing to add to a growing list of tasks.

He keyed himself through the security doors, placed his palm on his office security panel and keyed in his code. His office was as neat as he'd left it. He took a moment to try to see the space as Harriet must have seen it earlier that day, slowly taking in the blank walls, the lack of anything personal. It looked sterile and uninviting.

Scowling, Alex strode to his desk. Police departments weren't supposed to look inviting. They were strictly for work, where over-burdened officers solved crimes, not homey, comfortable rooms where you invited your friends for tea and sandwiches.

Leaning on the desktop's glossy black surface he powered up his comm system and found the WCD report. He settled back in his comfortably cushioned desk chair, put his feet up, and scanned the report.

There had been one hundred fifty-five people on the island at the time of Higgins' death. Alex sighed, tied his hair back, and began to read about each one.

It amazed him how, even with the advances in genetic engineering, crime couldn't be eradicated completely.

Science could eliminate even the worst birth defects in the womb. They had vaccines to prevent every disease known to man and unwanted pregnancy. They bred out undesirable traits; but they couldn't find the genes that turned people into drug addicts, made them steal, beat their spouses and children, or kill for pleasure.

Since the WCD prided itself on being thorough, he knew that a large percentage of the report would be useless. Traffic violations, stealing a candy bar as a kid–those offenders didn't interest him. As he read he crossed their names off the list he had showed to Harriet earlier.

An hour later, he had whittled the suspect list down to eight. Harriet and Solomon were at the top because they had motive and they had found the body.

He had only included the other six because he needed more suspects. None of the six had any previous connection to Bradley Higgins that he could find.

One had done time for jacking autos and assaulting a police officer when he'd been caught pulling a young mother from her car. Another had been charged with domestic violence but released on his own recognizance.

Two had been swept up in a gang bust and did time. Another one was an ex-cop retired involuntarily for using excessive force, and the last person of interest had been a collection agent with unproven accusations that he liked to break the fingers of those who didn't pay fast enough.

Alex took his feet off the desk and sat forward. Six men, none of whom knew Bradley Higgins, but all six had a violent incident in their past. How did they make it past the screening Mr. Wade had ordered on all personnel before hiring them? He would have recommended against hiring the six if he'd been asked to perform the security checks.

Ah well, water over the dam. They were here now and at least they gave him someone to look at besides Harriet and her friend. He made a mental note to keep an eye on the six and keyed in Solomon's name.

Harriet had been telling the truth about Solomon's aversion to violence. Judging from the number of times he'd been admitted to the ER, Solomon had withstood repeated beatings from a father who insisted his son prefer women and "manly" pursuits–not gardening and other fellows.

Solomon had finally run away at the age of seventeen.

Alex tapped his fingers together and thought about the lean, handsome gardener. No, Solomon was not Bradley's killer, he felt sure of it.

He keyed in Harriet Monroe. Caught shoplifting a bra at age sixteen. No known address. That jived with what she'd told him about running away and living on the streets. He felt a twinge of pity for the teenaged girl needing a bra and no money to buy one.

There was a note that Harriet's mother's sister and the sister's husband–Wendolyn and Arthur Wainwright–had taken custody of the young Harriet at the age of eight.

He skimmed the last of the report, wondered briefly why Harriet had run away from her aunt and uncle at the age of fifteen, and then laughed out loud when he read the last line.

"Well hot-diggity," he said to his empty office, grinning. He chuckled again–he couldn't help it. The last little tidbit, a piece of non-important information on Harriet, simply delighted him.

Harriet's parents had named their baby daughter Twinkle. Her aunt and uncle had legally changed her name to Harriet when they adopted her.

"Twinkle Monroe." Alex slapped his desk with his palm and shook his head, smiling. "I love it."

CHAPTER 14

The morning after Alex's visit, Harriet had showered, dressed, and eaten a slice of leftover pizza by the time Albie drove up to her cottage in a rugged all-terrain vehicle. To her relief she had slept well, and despite the bottle of wine she had polished off at Solly's, awakened refreshed and ready to tackle any problems the day might shove her way.

"Good morning, Albie." She smiled at the wiry, dark-skinned man who was rapidly becoming a friend. Albie flashed his bright smile in return and they were off.

"Where would you like to start today, Miss Harry?" he asked as he handed Harriet a go-cup of hot, fragrant coffee.

She sipped the dark, bitter brew and sighed with appreciation. Real coffee. She usually drank chicory root or mint tea because they fit her budget better, with the very occasional coffee splurge. The coffee boosted her spirits even further.

"I want to meet everyone who's on the island."

Albie looked at her out of the corner of his eye, one arm

draped casually on the wheel, the other holding his own go-cup. He looked very native in his usual bright, baggy, knee-length shorts and flat-soled flops on his feet.

"That's a lot of people. You thinking you should look for your boyfriend's murderer, Miss?"

"Bradley Higgins wasn't my boyfriend, Albie." She took another sip of the coffee while she contemplated how much to tell Albie.

"The truth is that Bradley was little more than my jailer," she said finally. The hard truth needed to be faced in the open or it would fester in her. "I was one of his possessions and he wanted me back where he could control me. I'm sure that's why he came to the island. To force me to leave with him."

When Albie said nothing she felt compelled to explain further. "And yes, I want to get a feel for the people here. I may not have loved Bradley anymore, but someone took his life and that person should be brought to justice. Alex told me that no one has left the island since Bradley's arrival so the killer is still here, hiding in plain sight."

"I heard Alex brought you dinner last night."

The change of subject had Harriet turning in surprise. She swallowed a too hot sip of coffee and winced at the pain. "How did you hear that?"

Albie merely raised his eyebrows.

Harriet faced front again with a scowl. "Never mind," she said, disgusted. "Island, right? Everyone here knows everyone else's business. Except me, because I don't know everyone."

"Nooo, I don't think it's general knowledge yet that Alex is keen on you, Miss Harry. I ran into Lana this morning when I was getting the coffee. Apparently she saw Alex leaving your cottage last night. She wanted to know if I knew why he was visiting you. I got the sense she had been looking for him and wasn't happy about where she found him."

Harriet flushed. "It's really none of her business," she muttered. "Alex came by to question me about Bradley. He brought pizza as neither of us had eaten dinner."

And he kissed me, she added silently. The memory of the heat in that kiss and her subsequent embarrassment made her face flush.

"What was Lana doing hanging around outside my cottage last night? She has an apartment over the kitchens, doesn't she?"

"That is correct, Miss Harry. Miss Lana and the head chefs all live over the kitchens."

Harriet pointed a finger at Albie. "Exactly. So why was she spying on me last night?"

"I don't think she was spying on *you*. She has a thing for Alex." They drove past the main complex and headed north.

"If it matters any," Albie continued as he stopped and waited for a large green iguana to cross the road, "Alex has never shown the least interest in any of the women on the island, including Lana, despite the fact that she's been throwing herself at him for the last month–ever since the day he arrived."

He shot a look at Harriet and raised an eyebrow. "If it matters."

Harriet hesitated, then huffed out a half-laugh, shaking her head. "Thanks, Albie. It-it might matter. I don't know yet."

"All right then. You're a nice person, Miss Harry and I believe Mr. Hayes is a stand-up guy."

The iguana disappeared into the bushes and they moved forward again. "We'll work our way up the west side of the island," Albie told her. "You've already seen

Kidd's Cove and met Mr. Douglas. He's the only non-employee on the island at this time."

Grateful for the change in subject, Harriet turned her attention to the beauty of the island. The all-terrain was open to the elements with no roof or windows except for a split windshield. They drove in an easy silence, enjoying the exotic scents carried on the breeze and drinking their coffees. The sea sparkled to their left. Formations of white gulls with black heads graced the sky, and colorful birds flitted through the foliage on their right.

Harriet took several deep breaths and felt lighter than she had in years. Maybe even since she'd been a young child. She had few memories of her life before her parents' death, only the occasional flash of running and playing with other children, or of her mother singing her to sleep. Her mother had been a contralto, she remembered suddenly, with a deep, raspy tone not unlike Harriet's own.

She cherished those brief glimpses of her childhood when they came, because other than the hologram of her parents, they were all she had left of her early life. Life before Aunt Wendy and Uncle Arthur.

Albie took the righthand fork, explaining to Harriet that it would take them to the resort's amusement park. He drove for three-quarters of a mile and pulled into a wide, shallow, sandy space backed with a tall cyclone fence. A sign indicated the space was set aside for guests to park their carts.

"We walk from here." Albie left his go-cup in the vehicle.

Harriet took a last sip and did the same. They followed the fence until they reached the lefthand edge of the parking lot where the wide entry gate stood open. There was no ticket booth as every activity on the resort was included in the package price.

Harriet trailed through the gate behind Albie, her head swiveling left to right and back again as she tried to take it all in at once.

The state of Maine didn't have any large amusement parks. She and Solly had once tried the mini-coaster, Ferris Wheel, and bumper cars at Old Orchard Beach, a tourist town located a short distance south of Portland that boasted a small amusement arcade.

They had saved the money they'd collected from recycling cans and bottles, skipped a few meals to save more, and had hitchhiked to the park, excited to get out of Portland's city proper.

The memories of the smells and giddy excitement of that day came rushing back to her. They had splurged on potato fries drenched in acidic vinegar and salt and drank lemon fizzies and wandered the long beach filled with vacationing tourists. It had been a fun adventure for two poor teens, but they'd never gone back.

The Island Resort's amusement park made that long ago one seem like a toddler's playground. The roller coaster track towered over the entire park, climbing and winding through and around the other rides, its high points so far above Harriet's head that it hurt her neck to look up at them.

"Wow."

"The coaster was especially designed by Aldous. He's supposed to be the world authority on historic parks."

"I can believe it. This is amazing."

"Come on, we'll look for Braxton. He manages the park." Albie led Harriet on a winding path through the rides, with the roller coaster a constant presence over their heads.

They passed a large water slide, with its labyrinth of twisting open and covered tubes and a waterfall that landed in a large pool designed to resemble a tropical lagoon. Water droplets shimmered and sparkled in the sunlight off the waterfall's spray and fractured into miniature rainbows. Tiny lizards and birds, vibrant with color, darted through the lagoon jungle.

To Harriet it looked enchanting and magical. She could imagine how a child might view it.

Instead of bumper cars, the amusement park had a speedway track that circled the park's perimeter. Sleek and colorful cars built to resemble rockets, sat empty at the starting line.

There were gentle rides for toddlers and wild, whirly-rides for older children, rides that whipped a person in circles and one that dropped the brave from a one hundred foot tower.

Harriet's stomach flipped over just looking at them.

"There he is. Braxton! Have a minute? I'd like you to meet someone." Albie took Harriet's hand and led her to the backside of a man working on the guts of a carousal. Brightly painted horses, lions, and giraffes smiled down at her as she waited for the man to extricate himself from the narrow opening.

Braxton pulled himself from the center of the carousel and jumped to the ground. He was one of the largest men Harriet had ever seen.

He stood seven feet tall and weighed at least three hundred fifty pounds by Harriet's guess. His beefy arms were covered with sweat and grease.

He pulled a grease-covered rag from his back pocket and wiped the sweat from his weathered face, leaving several smears of black behind. He had a large, fleshy nose, fleshy lips, the soft mocha-colored skin that told her he was mixed race, and the greenest eyes Harriet had ever seen.

His shaved head glistened with more sweat. The man was obviously not suited for tropical climes.

"Brax, this is my friend, Harriet Monroe. She's also the resort's new PR Director. Harry, this is Braxton Holliday, manager of the new Holliday Amusement Park."

Harriet smiled with pleasure at being called friend, and at Braxton's apt last name, although she didn't mention it. She knew how irritating it could be to be teased about your name. She'd been teased plenty about the old-fashioned Harriet and even more about her chosen nickname, Harry.

"I'm very pleased to meet you, Mr. Holliday," she said, extending her hand. "This looks like a frosty park you have here. Did you design the layout and choose the rides yourself?"

Braxton's smile transformed his whole face into that of a friendly bear. His enormous hands engulfed Harriet's as he took hers in both of his and shook it gently.

"Call me Brax, honey." His voice was a deep, pleasant rumble.

"I tracked down most of the rides from dead parks all over the world—amusement parks used to be a big deal, you know. All but the coaster, of course. That was specially designed for Mr. Wade by a friend of his named Aldous. My crew and me, we just built it according to Aldous's plan."

He looked up at the track overhead and shrugged. "Beats me why anyone would want to subject themselves to that, but it's Mr. Wade's money. He can spend it as he sees fit. Me, I'm just happy to see these things working again."

Harriet indicated the carousel and the inner workings showing through the open door. "This is absolutely beautiful. Are you having trouble with it?"

Braxton looked proudly at the ride. "She is a beauty, isn't she? I found her in pieces, the animals scattered to kingdom come, bought up by antique collectors so people could decorate their fancy houses with 'em. Took me two years to track down enough to fill the platform. I did all the res-to-ration work myself according to old photos I found. She's over three hundred years old and still grand."

He patted the neck of an ornate black horse with a gentle hand, a man obviously happy in his work. Harriet smiled at him and he winked as if reading her thoughts.

"She runs just fine," he assured her. "I just like tinkering on her. You come by when I'm running it for the guests and take a ride."

"I'd like that," Harriet responded, pleased by the invitation.

"So, Brax," broke in Albie, who knew the man could talk for hours about his carousel, "me and Harriet are trying to track down everyone who was on the island a couple days ago. Do you still have a crew here?"

"Did. Had two dozen guys help me set everything up. They were here almost nine months. The last of them left four days ago. The various ride operators showed up yesterday. They'll be here this afternoon to get up to speed. The food stalls will be manned by the kitchen. Why?"

He looked at them closely, his green eyes suddenly sharp with understanding. "You'd be wondering if I know anyone who might've killed that northern boy."

"Bradley Higgins," Harriet said. "His name was Bradley Higgins and I knew him."

"Sorry for your loss, lass, but there weren't nobody here but me and I been working day and night tying up the last loose bits so we'll be ready when the first guests arrive. I certainly didn't kill your friend."

"Oh, I didn't mean to imply that I thought you killed

him," Harriet said, embarrassed. "I just . . . crap. I'm trying to help Alex Hayes find the murderer," she finished lamely.

Braxton raised a sausage-like finger and wagged it in her face. "Take some advice from me and let Alex do his job. You go sticking your nose in where it don't belong and you might not like what happens."

"What do you mean?"

"I mean, you might wind up dead like your friend."

CHAPTER 15

Harriet and Albie rode in silence for several minutes after leaving the amusement park, still headed up the west side of the island. The scenery hadn't changed–there was the sparkling ocean, the birds, the jungle, the sunshine–but Harriet no longer felt like she was in paradise. Braxton Holliday's last words had shaken her.

"Why would Bradley's killer want to kill me?" she asked Albie, breaking the silence.

"Well, miss, I can think of two reasons."

"Two?" Shocked, Harriet twisted in her seat to look at her companion straight on. "You can think of *two* reasons for someone wanting me dead? That's–that's a little frightening."

Albie nodded. "Indeed it is. You need to be very careful, Miss Harry. Perhaps it would be best if I returned you to your office or cottage."

Harriet scowled. "Not until you tell me why someone would want me dead. What are your two reasons?"

Albie held up a slim finger. Not for the first time,

Harriet wondered how such a small, compact man managed to lift guests' heavy bags.

"Number one," he answered, "you are going around the island asking questions about the killer. As you should realize from the fact that I knew about Alex's visit to you last night, word gets around fast. What if you get too close to the killer and he panics? He will feel compelled to kill you to keep himself safe."

"So you agree the killer is a man."

"Yes." Albie gave a curt nod. "There are no women on the island strong enough to lift a grown man into the vines where you found him."

"Exactly!" Harriet slapped her thigh in agreement. "I think it's a man, too. That must eliminate a lot of people." She nodded. "All right, your first reason is valid. Obviously the killer doesn't want to be found. Asking questions could make him nervous. But killing me would only push Alex harder to find Bradley's killer."

"The killer could easily make your death look like an accident."

"How?"

"You haven't been on the island long, only a few short days. Not long enough to learn of the dangers here. The mangrove swamp can be very dangerous, for instance. What if you decided to explore it to take your mind off Bradley's murder? You could disappear inside the swamp and never be seen again. Eaten by a large predator."

Harriet's eyes widened. "There are large predators in the mangrove swamp?"

Albie rolled his eyes at her. "Saltwater crocs, Miss Harry. An adult male can weigh more than two thousand pounds. They're fast too. You'd never know what hit you until it was too late."

"Okay. I won't go exploring the mangrove swamp. How else could someone make my death look like an accident?"

"Well, say you decided to explore the east side of the island and go swimming, run into a riptide. . . "

Harriet made a disgusted sound. "I wouldn't be foolish enough to do either of those things."

"You don't have to be. The killer could knock you on the head and toss you into the sea alive. The tide and wave action would smash your body against the rocks so no one would ever know you were unconscious when you went into the water. Your lungs would be filled with seawater. The coroner will rule death by accidental drowning. Dirty deed done.

"Same thing with the mangrove swamp, only your body probably wouldn't be found there because it would be eaten."

Harriet didn't care for Albie's matter-of-fact tone talking about ways to kill her. And it didn't help that she could easily imagine either of the scenarios he had just described. She shuddered.

"I don't like it, but I can see how it could be done," she admitted. "And I have to say that I find it a little scary that you so easily came up with more than one way to bump me off. So, what's your second reason that the killer would want me dead?"

Albie pulled the all-terrain over to the side of the road and stopped. He turned to face Harriet. "Think about it, Miss Harry," he said gently. "We have no idea *why* your friend was killed. What if you are also a target? What if you are actually the *main* target and Mr. Higgins simply happened to be in the wrong place at the wrong time?"

A shiver ran down Harriet's spine despite the heat and sunshine. "That's—no." She shook her head. "No," she repeated more firmly. "I can't believe that anyone here would have a reason to target me. Why would anybody want to kill *me*? The only person I knew on the island before I came here is my friend Solly and he isn't a killer."

Albie shrugged. "Why would someone want to kill you? Why does anyone kill?"

"Jealousy, or, uh, money." Harriet shook her head. "I'm afraid I don't know much about murder. There must be more reasons than those two. I just don't know them."

Albie pulled back onto the road. "Greed, jealousy, hate, wanting to keep a secret . . . and I suppose there are still those who kill because they enjoy it."

Harriet's mouth dropped open. She snapped it closed. "How do you know so much about murder? Have you seen it before?"

"Yes, miss. There were two murders in two different hotels I worked. This was before the Palace, of course."

"Of course. No one would dare commit murder in the Palace," Harriet agreed dryly.

Albie completely missed the sarcasm. "That's true. The first murder was a jealous husband who caught his wife with another man. The second was committed by a pair of greedy siblings who couldn't wait for their mother to die to inherent her money so they helped her along. Both were solved immediately. They weren't the brightest of criminals."

"Wow. Who did the jealous husband kill?"

"Both the wife and her lover. Used a knife on the man and then choked his wife to death. Made an awful mess of the room. At the trial he said they deserved to die and he'd do it again but be more careful not to get caught next time. He'll be in a cage for the rest of his life."

"You were there?"

"The front desk sent me up to tell the wife she needed to vacate the room. She had only booked it for one day and it was the next day. She didn't answer the door so I used my master to see if she had left and forgotten to check out."

Harriet shuddered. "I can't imagine what a shock that must have been for you. I'm sorry."

Albie looked at her in surprise. "What are you sorry for, Miss Harry? You didn't kill them."

"I'm sorry that you had to witness such a terrible thing. I'll bet those images are still with you."

"That they are. It's been thirty years but I can still see that room as if it was yesterday."

"Was the mother's death as terrible?"

"It was terrible in a different way. The mother was a genuinely nice woman. She stayed with us several times and always had a kind word and a generous tip for those who served her. Her offspring couldn't have been more different. They poisoned her and tried to blame the hotel's kitchen. They were idiots and let their greed blind them. I felt bad about that one for a long time."

Harriet placed a hand on Albie's arm and squeezed gently. "I'm sorry for your loss. Even if the mother wasn't related to you, or a close friend, she was someone who impacted your life."

Albie patted her hand. "Thank you. You have a kind heart, Miss Harry."

"Your job is a lot more interesting than I imagined."

"It can be," Albie agreed. "It can also be dead quiet. Head baggage clerks tend to work in spurts, with downtime in between flurries of activity. I hate doing nothing so I always keep reading material on hand."

He shrugged. "After that first murder I got kind of hooked on them. I read a lot of mysteries and police procedurals, reports on murder trials. It's amazing how many people are driven to kill for the slightest and silliest reasons. That's why I'm afraid Brax was right–you could be next."

Harriet sat back in her seat. "Okay, I get your point. I'll be extra careful until Bradley's killer is found. But I have to try to help Alex. I might come across something important that he wouldn't see as important because he didn't know Bradley.

"So, where are you taking me next?"

"There's no point in checking out the carnival as it doesn't open until next month. You can just see the tent tops from here."

Harriet looked to her right. Through the trees she caught glimpses of bright white and yellow. Long, skinny resort blue banners fluttered in the breeze from the peaks of four tents.

"No one's there?"

Albie shook his head. "A crew came in to erect the tents and left last week. The carnies had another contract they had to fulfill so they can't start for another month. It's unfortunate that everything won't be up and running when the first guests arrive but it might actually work out for the better."

At Harriet's raised eyebrow he went on. "This way we get to concentrate on working out the kinks for everything else. There's always kinks with any new endeavor"–he gave Harriet a hard look–"and they won't be your fault. At the moment we have the guest hotel, cottages, kitchens, dining areas, spa, amusement park, and the marinas to fine tune."

"That seems like a lot."

"It is a lot. The hotel and guest cottages won't be a problem. The hospitality staff is highly experienced and we know what to do. The spas are part of a high-end chain belonging to Mr. Wade so he simply duplicated what works and added a few extra touches. They should run smoothly.

"The kitchens have been gradually building up to speed as more of the droids are brought on line, but head chefs are known for being divas so I suspect Lana will have a few minor glitches to handle."

"I didn't see any droids working when Lana took me through."

"The droids aren't activated until needed. The resort uses specialty droids for dish washers and line cooks–chopping and prepping, that type of thing. But all the hired chefs had to do their own prep work to start with in order to learn the dishes. That's probably who you saw in the kitchen. Lana will have moved the droids into most of those positions by now, although there will still be humans prepping for training purposes."

"I feel overwhelmed just listening to you," Harriet said. "I think the complexity and incredible scope of the resort is just starting to sink in." Afraid that Albie would think she wasn't ready to do her job, she hastened to explain herself.

"I mean, I knew Mr. Wade intended the Island Resort to be the ultimate vacation destination, and I read everything he sent me about what we offer, but . . . seeing in person what's involved in making it all happen is very different from reading about it. Like seeing Mr. Holliday fixing the carousel."

Harriet waved a hand. "Or take the roller coaster. I only saw a photo of the coaster track being built. You can't get the same sense of how awesome the ride is from a photo that you can by standing underneath it."

"That's exactly right, Miss Harry. You need to experience the resort to truly take it in and understand it. And that can't be done in one day. Not even in one visit. That should guarantee repeat visitors."

Albie smiled at her. "Fortunately you don't have to worry about how everything works. Your only responsibility is presenting us to the world in our best finery and coming up with ideas to lure visitors."

Harriet smiled then. "That shouldn't be too difficult. I have a lot of great stuff to work with."

They passed several roads leading down to private coves and more guest cottages. Albie explained that while each cove had identical sets of cottages, the coves themselves had physical differences that set them apart from one another.

Blackbeard's Cove was wide and deep, Black Bart's Cove had a partially submerged shipwreck that was great for snorkelers, Morgan's Cove was ideal for children with its large beach and shallow water.

Without saying anything, Harriet and Albie seemed to have had enough talk about murder. They discussed other things until they reached the island's largest marina.

Set approximately one-third down the island from the northern tip, the marina boasted four main docks. The two smaller docks had several dozen small finger docks jutting off them. Pairs of personal water jets were moored at half the finger docks, their custom painted white-and-resort-blue hulls bobbing gently in the water.

Florescent orange kayaks and sailboards were neatly piled upside down on the remainder of the small finger docks.

"Why are the kayaks and sailboards colored such a bright orange?" asked Harriet. "I thought the resort's equipment would all be the special blue Mr. Wade decided on."

"Not everyone knows how to kayak or sailboard well.

The marina manager told Mr. Wade it would be much easier to locate a lost guest if the equipment was brightly colored. The ski-jets and larger boats all have tracking devices because they're large enough to track individually on the map-screen, but the resort has seventy-five kayaks and fifty sailboards. Imagine if they were all out at the same time? Monitoring all those small boats would be an impossible job."

Harriet shook her head in sympathy. "I can't imagine what that would be like. Let's hope we never lose anybody. Is that the marina manager?"

Albie had pulled into a parking space near the marina office. A large man stood in the open office doorway and was watching them with an unfriendly scowl on his face. He sighed.

"No, that's Big Ed. Ed Whitfield. He used to be married to the resort manager, but they were divorced shortly after coming here to the island."

"Cassie was married to *him?*" Harriet couldn't hide her surprise. She couldn't picture the pleasant, well put-together resort manager coupled with the surly-faced man in the office doorway.

"Isn't that a little uncomfortable for them?" she asked. "Both working here and being divorced? Unless they both wanted the divorce, of course."

Albie grimaced. "From what I hear I'd go with uncomfortable. At least for Cassie. They were still married when they were hired. Rumor has it neither of them wanted to give up their new job. So here they are."

"He doesn't look very friendly."

Albie looked at Big Ed thoughtfully. "No, he doesn't look at all happy to see us. I wonder why that is?"

CHAPTER 16

Harriet looked around the marina before climbing out of the all-terrain under Big Ed's watchful eye. She saw several droids rigging sailboats down at the docks and no one else. Since these droids weren't built for interaction with people their faces were simple, frozen masks. She suspected they would be deactivated while guests were about.

"I don't think Big Ed wants company," she whispered, turning back to Albie. "Should we go?"

Instead of answering, Albie raised a hand and called to the man watching them. "Morning, Ed. I'm showing Miss Harriet around the island. Thought we should check out the marina."

Big Ed grunted a reply that made Harriet feel even less welcome. "I think we should go," she repeated.

"Nonsense."

Harriet followed her companion across the crushed shell lot to the office, aware that the expression on Big Ed's face hadn't changed. If anything, the scowl deepened as they drew closer.

"Ed, this is Harriet Monroe, the resort's PR Director.

Harry, this is Ed Whitfield, the marina's assistant manager."

"How do you do, Mr. Whitfield. I'm pleased to meet you." Harriet held out her hand. The assistant manager hesitated so long she thought he was going to ignore her, but then he grabbed her hand, gave a quick hard shake, and dropped it as if she'd given him an electric jolt.

"Not much to see." His voice sounded like icy, shallow water washing over pebbles—raspy, rough, and unwelcoming. Any exposed skin looked brown and tough like tanned leather, the skin of a man who spent most of his time on the water, unprotected from the sun. His hair and eyes also looked as if the sun had leached all color from them.

Harriet held her smile in place even though she would have preferred to turn around and leave. Big Ed's pale blue eyes stared at her without warmth or even the slightest interest. She took a deep breath and told herself not to let the man intimidate her.

"There's lots to see," she disagreed firmly. "I think the marina looks very inviting. So many different types of watercraft for people to choose from. Do you charter fishing trips from here as well?"

"Yes."

Harriet refused to give up. "Snorkeling and sightseeing too? I think sightseeing would be particularly attractive for families with older, less mobile, members and young children."

"Yes."

Well, that hadn't worked. Harriet looked at Albie, silently begging him for help.

"We must have caught you in the middle of something, Ed," Albie said easily. "Why don't I show Miss Harry the boats myself and let you get back to it."

"Suit yourself." Big Ed stepped back inside the office

and slammed the door, making the bell on it jangle in protest.

Harriet waited until they were well out of earshot before exploding. "That attitude certainly won't fly with the resort guests," she said. "I can't believe how rude he was."

"He was rude, I'll give you that. Beyond being introduced, this is the first I've spoken with him since I arrived. Fortunately the marina manager should be back by tomorrow."

"Where is he?"

"He had to go to the mainland unexpectedly yesterday."

Harriet grabbed Albie's arm. "What? What's the manager's name? Don't you think it's a little suspicious that he just happened to leave the island while Alex is looking for a killer?"

Albie flashed his bright smile. "The manager's name is Leonard Dixon and he had to rush his wife to the mainland hospital because the resort isn't equipped to deliver babies, although I think Mr. Wade might rectify that oversight now."

"Oh."

Deflated, Harriet turned her attention to the boats. She'd always had a soft spot for working waterfronts. As a young runaway in Portland she'd often whiled away her time hanging out on the docks, watching the fishing boats and container ships unload, and the ferries taking tourists out to the Casco Bay islands and sightseeing around Portland's harbor.

There had even been a few times when she managed to sneak through the gate to the yacht club's marina and wander its docks, admiring the luxury boats that belonged to Portland's upper crust.

The resort's much smaller marina didn't have Portland's fishing boats or container ships but it still fascinated Harriet.

The docks Albie led her to were much longer and twice as wide as the kayak and ski-jet docks she'd first seen, but they had the same finger docks jutting off each one. Power and sail boats in a variety of sizes and styles filled each berth.

The sailboats, ranging in size from small sailing dinghies for one or two persons to large overnight cruisers, occupied one entire dock. They rocked gently in the waves, their metal rigging clanging softly.

A seagull called overhead. For a brief moment the gull's cry combined with the softly clanging rigging and the smell of the sea and brought back Portland's waterfront so vividly that a wave of homesickness washed over her.

"Harry? Are you all right?"

Harriet gave herself a mental shake. She knew that the homesickness had nothing to do with wanting to return to Portland. Her life in Portland had left her with mostly bad memories. She'd been fortunate to escape.

She smiled at Albie. "I'm fine. Show me more."

Albie led Harriet down the powerboat dock, stopping to explain the functions of each one as they came to them. Harriet was amazed at the depth of his knowledge.

There were boats for sightseeing, boats for fishing and waterskiing or parasailing, even a few large pontoon boats for partying. Several boats had clear bottoms for the guests to explore the wonders of the coral reefs that surrounded the island without getting wet.

He explained that all of the resort's vehicles ran on small hydrogen reactors so the roar of the outdated fossil fuel engine didn't intrude upon the island's peace and to meet the stringent international pollution laws.

Harriet thought of the one engine she'd heard roaring around the island and felt her heart give a little flutter.

"Alex's motorcycle is pretty loud," she pointed out.

Albie grinned at her. "Alex refused to take the job unless he could bring his antique motorbike. Mr. Wade must have felt he was worth making an exception for. The rest of the resort's boats, scooters, carts, and all-terrains all run silent and emission-free."

Harriet turned to look at the boats, thinking. Small waves slapped at their hulls and against the dock boards under her feet. She smelled briny air and seaweed, saw the green fronds swaying in the water around the dock. Huge starfish and blue mussels clung to the dock's pilings.

Sunlight glinted off the sea beyond the marina. In the distance a thin, pale gray bank of clouds hung low on the horizon. She pointed at the clouds.

"Is that the mainland? Where those clouds are hanging? I read once that sailors of old used to find land by looking for clouds hanging on the horizon."

Albie shielded his eyes and looked where Harriet was pointing. "No. That's a small island. Not much more than a big rock jutting out of the sea with some shrubs and a few coconut palms. There's another smaller rock island between here and there that can only be seen when the tide is low. You'd need binocs to see it from here. The mainland is nearly four thousand kilometers to the northwest."

"Four thousand . . ." Harriet suddenly realized how isolated the resort was from civilization. She had not considered–not *realized*–what that isolation meant. "We're really on our own, aren't we?" she muttered.

Albie smiled. "For the most part. But Alex is in touch with the mainland at all times and Lana orders food from the mainland and everyone else gets their supplies from the mainland, so actually we aren't that isolated. Someone from the island picks up supplies a couple times a week by boat and the air shuttles run four times a day during daylight hours. Plus we have the helicopter for emergencies."

Harriet pursed her lips. "So. . . that means that the killer could have stowed away on one of the supply boats."

"It's possible."

Harriet turned around and headed back up the dock. "I want to talk to Big Ed again."

Albie hurried along behind her but wisely kept his mouth shut. He was learning that when Harriet set her mind to something it was best not to get in her way.

Harriet knocked once on the office door and entered. The office was surprisingly light and airy, with windows on two sides and the walls painted bright white with resort blue trim. A waist high counter jutted halfway into the room from the wall to her right. Shelves filled with items as diverse as fishing tackle, straw hats, sunshades, and umbrellas lined the back wall.

Big Ed sat at one of two blue metal desks set in the rear of the room. He rose and came to stand behind the counter. "Help you?" he asked when Harriet stopped in front of him.

"Yes." She flashed a smile, but Ed's expression didn't change. Definitely an unhappy man, Harriet decided, and felt a pang of sympathy. It couldn't be easy for him, living on the island with his ex, especially if he hadn't wanted a divorce.

"Could you tell me if you were working the day Bradley Higgins arrived on the island?"

"I already told Alex all I know."

"I'm sure you did, but I just thought of something, so, I wonder if you were here the day he arrived?"

"Yeah."

"Great! That's great. Was there also a supply boat here from the mainland when Bradley arrived?"

"No."

Harriet's excitement deflated. "Are you sure? A supply boat didn't show after Bradley arrived? Maybe later that day?"

"No. No boats. If that's all you wanted, I need to get back to work."

"Sure. I'm sorry I interrupted you."

Harriet turned away, then turned back. "Wait. Were any of the marina's boats missing?"

"No."

Harriet left the marina office disappointed. "I was so sure I was on to something," she told Albie as they climbed back into the all-terrain.

"It was a good thought. A supply boat would have made a handy getaway for your friend's killer. Less noticeable than stealing one of the marina's boats."

"Yeah, it would. How far is the air shuttle pad from here?"

"Not far. Mr. Wade had it built just north of the marina so the main resort wouldn't have air traffic flying overhead and disturbing the guests, reminding them of the outside world."

"Can you take me there?"

"Sure."

It wasn't far at all, Harriet saw, when they pulled onto the edge of the shuttle pad. She could see the marina through the trees.

Three blue and white air shuttles with *Island Resort* on their sides sat gleaming on the blue-gray crushed shell pad. Mussel shells for the landing pad, she noted. More utilitarian than the exotic pale pink and white shells used for the resort road and paths.

An attractive one story building squatted to one side of the pad–a waiting area for guests if the shuttles were all in use, Albie explained. The waiting area was open-walled and roofed with palm-leaves, with tables, cushioned chairs and a refreshment bar. Carts were lined up, ready to transport the guests to their cottages or the hotel.

A second long, stone building housed the mechanics area for any needed shuttle repairs. She learned that it also functioned as a hurricane shelter and was roomy enough to accommodate the carts, chairs, and other loose items from the lounge so they wouldn't be swept away. The shuttles had heavy duty tie-downs to keep them from being flipped in the event of high winds.

The weather had been so perfect since Harriet's arrival she couldn't imagine what a tropical storm would be like, but she was happy to learn that the infrequent storms had been taken into consideration during the design process.

She couldn't come up with any scenario that explained how Bradley had ended up dead and hanging in Solly's greenhouse and the killer vanished. Her ex had flown in on an early shuttle and that's the last anyone had seen of Bradley Higgins until she and Solly found him dead.

How had Bradley flown in when guests weren't slated to arrive until the next day?

She aired her frustration to Albie. "I think I want to go back to my cottage," she said. "I've seen enough for today. Thank you for taking me around, but I need a walk on the beach. I want to clear my head and get ready for work tomorrow."

"Does that mean you've given up trying to solve your friend's murder?" Albie asked as he headed toward the south end of the island.

"I guess. I don't have any ideas and no one has jumped

out at me and confessed, so, yeah. I'm afraid I'm done." She only wished that she felt better about giving up.

"It's probably for the best, Miss Harry." Albie reached over and patted her knee. "Hunting killers can be very dangerous work. I'd hate to see anything happen to you before you get a chance to show us all what a great PR Director you'll be."

Harriet looked at Albie's grinning face and felt a little lighter. She smiled back at him. "You are a wise man, Albion Aloysius Carter. If Mr. Wade keeps me on I promise you that I am going to be the very best PR Director this resort will ever have. Just you watch and see."

"I look forward to it, Miss Harry, I look forward to it."

CHAPTER 17

The long walk on the beach and a good night's sleep had helped Harriet's mood a great deal. It was tough to hang onto gloom and doom when you lived in paradise. Waking up to warm, salty ocean breezes and the sound of waves kissing the shore was a great way to start any day.

She dressed in the only summer suit she had brought with her, a pale pink linen skirt suit with a cream-colored silk tank under the jacket. The natural fibers had cost her an exorbitant number of credits but were worth the price. Her philosophy when it came to clothing was to buy the very best she could afford and own fewer pieces. Unfortunately the bulk of her wardrobe was chosen for the damp and cold Maine climate.

She'd have to see if she could make a trip to the mainland on her day off to shop for more office clothes. From what she'd seen, the staff's dress code was business casual, so coming up with a few items she could mix and match with the separate pieces of her linen suit and the silk tank shouldn't be too difficult–and hopefully not too hard on her dwindling finances.

Mr. Wade paid his employees on the first of the month and it was only the seventeenth. She had used a larger portion of her savings to fly to different cities than she had planned on and was dangerously short of credits. All for nothing as it turned out, since Bradley had easily tracked her to the island.

Fortunately room and board was part of her salary or she'd be sleeping on the beach and eating kitchen scraps.

The thought made her shudder. The memories of her early years living hand-to-mouth on Portland's streets were still easily recalled and better left forgotten. She pushed them away, put a smile on her face, and walked into the long, one-story building that housed her office.

A smartly turned out droid manned the high reception desk in the center of the lobby. He hadn't been there the last two days. A new addition in response to the murder?

The droid wore a smile on his handsome face and a white linen suit with a resort blue shirt. The corner of a neatly folded matching blue hankie peeked from his breast pocket.

"How may I direct you today, miss?" Harriet caught the faint trace of an upper class British accent in the droid's smooth voice.

"I'm Harriet Monroe. Today is my first official day of work."

The droid check his comm unit. "Yes. I see you here. Public Relations Director. May I see your i.d. tag, please?"

Harriet handed him her photo i.d. He scanned the tag, his face going blank for the few seconds it took, and checked the results against his internal database. "Do you need directions to your office, Miss Monroe?" he asked, handing back Harriet's tag

Harriet slipped the tag back inside her bag. "Thank you, no. I know the way."

"In that case, enjoy your day, Miss Monroe. If you need anything please dial seven and let me know."

Harrie turned to walk away, then turned back. "You're new, aren't you?" she asked.

"Yes, miss. There are several of us, installed today as an extra layer of protection upon Mr. Hayes' request."

"I see. Do you have a name?"

"You may call us Jeeves, miss."

"Jeeves?"

The droid's face remained impassive. "I believe it is a joke, miss. You would have to ask Mr. Hayes."

"I'll do that," Harriet mumbled as she headed for her office. Her heels clicked smartly on the wide hall's creamy white tiled floor. Wide-bladed fans already twirled lazily overhead. Tall, narrow windows spaced evenly along the left hand wall looked out on the crushed shell road and the kitchen building situated opposite.

Frescos of island life covered the righthand walls. Albie had told her that the frescos were painted by a renowned island artist. Harriet thought they were quite good. She recognized the mangrove swamp with its flock of brilliant flamingos and the three mountains in the island's center.

The door to her office was neatly camouflaged at the base of the center mountain, the security panel hidden in a slim waterfall.

She placed her palm on the security reader and keyed in her personal code. The door slid silently open and Harriet entered her office with a mixture of thrill and determination. Damage control had to be done before the fallout from Bradley's murder caused too many cancellations and it was up to her to see to it.

The first thing she did was kick off her heels and open the doors to the lanai to let in the sea breezes, taking a moment to enjoy the view. The white beach, empty but for a trio of black-headed gulls, stretched in both directions. By later that afternoon the island would no longer feel like a private paradise, she realized. There would be guests on the water and the beach.

She walked to the wall of shelves and picked up the holo of her mother and father and wished them peace and happiness, a daily habit she had started as a child–her way of trying to maintain contact with her dead parents.

Setting it back, she decided it was time to get a still made from the holo so she could have her parents with her in her cottage as well as in the office. She could see to it when she went to the mainland to shop for clothing.

The holo was all she had left of them. She had never thought to ask her Aunt Wendy why there were no other mementos of her mother and father and her aunt had never offered any.

She recalled shedding a lot of tears when she first went to live with her aunt and uncle and begging them to let her see her parents.

She couldn't remember anything about her parents from before that time, other than brief, chaotic flashes of memory. One day her aunt had shown up with a man and a woman, both dressed in matching uniforms, to take Harriet away. There had been an accident, her aunt said, and Harriet had to go with them.

Her aunt had told her that her parents were dead, that there could be no going back, and Harriet's life was with them now. An accident, was all she would answer when Harriet pressed for more information.

She suddenly had a vague memory of sitting in her father's lap with the others in a large, happy circle. Somehow she knew it was a happy moment. Because they were singing? Harriet remembered pressing her ear against her father's chest to feel his deep voice rumble there. They must have had a lot of friends because there were always other adults around and lots of children to play with.

She tried to push for more of the memory but a sharp pain stabbed through her head. Damn migraines. She'd started getting them after going to live with her aunt and uncle. Fortunately the type she was afflicted with never lasted long.

The sharp pain morphed to a dull throb that beat low inside the back of Harriet's skull. She rubbed the back of her neck and forced her mind to concentrate on more important, more *current* matters.

She still thought the murder-themed dinner theatre idea was a good one. She simply needed to find a way to convince Lana to give it a shot.

Harriet settled at her desk and engaged her comm station. She went to work collecting testimonials and researching data on the old dinner theatre tradition. Several hours passed. She was glad for the interruption when Solly came in with a large, colorful bouquet of flowers for her office.

"I didn't see you yesterday or last night," he said, kissing her cheek. "Are you all right?" He carried the flowers to the conversation area and set it in the center of the table.

"The flowers are beautiful, Solly. Thank you. And yes, I'm fine. Albie took me on a tour of the resort yesterday. I was pretty beat by the time I got home so I crashed early."

"Yeah? What'd you see?"

"He took me to the amusement park, which is pretty incredible. The antique carousel is amazing." She pointed a finger at him. "And don't even dare to think you'll ever get me on that coaster."

Solly flashed a grin, showing that he remembered their trip to the amusement park all those years ago. "Are you daring me to try? I got you on the mini-coaster, didn't I?"

Solly could be relentless if he thought she had issued a dare. Since Harriet had no intention of ever riding the resort's roller coaster she ignored him and changed the subject. "I met Braxton Holliday. He's like a big human bear."

"Brax is a good guy. A little scary to look at maybe, but he knows his ride attractions inside and out. You can bet there will never be an accident while he's managing the park." Solly walked over to Harriet's chiller and pulled two waters.

"Where else did you go?" he asked, handing her one.

Harriet cracked open the water and leaned back against her desk. "We went to the marina. A crew of droids was rigging the sailboats. Reminded me of Portland Harbor. Remember all the times we'd roam around the docks looking for food or just watching the fishing boats?"

"I do, although it's a mixed bag of memories. We were desperately hungry more often than I care to remember during that time." He took a thoughtful sip of his water. "Is Dix back with his wife and new baby yet? I need to take Dorinda some flowers."

Harriet made a face. "If you mean Leonard Dixon, no. At least he wasn't back yesterday. I met his assistant manager though. Big Ed. He was not at all friendly. Not at all."

"Ed is not a happy man. His divorce is about to go through, as soon as Cassie signs the final settlement papers."

"Albie thought they were already divorced."

Solly shook his head. "Nope. Ed's been stalling, but I don't think he has any more moves left." He shrugged. "I feel a little sorry for him. For both of them, actually. But it isn't any of my business."

He fed his empty water tube into the recycler and gave Harriet a quick hug. "Gotta run. Want to come over for dinner tonight?"

"Sure. I'll bring the wine. It seems to be the only thing the Mermaid is stocked with."

After Solly left, Harriet had barely settled behind her desk again when she heard another sharp rap on her door. "It's open," she called out.

Lana stepped into the office carrying a small pitcher of lemonade. "I thought you might like some refreshment on your first official day."

"That's very thoughtful of you," Harriet replied, puzzled. Was Lana a Jekyll/Hyde type of character? Sweet kitchen manager one day, jealous bitch the next? She decided to take advantage of Lana's seemingly friendly mood.

"I've looked further into the dinner theatre thing and I really think it could work for us, Lana. It was hugely popular in the late nineteen hundreds and some of the better restaurants even charged customers extra to participate.

"Now I realize we couldn't charge extra," she added quickly, holding up her hand to stop Lana from interrupting. "I know the resort fee is all-inclusive, but maybe we could have a nightly drawing to see which guests get to play a part. Anyone interested could put their names in a hat."

She took the pitcher from Lana's hands and set it in the chiller. "And maybe we could offer some sort of prize," she added, thinking aloud. "Maybe have the other guests vote for their favorites. Or something like that. I think it could get to be a big deal, with bragging rights, you know?

Guests would boast to their friends back home that they got to play the part of the murderer."

"I'll consider it."

"You will?" Harriet couldn't quite disguise her surprise. "That's great. I'll print out a hard copy of my research for you to look at and bring it over later so we can figure out how to set it up." Her smile turned to a frown when she saw that Lana looked upset.

"What's wrong? Is there something I can do to help?"

"I don't know if I should tell you this," Lana began, "but Alex came to see me yesterday. He was . . . upset. He said that you threw yourself at him the other night and embarrassed him. He wants you to keep away from him but he doesn't want to hurt your feelings because you're new here."

She reached a hand toward Harriet, a beseeching look on her face. "I just thought you should know before you embarrass yourself any further." She gave Harriet a serious look. "So, now you know. I'm sure you can understand that you need to give Alex a break. He's too polite to say anything and it's important to keep the peace among us co-workers."

Lana turned and stepped to the door and then turned back with a bright smile. "Well. I guess I'd better get back to the kitchens. We have guests arriving any minute and I'm sure some will be hungry."

She hurried out of Harriet's office. The door quietly slid shut behind her.

Harriet stood gobsmacked in the middle of her office, looking at the closed door. *Alex* was embarrassed? He was the one who initiated the kiss! How–how . . . infuriating. And how embarrassing that he had told Lana about it.

She fisted her hands and whirled around. Whirled back. Why hadn't Alex spoken to her directly instead of going to

Lana? The *coward*. See if she agreed to have pizza with him again.

She ignored the dull pain in her heart and threw herself into pulling together the dinner theatre information for Lana.

CHAPTER 18

Harriet kept her nose to the grindstone after Lana left, forcing herself to concentrate on her work so she wouldn't think about Lana's visit. She snacked on fruit and skipped lunch because she didn't want to risk running into Alex in the employee dining room. Her work kept her focused, but she could still feel her anger and shame simmering beneath the surface.

Cassie interrupted Harriet mid-afternoon to fill her in on the latest resort news. While half the early reservations had been cancelled, plenty of people had stepped up to take their place. Apparently murder was a big draw.

Harriet wasn't surprised and was pleased by the crop of new reservations, but found she felt a little disgusted by the murder ghouls. Cassie, however, was pleased as could be and hyped that they hadn't lost any business so Harriet kept her feelings to herself. The fact that Bradley's murder was a definite draw only solidified her determination to make the murder mystery dinner theatre happen.

She tried to think of a subtle way to bring Cassie's husband Ed into the conversation, but she couldn't come up with a polite way to say,"Hey, I hear you're getting a divorce. Good move, your husband is a jerk."

Bottom line, it wasn't right to ruin Cassie's good mood with a topic that had to be unpleasant for the resort manager. Besides, what business was it of Harriet's? And what did it matter?

Big Ed was a jerk, sure, but that didn't make him a killer. He had no reason to kill Bradley, unless he had snapped and killed to release some of his frustration over the impending divorce.

Harriet mulled that angle over for several minutes before discarding it as too far-fetched. She wondered how Alex was getting along with his list of employees and immediately shut down that train of thought.

As long as Alex didn't try to pin Bradley's murder on either Solly or herself she no longer cared what he did. She intended to stay as far away from Alex Hayes as possible. He would never again be able to complain that she was throwing herself at him. She still couldn't believe he had complained to Lana of all people.

At last Harriet felt she had done all she could for the day and shut down her comm system. She slipped on her heels, then changed her mind and pulled her trainers from her bag and put them on instead. The work day was long over and she had no meetings and no one to impress. She might as well walk back to Mermaid Cottage in comfort.

The late day sun cast warm, golden shafts of light on the water as Harriet made her way back to her cottage. The narrow shell service road was empty but for her, although in the distance she saw a couple of solitary guests walking the beach down near the low tide mark. They reminded her that the resort was officially open for business, making it much more difficult for Alex to find Bradley's killer.

Maybe they'd never find the killer. Harriet frowned

while she considered that possibility. Other than the fact that Bradley had left her everything, there was no clear motive for his death. And she knew she hadn't killed him. And there was no way that Solly knew about Bradley's will so Solly hadn't killed him.

What other motive could there be?

She mulled over the problem until she reached Mermaid and keyed in the front door code. "Honey, I'm home!" she called out to the empty cottage, a habit she and Solly had developed over the years of living together. The memory made her grin as she headed to the bedroom to change from her office attire to clothes suitable for relaxing.

It took Harriet a a full minute to take in the destruction in her bedroom. Her clothes–her two spare work suits, her sweatpants, tops, everything she'd brought with her–lay in tatters and strewn around the room.

Not quite believing her eyes she picked up a pair of capris. The legs had been slashed to narrow ribbons, a large hole cut out of the rear. She laid them on the bed with trembling hands and looked at the complete devastation of everything she owned.

"Oh no." Harriet ran from the bedroom to the living room and stopped in front of the table where she had lovingly set out her prized wooden hippo collection only the night before. They lay in a massacred jumble of legs, heads, and bodies.

She pressed her fingers to her eyes to stop the hot tears that threatened to fall.

Why? Who? How?

She walked back into the bedroom and checked the lanai doors. Locked. The front door had been locked because she'd used her code to get in. She moved to the bathroom. The lanai door behind the slipper tub stood open. She knew she had closed it after her shower that morning, but had she remembered to lock it?

Harriet sunk to the edge of the tub, her knees suddenly too weak to support her. She felt dizzy, whether from lack of food or because of the viciousness of the attack on her belongings, she didn't know.

Her pocket link chimed and she answered it without thinking.

"I thought you were coming to dinner. Did you get hung up at work?" Solly sounded his usual chipper self.

Harriet tried to answer but discovered that her throat had closed tight with tears and she couldn't speak.

"Harry? What's wrong?"

"Solly."

'I'll be right there."

Harriet dropped her link back in her pocket. Solly was coming. He'd know what to do.

In less than a minute he found her sitting on the tub. He sat beside her and put his arm around her shoulders. "What's wrong, sweetheart? Did something happen at the office to upset you?"

Harriet shook her head. "The bedroom."

With a puzzled look, Solly stood and went into the bedroom. She heard him cursing moments later. He came back into the bathroom, his eyes glittering with anger, his link already in his hand.

"I'm calling Alex," he said. "This isn't just a prank. This is serious." His eyes never left Harriet's face as he placed the call.

"Alex? We need you at Harry's right away. No, just come. You'll see when you get here." He put his link away.

Taking both of Harriet's hands he pulled her to her feet

and supported her with an arm around her waist. She leaned on him, still too shaky to stand on her own. She felt foolish, acting like a weepy, weak girl, but that's exactly how she felt.

"Come to the kitchen. Let's get you a glass of wine."

"I don't need wine."

"Well I do. Alex should be here in a few minutes."

Harriet averted her eyes from the mutilated hippos as they passed through the living room. Once in the kitchen, Solly helped her onto a stool and rummaged in the chiller for the wine. He poured two glasses and set one in front of her.

She'd taken only a small sip when Alex's motorbike roared up, followed by the pounding of his fist on the door. "Harriet? Solly? Dammit, open the door."

Before either of them could move Alex came striding into the kitchen. "What's wrong?" He took in Harriet's wide, glassy eyes and her pale face and cursed. "What happened?"

"Check the bedroom," Solly answered. "Then you tell me."

After Alex left the kitchen to inspect the damage, Harriet made an effort to pull herself together. She would not appear weak in front of him. She reminded herself of Lana's visit earlier that day and forced herself to feel angry again. The anger felt better than feeling violated and help-less so she fed it. By the time Alex returned to the kitchen she was furious with him.

"When did this happen?" he asked, looking grim.

"While I was at work."

Alex was pleased to note that the glazed look was gone from Harriet's eyes although he didn't care for her clipped tone. "Do you know how they got in?"

"The bathroom lanai door was open. I may have forgotten to lock it after I showered this morning."

An image of Harriet in the shower stopped Alex's thoughts. She showered with the lanai door open? The picture that made in his mind unsettled him. He made a conscious effort to force his thoughts back to the problem at hand and frowned at her.

"Are you up to inspecting the bedroom with me? Did they destroy everything?"

Harriet stood stiffly. "It looked like everything. I didn't bring much with me." She looked down at the linen suit she still wore, wrinkled and tired looking now, then looked at Solly. "Can I borrow some stuff until I can get new clothes?" she asked.

Replacing her wardrobe was going to wipe out every last credit she had. She suddenly felt the tears pressing against the back of her eyeballs again and willed them away.

"Of course you may," Solly answered. "Anything you need, you know that. Let's help Alex get through this first and then we'll head next door. You'll stay with me tonight."

Harriet gave her friend a grateful smile, then turned to Alex. "Let's get this over with," she said stiffly.

She led the way to the bedroom and stopped just inside the door, suddenly unwilling to go further. Solly pushed past Alex and took her hand. "Had you unpacked all your clothes?" he asked gently.

"Yes." She opened the closet door. Every hanger was bare, the clothes in a heap on the closet floor. She picked up several short sleeve tops. The ribboned fabric fluttered in her hand.

Harriet dropped to her knees and dug through the clothing for her shoes. She picked up her remaining two pair of dress shoes. All four heels had been hacked off.

"Guess it's a good thing I had to go to work today. At least I have one outfit left," she said with a sigh. She got to her feet and turned around to find both Alex and Solly staring at her bed.

"What? What is it?" She stepped to the bed and looked down, expecting to find more destroyed clothing, or maybe a bottle of catsup emptied on her sheets. Instead she saw a piece of paper pinned to the center of the mattress with a long, slim-bladed knife.

"Oh." Harriet swallowed. "What does it say?"

Alex pulled on a pair of thin gloves and plucked the knife and paper from the mattress after snapping a photo with his link.

"It says, 'Leave the island or you'll be next,'" he read grimly. He turned to Solly. "You didn't see anyone around here today?"

"I wasn't here. I left for the greenhouse early–before sunrise–to get a jump on the flowers for the guest cottages." He gripped Alex's arm. "Do you think whoever killed Bradley Higgins is after Harry now?"

"It looks that way. I have a small lab attached to my office. I'll check for prints on the knife and see if anything pops." He turned to Harriet. "I want someone with you at all times until I nail whoever did this."

Harriet's spine stiffened. "You don't have to worry about me. I can take care of myself. And you certainly don't have to worry about me throwing myself at you. Trust me, I want nothing more to do with you."

Instantly she wished she could call the words back. Even if they were true she hadn't meant to speak them aloud, but her fear, anger, and embarrassment were creating a toxic stew in her brain and the words had popped out.

Alex furrowed his brow. "Throwing yourself at me? What? What are you talking about?"

"When you kissed me. In the future, if you have something to say to me say it to my face. Don't hide behind your pal Lana. It just pisses me off."

Harriet turned and stalked out of the bedroom and out of Mermaid Cottage.

CHAPTER 19

Harriet slammed out of her cottage. She was shaken by the destruction, fuming with anger at Alex, and embarrassed by her outburst. Instead of coming off as a cool-headed woman who could take care of herself, she had acted like an over-wrought teen-aged fool. Idiot.

She headed next door to Solly's and waited for him on his lanai, staring at the dark water with unseeing eyes. A billion stars glittered overhead but she barely noticed them.

Stupid. Why couldn't she remember to engage her brain before she spoke? She'd never be able to look Alex in the eyes again. She should have treated him with a cool distance, shown him that what he told Lana didn't matter to her.

To make it worse, she now had a witness to her humiliation. At least it was only Solly. He might tease her but he wouldn't gossip about her with others.

She shivered and wrapped her arms around herself. The air was still warm but the adrenalin from the shock of what had been done to her things was wearing off and leaving her shaky. She sank into a cushioned lounger and wished Solly would hurry up. She wanted to get out of her work suit and into something warm and comfortable.

Several more minutes passed before she heard the roar of Alex's motorbike taking off and Solly calling her name.

"Out here," she answered.

Solly appeared in the lanai door. "Be right back." He disappeared and reappeared with two glasses of wine and a blanket. He handed Harriet a wineglass and dropped the blanket over her bare legs.

Grateful for the warmth, she worked the blanket around her body with her free hand. "I'm an idiot," she moaned before he could say anything.

Solly dropped into a nearby lounger. "More than I realized. First I find out you've been living with an impotent man you didn't even love–something I'll never understand–and tonight you reamed Alex for . . . I don't know what for. What the devil was all that about?"

Harriet took a large gulp of the wine. Her shivers were subsiding. She loosened her hold on the blanket and began to pluck at it nervously, too embarrassed to look at Solly.

"I–. Well." She huffed out a big breath. "Remember I told you that Alex kissed me the other night and I, um, I responded?"

Solly arched his eyebrow at her. She hated when he did that. It meant he was going to put her in her place and she usually deserved it.

"Of course I remember. Grow up, Harry. If you jump down a guy's throat like that for kissing you it's no wonder you've only had one boyfriend. What gives?"

"I didn't jump down his throat for the kiss. I jumped down his throat for what he did after the kiss."

Solly leaned forward. "There was more? Do tell. Since

I'll never get a shot at Mr. McDreamy I'll have to be satisfied with secondhand details."

Harriet scowled at her friend. "Stop calling him that. He's not that dreamy, believe me. Lana came to my office today. She told me that Alex felt uncomfortable because I'd thrown myself at him and he didn't know how to tell me that he didn't like it."

The tears were threatening again. Harriet pressed her palm against each eye and sniffed. What a lousy day. She wanted nothing more than to ball up in her favorite sweats and have a good cry. Only she couldn't because her favorite sweats were nothing more than tatters. With a big hole in the ass.

"You believed Lana? Knowing that she's been chasing Alex ever since he arrived? Really, Harry, I thought you were smarter than that. She was just trying to manipulate you so you'd stay away from Alex. And apparently she succeeded." Solly sounded disgusted.

"At first I thought that too, but–how did she know about the kiss, Solly? She couldn't have known unless someone told her. So Alex *must* have told her because I only told you about it and you wouldn't say anything to anyone else, right?"

"Don't be ridiculous, of course I wouldn't tell anyone else." Solly frowned. "It's hard to believe that Alex would confide in Lana though. I had him pegged as more of a "go straight at 'em" type of guy. If he didn't like something he'd deal with it directly."

Harriet slumped back in the lounger. "I know, right? That's what I thought. Imagine my surprise and embarrassment when Lana came to me today and told me I shouldn't throw myself at him anymore because he didn't like it. Then I come home to my cottage and find everything I own destroyed. Oh, Solly, my hippos."

This time she couldn't stop the tears.

Solly set down his wine and joined her on the lounger. Turning her toward him, he gathered her in his arms and held her while she cried. "Shhhh, honey, we'll get to the bottom of this. We'll get you a new wardrobe and start a new hippo family, I promise."

It took several minutes for Harriet to pull herself together. She rubbed her face on Solly's tee shirt and pulled back. "Sorry. I couldn't hold it in."

"No need to apologize. What're a few tears between best friends?" He pulled his shirt away from his chest. "Well, maybe more than a few–my shirt is soaked." As he hoped, that elicited a choked laugh. "I think I'll change and finish making dinner. You need to eat, and while we eat we'll discuss what to do."

Harriet sniffed and gave Solly a watery smile. "Thanks. What would I do without you?"

"You'd manage. You're stronger than you give yourself credit for, Harry. I'll be in the kitchen. Come in when you're ready. I'll pull out something comfy for you to wear."

Back at the security office, Alex acknowledged Mary with a curt nod. The droid saluted and stood at attention, eyes focused straight ahead.

"At ease, Mary. I have some work to attend to."

"Yes, sir." She reclaimed her stool, prepared to wait all night for any guests who might request help. In the morning an identical Mary would take her place while she remained in standby mode.

Alex thought whoever had named all of the security droids Mary should be fired. As soon as he had the time he intended to reprogram them to be a little less formal in manner and rename them.

He keyed in the code for the wood-simulated double metal doors that protected his office, lab, and the interrogation room. It took him three angry strides to reach his office door, but it took him two tries to key in his security code and open the door.

This wouldn't do, he told himself as he called for his office lights. He had a killer loose on the island. He needed a cool, emotionless head to find him. He couldn't let his attraction for Harriet get in the way of doing his job.

He stood in the center of his office with the bagged knife and note in hand and forced himself to take several deep breaths.

He liked Harriet. Liked her a lot if he was honest with himself–and Alex prided himself on always being honest with himself. There was the potential for more with Harriet–he felt strongly attracted to her. Unfortunately his feelings were muddling his thinking.

He looked down at the knife, still stabbed through the note, and felt sick. At least he could eliminate Harriet from his list of suspects. She'd been at the office all day, and unless she'd destroyed her place before she left for work– no. He'd seen the glassy look of shock in her eyes. Harriet had not destroyed her own things.

Alex stepped over to a door set in the righthand wall and placed his palm against a hidden plate. The lab door was difficult to see if you didn't know it was there, its flat surface painted the same off-white as the rest of the office. Unless a person put their nose right up to the wall they'd never see the thin lines that showed the door's shape.

The palm plate lit a soft orange glow and requested his code. He recited it slowly and the orange glow flashed green. A moment later the door slid silently open. Alex stepped inside and the door slid closed behind him.

The lab was small, with only room for one person to sit at the work station, but it was well lit and well equipped. Alex slid onto the single round, wheeled stool and lay the bagged knife on the workbench.

He pulled on gloves and went to work. It only took a few short minutes to determine that there wasn't a single print on either the note or the knife. The fact that the note had been computer generated and printed added to his frustration.

Alex knew the knife was a filet knife commonly used by fisherman to gut and filet fish. There were dozens in the resort's kitchens. At least that many more owned by employees. Fishing was a popular pastime on the island.

Frustrated, he pushed back from the workbench and stood. Maybe it was time to call in outside help. Four days had passed since the murder and he was no closer to finding the killer.

He shut down the lights and closed the lab, tried to sit at his desk but sprang up again to pace his office, too restless to sit still.

The big problem with trying to solve the murder was identifying the motive. The only person with a clear motive was Harriet and she wasn't on the island when Bradley Higgins had been murdered.

Solomon Ayers had the second strongest motive but Alex couldn't see the head gardener killing for a friend, even one as close as he and Harriet appeared to be. His gut told him that Solomon was not a killer–although he'd seen enough murders to know that anybody could kill if driven to it.

The other problem with hanging the murder on Solomon was that he had an alibi for the time of death–

he'd been seen by at least three resort employees while Higgins was being strangled and hung in the specialty greenhouse.

Alex strode to his desk and picked up the list of six employees with records. He needed to interview them as soon as possible. It was time to get their alibis for the time of the murder and the destruction of Harriet's cottage.

No, that wasn't right. Frowning, Alex set the list down. The only things in the cottage that had been destroyed were Harriet's personal belongings. The cottage itself had been left alone. Not even a glass had been broken. Nothing spilled or dumped like he would see with wanton vandalism.

The attack on Harriet's things had been personal and very, very angry. Out of control angry. Someone hated Bradley Higgins and Harriet Monroe. The realization chilled him. Was the perpetrator angry enough–hateful enough–to kill again?

He was afraid the answer to that was yes.

CHAPTER 20

The following morning Harriet borrowed a pair of long khaki shorts and a man's white shirt from Solly to wear to work. She rolled the shirt sleeves to her elbows and tucked in the tails, then found a belt to hold up the slightly too large shorts. Shaking her head at her image in the bathroom mirror, she pulled on her trainers and called it good.

It was the best she could do under the circumstances.

She would have to hunt up Cassie later and get the names of clothing shops on the mainland, she decided. She'd have to make the clothes shopping trip sooner than she'd planned but it couldn't be helped. While she could get by wearing Solly's clothes at home, she needed appropriate clothing for work.

The shopping would wipe out her savings but if she focused on work outfits she could put off a shop to replenish everything until she had at banked at least two paychecks.

She still felt a little hollowed out from the previous night. Worried about her being alone, Solly had held off going to the greenhouse, hovering over Harriet until she finally pushed him out the door with a promise to call him as soon as she arrived at her office. She appreciated her friend's concern but needed a little alone time to think.

The walk to her office was pleasant. The sun sparkled on the aqua-blue water, birds sang in the trees, a large green and blue iguana with red eyes peered at her from a group of shrubs beside the road before withdrawing in silence.

It looked like another glorious day in paradise. She resolved not to let some crazy person ruin that for her. The position of PR Director was the job of her dreams. No one was going to take it away from her–unless of course Mr. Wade personally sacked her for bringing trouble to the island.

She pushed that depressing thought from her mind, breathed in the heady mix of salt air and fragrant flowers and smiled. A hot meal and a good night's sleep on Solly's couch had done wonders for her spirits. While not one hundred percent, she felt that she could face most anything today.

Anything except maybe another murder.

Don't go there, she scolded herself. Focus on the day's to-do list. Harriet had made lists for as long as she could remember, both mental and when she could afford to buy one, in her personal notebook. Lists helped her stay organized and gave her a sense of control over her life.

More important, they gave her a way to keep score. It felt satisfying to cross an item off a list, to know that she had accomplished something she had set herself to do.

"Harriet!"

Harriet looked up from keying an idea into her notebook and realized she had reached the office building. Cassie stood out front, waiting for her.

"Good morning, Cassie." Harriet smiled as she slipped

the notebook into the rucksack she carried instead of a handbag. "I was coming to see you later today."

Cassie held open the wooden door with its swirl of blue stained glass inserts and indicated that Harriet should enter first.

"I heard what happened to your stuff," she said, eyeing Harriet's outfit. "It's just terrible."

Harriet stopped walking. "You heard? How did you hear?"

"I saw Lana on my way in and she told me."

Despite her promise to herself not to let Lana bother her, anger and hurt warred inside Harriet's chest. Alex must not have wasted any time informing Lana last night. Which meant they'd been together. Not that she cared. And of course Lana had passed the gossip on. She wondered if everyone on the island knew about the destruction of her things.

Cassie placed a hand on Harriet's arm. "I know we aren't anywhere near the same size, but I might have a few pieces you can borrow until you get the chance to shop."

Unexpected tears at the friendly offer pricked at Harriet's eyes. She blinked them back and took Cassie's hand, squeezing it gently.

"Thank you, that's very generous of you. That was one of the reasons I wanted to look you up later. I'm hoping you can give me the names of some decent clothing stores that won't bankrupt me. I'm living on the last of my credits until payday."

"No problem. I'll make a list of shops and addresses and have it ready for you by end of day. What was the other reason?"

"What?"

"You said that was one reason you wanted to see me later. What was the other reason?"

"Right. Sorry. My brain seems to be a little frazzled still." Let Cassie think the frazzle was all due to the attack on her belongings and nothing to do with Alex Hayes and Lana. The jerk.

"I wanted to run some ad ideas by you. Albie took me to the amusement park day before yesterday and I'm thinking of creating an ad campaign that focuses exclusively on Braxton Holliday's park. I thought we could run multiple series of ads focusing on different aspects of the resort, then maybe mix them up later."

Cassie's eyes lit up. "I like it. Bring me what you have later today and I'll see if I have anything useful to add to your ideas."

Cassie's enthusiasm boosted Harriet's confidence. She knew she had some good ideas, she just needed to get them organized and figure out the parts she wanted to video.

"Good morning, Miss Montgomery, Miss Monroe. How are you ladies this beautiful morning?" The British droid looked smart in a pale beige suit with a blue shirt and tie.

"Good morning, Jeeves," Harriet answered. "I'm doing remarkably well, all things considered." She wondered if even the droids had heard the gossip about her.

"Could you please tell any visitors that I'm unavailable today? I need some uninterrupted alone time to get a project going."

"Yes, Miss Monroe, I certainly can."

Harriet started through the hall door after Cassie, then stopped and came back to the receptionist. "That includes Lana Tso, even if she's bringing me lemonade," she said in a whisper so Cassie wouldn't overhear.

"Very good, miss." Jeeves winked at her. "Don't you worry. You'll get your privacy."

Harriet flashed the droid a smile and received one in

return. She hurried after Cassie but the resort manager had already disappeared into her office. Harriet keyed herself into her own space, wished her parents' holo a good day, and went right to work.

She was sketching her vid ideas for the carousel ad when her office link buzzed.

"What?" she answered, without bothering to see who it was. There was silence, then she heard someone clear their throat.

"Is this Harriet?"

"Yes, it's–" Harriet looked at the link display. "Oh, Mr. Douglas, it's you. I'm sorry. I have a tendency to get lost in my work. What can I do for you?"

"I stopped by to see if you would have lunch with me, but Jeeves insists you are not to be disturbed. I had to remind him that humans need to eat and threaten to shut down his circuits if he didn't let me at least call you. "

"Lunch?" Harriet frowned, then checked the time. It was well after the lunch hour and she suddenly felt famished. "I didn't realize it was so late. I'd love to have lunch with you. Where should I meet you?"

"I'm in the lobby. Why don't we walk over to the employee canteen together and see what we can scrounge up?"

"I'll be there in two minutes." Harriet cut the link and headed for her door. She looked down at Solly's clothing and sighed. There was nothing she could do about her appearance. Hopefully Mr. Douglas would understand.

As it turned out, Mr. Douglas not only understood, he had some great news for her.

They sat at a small, round, bamboo table under the vine-covered lanai, away from the few employees still eating in the dining room. Harriet was enjoying a spicy rice and fish dish while Mr. Douglas ate a shrimp salad.

She marveled at the way he made even casual resort wear look elegant on his tall, lean body. His thick, white hair was brushed back from his forehead and his blue shirt accentuated his pale blue eyes.

"I heard about what happened to your possessions," Mr. Douglas said after they had made a good dent in their meals. "I'm very sorry to hear that you're being targeted."

So, even some of the guests had heard about her misfortune. Wonderful. Harriet gave a grim smile. "I'm sorry too, but I don't know what I can do about it. Thank you for your concern though, Mr. Douglas."

"Please call me Payson. If we become friends, as I hope we will, calling me Mr. Douglas is going to become tedious very quickly." He flashed a smile that lit his face.

Harriet smiled back. "All right, Payson, but you must call me Harry as my friends do."

They made easy small talk while they finished their meals. Harriet found Payson Douglas an interesting, intelligent, relaxing companion and she enjoyed her time with him. She was about to push back from the table and make her excuses to return to work when Payson stopped her with a hand on her arm.

"I talked to Douglas Wade last night and told him what happened to your things. I hope you don't mind, but it *is* his resort and he's quite protective towards it and his employees. He was understandably upset and asked me to tell you that the resort will cover the cost of a new wardrobe and replace anything else that was destroyed."

Harriet's mouth dropped opened. "Oh, that's–" she shook her head. "That's very generous of him, but I can't accept. I don't think that would be right. Mr. Wade isn't the one who destroyed my things. He shouldn't be the one who pays to replace them. Please thank him for me but I can't let him do that."

Payson's hand tightened on Harriet's arm, keeping her in her chair.

"Harry, Doug spends more on a single suit than he would on the cost of a wardrobe replacement for you. Accept the offer. If you don't he might just take it upon himself to buy you new clothes and send them to you. This way you can buy what you prefer."

At her still-skeptical look he added, "Trust me. I know Doug. He won't let this go until you accept."

Harriet patted Payson's hand on her arm. "All right. If you're sure. I won't deny that I was wondering how to pay for a new wardrobe. I'm pretty much living on fumes until payday."

"I'll call Douglas tonight and let him know. Shall I suggest that he simply transfer some credits into your account and you can draw on them as you need them?" Payson looked at her expectantly.

Harriet smiled. "That would be wonderful. Please convey my gratitude to Mr. Wade and tell him I'll return any credits I don't spend." What a huge relief. She would be able to replace her clothing as soon as the credits showed in her account.

Harriet stood and dropped her napkin on her empty plate. "And thank you so much for taking me out for lunch. I would have worked all day without stopping if you hadn't called."

Payson stood too. "It was my pleasure, Harry. I'd like to do this again. Want to set a date for next week?" He broke out in laughter at the look on Harriet's face.

"Not a date-date, my dear. Trust me, I know that I'm far too old for you, although if I was a younger man I would certainly try to woo you, Harry. No, I just meant pick a day and we'll plan on a lunch date."

The tension visibly drained from Harriet's body even

though the compliment made her blush. She liked the old-fashioned term 'woo'. Did men actually still woo women? It was a lovely concept.

"I'd like that, Payson. How about Thursday? You can always call me to cancel if something comes up."

"Thursday it is. When will you head to the mainland to shop?"

"I'm thinking day after tomorrow if I have the credits. I want to get the first ad campaign nailed down tomorrow and I need to check the air shuttle schedule so I can get to the mainland and back."

"The credits will be there," Payson assured her. "Thank you for the lovely company my dear, and please try to steer clear of any more trouble."

Harriet gave a half laugh. "I'll do my best." She hesitated a moment before deciding to ask Payson if he knew how upset Mr. Wade was over the trouble she'd brought to the new resort.

Payson laughed. "Doug's not at all bothered, my dear. He's dealt with much more annoying bullshit, I assure. Don't worry your pretty head about your job."

Harriet thanked him and headed back to her office.

She found Lana arguing with Jeeves when she entered the lobby. Jeeves stood in front of the hall door refusing admittance while Lana railed at him, obviously steaming mad.

When she saw Harriet the kitchen manager rushed over to her and placed a hand on Harriet's arm. Deep purple seemed to be the color theme of the day, from Lana's purple curls and eyes to her long purple fingernails and shiny platform shoes.

"Harry, I'm so glad I caught you," Lana gushed through purple lips. "It's just *terrible*. I rushed right over as soon as I had the chance, but this clown wouldn't let me in to your office. You must be *so* upset."

Harriet looked down into Lana's face and saw the glee mixed with malice in the woman's eyes. She pried Lana's hand off her arm and let it drop.

"I'm fine, Lana," she said coolly. "Thank you for your concern. I have a lot of work today and asked Jeeves not to let anyone in." She headed for the hall door where Jeeves still stood guard.

"Thank you, Jeeves. I'm heading back to my office. Please continue to see that no one disturbs me."

"Very good, Miss Monroe." Jeeves winked at her as he let her through the hall door. She heard him re-engage the door lock and smiled. Lana might be Alex's confidant but she was certainly no friend to Harriet. She could see that clearly now.

Harriet had never been very adept at playing the games other people played with one another. She preferred relationships to be straightforward. If she liked a person it showed. If she didn't care for someone, she didn't pretend otherwise.

And she definitely didn't care for the likes of Lana Tso.

CHAPTER 21

Harriet spent the night at Solly's and arrived at the resort's air shuttle pad with time to spare.

Mr. Wade had made good on his offer to replace her damaged belongings. A surprising amount of credits had appeared in her account soon after her lunch with Payson. Harriet figured she could easily replace her wardrobe and even buy a few extra pieces to replace what she had left behind in Portland–and still not spend half the amount posted to her account.

She would return the remainder to Mr. Wade with a thank you note as soon as she returned to the resort, she decided. And then she'd move back into her own cottage.

Solly would let her live with him as long as she needed or wanted, but she couldn't hide from whoever was stalking her forever. The longer she hid the more her fear would take control. Feeling fearful all the time was no way to go through life.

Whoever destroyed her things was definitely a stalker– a different type of stalker from the way Bradley had stalked her–but still a stalker.

The fact that she hadn't realized that Bradley had stalked her until recent events had made it painfully clear made her feel stupid. How could she not have known that her ex had gone to great–and even illegal–lengths to keep tabs on her?

Don't go there.

She entered the shuttle pad waiting area, an open-to-the-air room with no walls, a woven palm frond roof, small round bamboo tables, cushioned seating, and a refreshment bar for travelers waiting for the shuttle.

Several people sat with drinks in front of them, furiously working their links or personal pcs. Business people, Harriet decided, noting the pressed suits. Probably called back to their offices after only two days of vacation to handle some pseudo-crisis, poor sods.

She wondered how many spouses or lovers had been left back in their rooms or cottages, disappointed or even angry at the interruption of their holiday.

She ordered a pineapple smoothie from the refreshment bar and found a comfortable seat away from the others. Pulling out the list of shops Cassie had provided her, she ordered them in her mind to make the most efficient use of her visit to the mainland.

Shopping was not something Harriet particularly enjoyed. She wished Solly had been free to join her–he loved to shop for clothes and would have breezed through the chore, but she hadn't asked him because he was swamped with work now that the guests had arrived.

She sighed and told herself to buck up. Most women would be ecstatic over a shopping trip on someone else's credits.

Resigned to the task ahead of her, Harriet blanked her mind and drank her cold smoothie, savoring the tart and sweet pineapple flavor while she idly watched the activity on the shuttle pad. The sleek blue and white air shuttles gleamed in the sun against the dark gray pad. Droid mechanics with blank faces were doing a visual inspection on two of the shuttles. A third shuttle sat under a canopy off to the side.

As she watched, a large man came out of the maintenance building and took the place of the droid inspecting the smaller shuttle. After inspecting the shuttle carefully the man went back inside.

What was that all about?

"Shuttle Resort Three is ready for loading." A trim, female droid stepped into the waiting area with a small screen in her hand. "My name is Allison and I'll be seating you. I need Mr. Burrows, Mr. Geelhood, and Miss Jacobs to follow me. Please have your identification tag ready. I'll return for the rest of you in a few minutes," she added in a clipped British accent.

The three people called followed the droid and disappeared inside the shuttle. She returned twice more, always taking three at a time, until nine people had been seated and the waiting area was empty but for Harriet.

Harriet slipped Cassie's shop list into her rucksack and carried her empty smoothie pouch to the recycler. She stepped to the edge of the waiting area, ready for Allison's return, but saw no sign of the seating droid.

"Where'd she go?" Harriet did a slow turn but saw only the male droid working the refreshment bar. She took a step toward the shuttle just as it lifted into the air.

"Wait! I'm supposed to be on that shuttle!" she cried, but it only rose higher and then zipped out of sight.

Harriet's shoulders slumped. "Great. Freaking bloody great."

No point in whining about it, but oh, how she wanted

to! She'd just have to take the next shuttle and shop faster in order to make the last daily shuttle back to the island.

"Miss Monroe?" A short, dark man in a military-style resort-blue uniform approached her. When he got close enough Harriet saw that he wore a pair of silver wings pinned to his uniform lapel. A pilot?

"I'm Harriet Monroe."

The man held out his hand. "Pleased to meet you. I'm Captain Rodman. If you'll follow me I'll take you to the mainland."

Harriet shook the offered hand. "I don't understand," she said, hurrying after Captain Rodman. "Did they mess up my booking?" The Captain moved fast despite his much shorter legs and she had to work to keep up with him.

"No, miss. Mr. Wade requested his personal shuttle for you. Watch your step, please."

They had reached the bottom of the smaller shuttle's stairs. Harriet looked up. This was the second shuttle she had watched the man inspect when he replaced the droid mechanic.

Understanding dawned.

"Mr. Wade thinks–" she stopped, her throat closed with fear. She coughed and tried again. "Mr. Wade is worried someone would try to harm me on the shuttle?"

Captain Rodman smiled, his teeth white against his dark face. "I don't know about that, Miss Monroe. I'm only following orders. Your companion is waiting inside for you. If you'll just get in and fasten your seat belt I'll get you to the mainland in no time. This baby flies faster than your typical commercial shuttle."

Companion? Had Payson decided to join her? Delighted with the idea, Harriet stepped onto the stairs.

The pilot took her elbow to help her up the steps and

Harriet found herself propelled into the main cabin before she could ask more questions.

Harriet stopped at the door, causing Captain Rodman to nearly walk into her.

Sorry," she muttered, embarrassed.

Mr. Wade's private shuttle was all jaw-dropping opulence. Unlike the commercial shuttles that packed riders in elbow to elbow in hard plastic seats, the private shuttle held only a dozen deep-cushioned reclining seats, each with a small table set beside it.

She stepped further inside the cabin and sank into thick blue carpet. The walls and ceiling were padded white leather. She could see a large bed through an open door in the rear of the cabin.

The captain passed her off to the human flight attendant and went forward to the cockpit.

Harriet looked around the cabin but didn't see anyone else. Had Captain Rodman been referring to the flight attendant when he said "companion"? She gave the attendant a quick study—compact and pretty and as dark as the captain. Were they a husband and wife team?

"Welcome aboard Wade One," the attendant said with a wide smile. "Please choose any seat you wish, Miss Monroe. My name is Amaryllis and I'll be serving you today. Can I get you a drink while we wait to take off?"

Harriet felt absurdly pampered. First the credits. Now one of Mr. Wade's personal shuttles? She smiled back at Amaryllis. "I'm all set, thank you. I think I'll sit by the window over there." She moved to her chosen seat and settled in.

"If you need to contact anyone you'll find a link in the seat arm." Amaryllis leaned over to show Harriet how to slide the arm open to reveal not only a link but a miniature comm unit and pc.

"Wow. Thanks, but there's no one I need to call." She closed the arm and fastened her seatbelt. What a treat. She had never been in such an opulent, comfortable shuttle in her life. Mr. Wade really knew how to travel in comfort and style.

Other than the resort shuttle from the mainland to the island–which had been comfortable but paled in comparison to Wade One–Harriet had only ridden the air shuttles commonly known as cattle cars when she left Portland to take the resort's PR job.

She took a deep breath and noticed the fresh bouquets of flowers set in vases attached to the cabin walls and wondered if Solly had provided them.

Of course he had. Where else could they have come from? She bet Solly installed the bouquets personally so he could check out the Wade One.

"Pretty nice, huh?"

A large male body dropped into the seat next to Harriet's. She looked, first in disbelief, then in anger.

"What are you doing here?" she asked between gritted teeth.

"My job. I told you I didn't want you to be alone until I catch whoever killed your boyfriend and destroyed your things."

Harriet's scowl seemed to have no effect on the security manager. Alex fastened his seatbelt, stretched his long legs out in front of him, and settled back into his seat.

He smelled good. Like fresh air and musky male. He looked good, too, his blue chambray shirt sleeves rolled to his elbows, revealing tanned, muscular forearms. The shirt color intensified his blue eyes.

Harriet folded her arms across her chest and tried glaring at her unwanted companion. "I don't need a babysitter."

"I'm not letting you travel around the mainland alone, so get used to the idea." Alex reclined his seat and closed his eyes. His thick, black lashes looked like smudges of soot on his sharp cheekbones.

Harriet felt an irresistible urge to hurt him in some way. She wanted to pull his thick long hair, bite his sensuous bottom lip–no! She almost groaned out loud but caught herself in time.

Bite his lip? She felt her face flame as she turned away to stare out the window.

She didn't see Alex slit his eyes open to watch her. Nor did she catch the slight smile on his face. He was feeling pretty smug. Arranging permission to leave the resort and keep an eye on Harriet had been easy. Wade wanted her protected.

He knew she would have cancelled her shopping trip if she had known he was to accompany her so he'd snuck on board the shuttle while the Resort Three was loading. He had no doubts that he'd taken her by surprise.

He did have doubts about how she felt about him and he found that irritating. Alex knew he was no beauty, but he had never had a problem attracting women. He tended to have the opposite problem–how to make them leave him alone.

Harriet was another story. There was something about her that tugged on him. He inspected the sharp blade of her cheekbone and the set of her firm jaw as she stared out the shuttle window, the honey-colored hair with so many shades of blonde it dazzled the eye. The small bump that gave her nose character.

How did she get that bump? he wondered. He bet there was a story behind it. He knew if she turned to look at him that her silver-blue eyes would be filled with intelligence and whatever emotion she was feeling.

Harriet was terrible at hiding her feelings. There was a kind of innocent honesty about her in spite of having lived on the streets at a young age. Despite what she must have seen and experienced she still seemed to possess a belief in the innate goodness of man.

He knew he'd pissed her off with the underhanded way he'd wormed his way into her shopping trip.

He also felt fairly certain that he'd seen lust flash in her eyes before she turned away. That cheered him immensely.

Yes, Harriet Monroe was different from other women and he fully intended to get to know her better.

But first he had a murderer to find and put away.

After they shopped for clothes. Alex grinned to himself. He was going to enjoy this.

CHAPTER 22

Harriet kept her eyes focused on the view below during the entire flight, uncomfortably aware of the large man seated next to her while trying to ignore him–an impossible task. Alex's presence seemed to envelop her in a cloud of essence of strong male. The fact that she was secretly grateful for his company only added to her irritation.

The Wade One landed forty minutes after taking off from the island on a private air pad on the outskirts of Miami.

They were quickly whisked through security and deposited in the traveler's long term parking lot. It was only then that Harriet realized she had no transport. For the guests' convenience, the resort shuttles used the central Miami air port with its surrounding modern public transport system. She had planned to take an airbus from there into downtown Miami and shop only the stores she could easily walk to.

The hot sun beat down on them, reflected and magnified by the quiet paved lot. The light cotton shirt that Harriet had borrowed from Solly the day before and had worn again that morning was already sticking to her back. She felt a desperate need to power through this shopping trip and get back to the island as quickly as possible.

Harriet reluctantly turned to Alex. "I was expecting to land at the Miami Air and Sea Port and take an airbus from there," she said stiffly. "I don't have a ride here."

"Not a problem." Alex grabbed her hand. "Mr. Wade arranged for a vehicle for our use today." He scanned the lot. "I see it over there." His heart did a happy dance when he saw the sleek sports car in the familiar resort blue.

He led Harriet to the car, ignoring her attempts to pull her hand free. "Here we are," he said, smiling. He disengaged the locks and security and opened the passenger door for her.

Harriet looked at the sporty two-seater and tried not to show her excitement. The car was a honey, a sleek road rocket that she imagined handled like a dream. Too bad she had never been licensed to drive.

When other teens were getting their learner's permits she was struggling to pay for food and find a place to safely sleep. By the time she finally made enough money to consider owning a car she hadn't needed one. Portland was a small city and she could walk or bus anywhere she needed to go. Buying a car and paying for a parking slot made no economic sense.

She slid into the tan leather seats and wiggled her bottom. The seat fit her like a glove. Since he couldn't see her, she took a moment to ogle Alex as he rounded the front of the car. The man was built and gorgeous. Ignoring him on the flight had taken a great deal of effort. She had forced herself to stare out the window so he wouldn't see the lust she felt sure showed on her face.

He slid into the seat beside her and moaned. "Oh, baby. This is going to be fun. Where to first, my lady?"

Harriet took the list of shops from her bag and chose one at random. Now that she wasn't walking she could take them in any order.

Alex started the car. The engine purred. "Navigation program," he commanded.

"Navigation engaged. Please state your destination." The car responded in a husky female, somewhat British voice, similar to the resort's drones.

"Mr. Wade sure likes his British accents, doesn't he?" Harriet murmured.

Alex looked at her and grinned. The dimple in his right cheek appeared and Harriet felt her tummy flop. She fought to put a scowl on her face. Resisting Alex's charms was going to make for a long day. She reminded herself of the way he ran to Lana and confided her and Harriet's mood soured.

"Are we going to sit here all day?" she grumped.

Alex's grin only widened. He fed the address to the navigation system and hit the gas. The car lived up to its sleek appearance. They shot out of the private air pad and onto the highway heading downtown.

Traffic was horrendous. All lanes leading into downtown were jammed, but somehow Alex managed to find the spaces and sneak the little sportster forward. Before long they were looking for parking.

"We'll never find a slot," Harriet commented, after they'd circled a three block section twice.

"Never give up. There's a spot, where that red SUV is pulling out." Alex whipped the car into the vacated slot almost on the bumper of the SUV.

"Well done." Harriet unfastened her seat belt. "Did you want to find a coffee shop or smoothie bar to wait while I shop? We could rendezvous in, say, two hours?"

Alex unhooked his own seatbelt and leaned toward her

so his nose was practically touching her own. "Not a chance, sweet cakes. I'm sticking to you like a barnacle to a rock. If anything happened to you while I'm supposed to be looking after you it would cost me my job. I happen to like my job. So relax and enjoy my company."

Harriet grimaced at him and crossed her eyes.

Alex laughed and tapped the tip of her nose. "We'll have a fun day, I promise. You might even find that you like my company."

"I doubt it, but I don't seem to have much choice," Harriet snapped back. She climbed out of the car. "You know how to set the security on this? I'd hate to have it stripped while I shop."

"No problemo." He pushed a button on the key fob and dropped the key into the pocket of his khakis.

Taking Harriet's hand again, Alex set off down the sidewalk. She tried to pull away but he only tightened his grip. She hated to admit that his hand felt big and warm and strong and she liked that he held her close while they walked down the crowded sidewalk.

Remember what Lana said, she reminded herself. Don't be taken in by Alex. He might be an attractive man but he has a serious fault. He takes everything you say and do and shares it with that bitch Lana.

Downtown Miami was a noisy place. Billboards plastered to the sides of buildings squawked over her head. "Buy now!" "One Day Sale!" "Special Rates!" The talking billboards competed with music piped from the store fronts onto the streets, traffic horns and engines, and food cart vendors hawking their wares.

The mixture of sound reached a decibel level Harriet had never experienced in the smaller, quieter, Portland. She wondered how people could think with all the noise.

She smelled coconut sunscreen on passing pedestrians,

grilled pineapple and soy dogs from the food carts that graced every corner, and exhaust fumes from the rumbling city buses. Beneath it all was the faint scent of salt air, reminding everyone that Miami was a coastal city.

Relief swept through Harriet when she spotted the store they sought. She pulled on Alex and hurried through its door.

"It's like a carnival out there!" she said as the door closed behind them, cutting off the deafening cacophony. She pulled her hand free from Alex's hold and moved further into the narrow store, carefully eyeing the layout and offerings.

Shirts and jackets of every hue and style hung on upper racks along both sides of the store with skirts, shorts, and pants on lower racks beneath them. Dresses, skinsuits, and a variety of accessories were displayed down the center of the floor.

Harriet huffed out a breath and relaxed slightly. She should be able to purchase most of what she needed right in this one store. She got busy, pulling items to try on. A sales droid carried her selections to a dressing room in the rear. By the time she reached the dressing room she found Alex seated comfortably with an iced drink, waiting for her.

"I'm going to enjoy this part," he said, wagging his eyebrows at her.

Harriet sniffed. "I don't see why. You certainly aren't coming into my dressing room."

"True. But the only mirrors are out here. I checked." He indicated the triple-mirror viewing area just outside the dressing room. "If you want to see how something looks I'll get to see it too. I'll be more than happy to give you my opinion."

"Bite me." Freshly irritated, Harriet stalked into the

large dressing room. The ample supply of wall hooks had been neatly filled by the sales droid with Harriet's selections. Alex was right–there were no mirrors.

"Dammit." She had no choice but to parade the clothing in front of Alex since she wouldn't buy anything without checking how it fit. Maybe she could put off buying clothes until after Alex found the killer. Come back to Miami by herself to shop.

She picked up the bag she'd dropped on the dressing room bench and turned to walk out but stopped. She'd worn Solly's borrowed shorts and shirt for two days now. She desperately needed new clothes. The shopping couldn't be put off.

She set her rucksack back on the bench and sat to remove her shoes. Best to get it over with. She'd simply have to suck it up and do her best to ignore her escort.

Ignoring Alex turned out to be much more difficult than Harriet had anticipated. Downright impossible, in fact. He had opinions about everything–fit, color, fabric–and double-dammit, Harriet found his opinions insightful and useful. She still argued with him, determined not to let him think he was influencing her, and even tried on the selections he sent into the dressing room.

By the time Harriet worked her way through the items they'd picked to try on, she had a workable selection of office and leisure outfits. The fact that she had agreed with Alex about everything only pissed her off more because she knew he would believe she had made her choices based on his input.

She was practically snarling by the time they left the store. She turned left because Alex turned right, and took off down the sidewalk. It took him less than a minute to catch up with her.

He grabbed her arm and hauled her into a narrow dirt

alley. The noise and people continued to stream by. Behind them she could smell a recycling bin that needed emptying.

"What's wrong with you?" he demanded. His eyes were dark with anger. "Most women would be deliriously happy after a shopping spree like you just had. You act as if you've been insulted. I don't get it."

Harriet pulled her arm free and glared at him. "Of course you don't get it. You probably think I bought the clothes I chose because *you* liked them or because you picked them out." It had galled her to discover that several of the pieces Alex had chosen looked great on her.

Alex furrowed his brow. The scar over his right eyebrow puckered white against his tanned face. "Well, I hope I was helpful, but no, I figure you bought what you bought because you liked the clothes. Is that why you're so mad? Because I liked the clothes you bought?"

He took a step back and looked at Harriet. "You're a strange one, you know? I don't understand you."

"No? Well maybe you can just run to Lana when we get back to the resort and tell her all about our little shopping trip and have her explain it to you."

Much to Harriet's embarrassment, tears welled up in her eyes. She dashed them away with the back of her hand and turned away from Alex.

She would not cry.

"Oh, lord. Please don't cry, Harriet. I'm trying here. I really don't understand. And what does Lana have to do with our shopping trip? I was having a great time. It was fun, watching you try on clothes. You're tall and slim, have an athletic build, and you looked great in everything. It reminded me of shopping with my sister."

Harriet sniffed but didn't turn to face him. She kept her eyes on the people walking by the mouth of the alley.

"You have a sister?"

"Had." His voice was so quiet Harriet had to strain to hear. "Allysa was killed by a mugger who wanted her new trainers. That's why I became a cop. I wanted to put away the bad guys." He sighed. "Turns out there's an endless supply of bad guys. After eight years of putting them away I burned out. And here I am."

Harriet took a deep breath, let it out. Everyone had a story, she reminded herself. "You shopped with your sister?" she asked, still not looking at him. She was beginning to feel like an over-sensitive fool.

"Yeah, I did. Allysa was a clothes hound but I always had better taste than she did and she knew it so she'd bribe me to shop with her." The memory of his vibrant older sister brought a small smile to Alex's lips. He had loved his sister unconditionally. Her senseless murder had devastated him. Sixteen years had passed since her death and he still missed her.

Harriet wiped the last of her tears away and turned around. "What did she bribe you with?" Alex's sudden wolfish grin made her belly do several flops.

"She'd let me sneak a peek in the family room when she had a sleepover. What fifteen year old boy wouldn't love seeing a bunch of seventeen year old girls in their pajamas?"

He flapped his hand over his heart. "I must have fallen in love with at least half of her friends at one time or another."

Harriet couldn't help herself. She smiled at the image of a teenaged Alex lusting after his sister's friends. "I'll bet she loved you."

The smile disappeared. "Yeah. Yeah, she did. So, are we okay now?"

Harriet nodded. "I'm hungry. Let's find someplace for lunch."

"I was hoping you'd say that."

They locked the one outfit Harriet had carried with her from the store in the boot of the car and strolled down side streets until they found an open-air restaurant offering spicy food. They kept their lunch conversation light and ended the meal in a companionable silence.

After lunch Harriet hit two more stores on Cassie's list for footwear, underwear, casual wear, and accessories. She included Alex in her decisions and found herself enjoying the remainder of the day. She found Alex easy to be with. He ignored the admiring glances other women cast in his direction and focused his attention entirely on Harriet. It made her feel . . . special.

It wasn't until they were back on Wade One that Alex brought up Harriet's outburst. "In the alley," he began . . .

Harriet tensed.

"What did you mean when you told me to go ask Lana about you? That didn't compute for me."

Harriet rested her head on the cushioned seat back and kept her gaze focused out the window. She didn't want to talk about Lana. It spoiled what had turned out to be a lovely day.

"You seem to run to Lana with everything." She shrugged. "It pisses me off."

Alex frowned. "I don't run to Lana with anything unless it has to do with Lana. What are you talking about?"

Harriet rolled her eyes at him. "Don't lie. Lana came to me the morning after you-we–the day after we kissed. She told me what you said about not liking the way I came on to you. She also told me that you asked her to convey a message. Consider the message conveyed."

"What message?"

"Really, Alex, I understand. I'd rather not discuss it anymore. It's embarrassing for me, okay? I kissed you back because I thought you wanted to kiss me. I misread the situation. I'm sorry. It won't happen again."

Alex cupped her chin firmly and forced her to turn and face him. "Just what was that message?" His voice held the chill of a brisk winter's day. The look in his blue eyes hardened. "Tell me."

"She said you didn't want to see me anymore but you also didn't want to hurt my feelings by telling me that." Tears pricked at the back of Harriet's eyes. Jeezus, she wasn't turning into one of those women who cried all the time was she?

She forced as much coolness into her voice as she could muster. "So, for the record, my feelings aren't hurt. You don't have to see me anymore, or at least you won't once you find the killer."

"Lana lied to you."

"What?"

"I have never discussed you with Lana. Not once. Nor would I ever."

"I . . . if that's true, how did she know that you kissed me? I only told Solly and he's like a gold vault. He'd never repeat gossip about me."

"That's a very good question. One I intend to get an answer to as soon as we land."

He brushed his lips lightly over hers and slid his palm up to gently cup the side of her face. "For the record, I enjoyed our kiss very much. And I definitely want to see you again."

CHAPTER 23

At Harriet's request, Alex dropped her off at her office so she could check on any messages. There were two; one from Cassie with a couple of small suggestions for Harriet's upcoming ad campaign, and one from Payson wanting to know if she had found everything she needed during her shopping trip.

Harriet left a message for Cassie thanking her. She put off calling Payson. She wanted to thank him in person for making the shopping trip possible. If he hadn't called his friend Mr. Wade Harriet wouldn't have had the credits necessary to replace her wardrobe.

Everything else could wait until tomorrow, she decided. She grabbed her rucksack and the shopping bag containing one new work outfit and locked her office.

"Goodnight, Jeeves. I'll see you tomorrow." Harriet gave a little wave as she crossed the building lobby.

"Goodnight, Miss Monroe. I look forward to it."

Harriet was nearly to the door when Jeeves stopped her. "Miss Monroe, Miss Tso was looking for you today.

She came by twice asking where you were. As I didn't know, I was unable to answer her question."

The reminder of Lana took a little of the shine off Harriet's day.

When she stepped outside and saw Lana loitering outside the office building door she groaned. She had zero desire to talk with the bitchy kitchen manager, especially after the wonderful day she'd had.

"Hi." Lana turned and walked with Harriet. "I was looking for you earlier today. Where were you?"

Harriet stopped walking and looked down at Lana. She hadn't changed yesterday's purple enhancements but her normally bouncy curls hung like limp rags. Her purple polish had begun to flake off her fingernails and Harriet saw that the nails had been chewed down to the quicks. Lana smelled of fried food and unwashed body.

"I'm sorry, Lana," she said gently, "but I don't really see where my whereabouts are any of your business. If you'll excuse me, I need to get to Solly's."

"You think you're really something, don't you?"

The venom in Lana's voice sent shivers down Harriet's spine. "I don't understand what you mean."

Lana flicked a hand in Harriet's direction. "Tall and slim and blonde. You think you can waltz in and take a woman's man just because you want him. Isn't Solly enough for you?" she sneered. "Do you have to go after my man too? You're nothing but a whore."

Harriet took a step back. The purple contacts coloring Lana's eyes did nothing to hide the gleam of pure hatred she saw there.

"I'm not chasing any men, Lana. I don't have time for men. I have a new job that requires all of my energy. Now if you don't mind, I'm tired. I want to get home and take a shower."

She started off again but Lana leaped in front of her, her hands fisted at her side.

"I know you followed Alex to the mainland today. You can't deny it. I saw you enter that air shuttle after he went aboard. You trapped him on that shuttle."

Lana shook her fist in Harriet's face. "I warned you about chasing Alex. You leave him alone or next time you'll find the knife in your chest." She whirled around and stormed away.

Harriet stood frozen to the spot. For several long moments her mind remained blank before it kicked into gear again. *Lana* had destroyed her things? It was Lana? Not the killer?

She felt weak and dizzy and leaned against the front of the building. Jeeves must have heard or seen her with Lana because he came out of the building and took her elbow.

"Miss Monroe, please let me help you inside where you can sit. Can I call anyone for you?"

"Thank you, Jeeves, no. I'll be all right in a minute. I just had an unexpected shock, that's all."

"If you don't mind me saying so, Miss Monroe, you look awfully pale. I think I should call a medic."

"No." Harriet placed a hand on Jeeves' arm. He was cool to her touch, a reminder that he was a droid, programmed for certain responses.

"Thank you, but I'll be fine in a minute. Really."

What should she do? She really had only one choice. She needed to tell Alex that it was Lana who had broken into Mermaid Cottage and destroyed her things. Not the killer.

Unless Lana was the killer? She thought about Lana's size. While the kitchen manager was certainly strong, she was too small to have lifted Bradley's body into the greenhouse vine.

How was she going to tell Alex about Lana without tipping Lana off? The woman obviously kept a close watch on Alex. She closed her eyes and thought.

She couldn't ask Alex to come to her cottage–or Solly's cottage. She couldn't ask him to come to the office because Lana would know he was meeting her. The public dining rooms were out. In fact, anywhere the public would see them was out as Lana would see them as well.

Then she had it. She hurried back into the building to make a call.

CHAPTER 24

"Thank you, Payson. I know this seems odd, but trust me, it's necessary. I apologize for intruding on your privacy but I couldn't think of anywhere else to do this."

Harriet sat in Payson's living room on a comfortable couch. Payson sat across from her, his tanned bare feet up on the low coffee table, a glass of cold sweet tea in his elegant hand.

He had greeted Harriet with a reserved welcome when she knocked on his door, and asked no questions when she explained that she needed to meet Alex there, out of sight of any other employees. They were waiting for Alex now.

Harriet took a sip of her lemon water and looked around the space with appreciation. Payson's cottage was larger than her own Mermaid, with two bedrooms and a larger living room.

While it had the same luxurious standard of furnishings she had come to expect from the resort, she could see that Payson had added his own touches to the space. This cottage was obviously used by no one else.

A collection of finely carved wooden masks dominated

the room, reflecting every human emotion along with several non-human faces that fascinated Harriet. She itched to get up and inspect them much more closely, but she was acutely aware of the imposition her barely-announced visit made on her host and didn't want to take advantage any more than she already had.

Several antique, hand-knotted rugs in blues and tans covered the floor. The doors to the two bedrooms were closed. Harriet idly wondered if Payson had converted one to an office so he could work from the island.

Fortunately she didn't have long to wait for Alex. Less than ten minutes had passed when he roared up on his motorcycle and, tapping lightly on the door, let himself in.

"Payson? You needed to see me?" He stopped short when he saw Harriet. His eyes narrowed. "What are you doing here?"

"I had to talk to you as soon as possible and it needed to be somewhere where we wouldn't be seen. This was the only place I could think of."

Payson stood. "Why don't I step outside while you two talk."

"No." Harriet reached out and grabbed Payson's hand. Horrified by the familiarity of the gesture she hastily dropped it. "Please stay. Really. It's nothing you can't hear. In fact you might have an idea of what to do."

"All right then. If you want me to stay, I will." He took his seat again and waited expectantly.

Harriet watched Alex. "Lana came to see me at the office after I returned to the island. Oh, that reminds me."

She turned her attention to Payson. "Thank you for telling Mr. Wade about losing all my things. Please thank him for the generous credits. I replaced everything today and what I didn't spend I'll return to him tomorrow. I'm sure the bank can just reverse them back into his account."

Payson's pale blue eyes sparkled. "You're quite welcome, my dear. And may I say that I look forward to seeing one of your new outfits when we lunch next week."

Harriet smiled at him and turned back to Alex, her expression serious again. "Lana was upset that we flew together to the mainland. She told me that she watched me get on the shuttle after you boarded. She accused me of chasing you. Alex, I think Lana is stalking you."

"If she is it's nothing I can't handle. Is that why you dragged me out here?" He sounded more irritated than grateful for the warning.

"No. There's more. She threatened me. She said that if I don't stay away from you then next time I'd find the knife in my chest."

Alex huffed out a breath. "That's a lot more serious." He gave Harriet a speculative look. "You think Lana might be the person who destroyed your things?"

"It makes sense. She's warned me three times now to keep my distance from you. She claims that you . . . that you are her man. Think about it, Alex. If you didn't tell anyone, and I didn't tell anyone that we kissed, how did she even know? She must have followed you to my cottage that night."

Harriet's hand flew to her mouth as she felt the warm blush creep up her neck. But when she glanced at Payson he merely winked at her and smiled.

"There's nothing wrong with two people feeling attracted to each other, my dear."

Alex leaned back in his chair, stretched out his long legs, and steepled his fingers. Harriet was beginning to recognize this as his thinking mode.

"What you're saying is you think that because Lana knew we flew together to the mainland today and also knew we kissed, that she must be stalking me."

"It makes sense," Harriet said stubbornly. Couldn't Alex see what was blindingly obvious to her?

"It does make some sense," he admitted, watching her, "but there could be another, simpler explanation."

"How else can you explain it?"

"Maybe she was walking the beach past your cottage and just happened to see us."

"Fine. What about seeing us board the shuttle today? She had no reason to be at the air shuttle pad. And what about the crack she made about the knife?"

Alex tapped his finger tips together several times. "Like everyone else she heard what happened to your things. She was upset and seized on that to threaten you."

Harriet stood and pointed her finger at Alex's chest. She was starting to feel angry. "How did everyone know about what happened to my things? Solly knew. You knew. I knew. And Payson knew. I've told you before Solly is like a vault. He would never, never ever, gossip about my personal business. Ever. So that leaves you. You must have told Lana about the knife and the destruction of my clothing and hippos."

Alex shook his head. "No. I didn't say a word. But people seemed to know. It was all over the resort."

Harriet threw her hands in the air. "That's what I'm trying to tell you. How, Alex? *How* did they know? The only other person—besides the four of us—who knew about the knife was the person who put it there."

They glared at each other for several beats. Harriet dropped back into her chair. The day's activities and travel were catching up to her. She felt ragged, tired, and hungry.

"Okay, let's think about this. Neither you nor Solly told anyone about the knife." Alex's voice sounded calm.

"Right."

"I told Payson about the knife." He turned to Payson. "And you–?"

Payson held up a hand, palm out. "I never said a word to anyone."

"Except to Mr. Wade," Harriet pointed out.

"Yes, of course. That's right."

"I feel reasonably certain that Mr. Wade has more on his mind than spreading gossip around the resort," Harriet pointed out dryly.

"Right. So if none of us talked about it, that would mean that the person who left the knife in your mattress started the gossip," Alex stated. "Okay. I agree with you Harriet–that makes the most sense."

He tapped his fingers while he thought. "The trouble is nailing down exactly where the gossip started. Half the people who passed it on won't remember who they heard it from."

"Cassie told me that she heard it from Lana."

"All right, I can at least ask around. And I'll have a serious talk with Lana about threatening you. I find it hard to believe that she's stalking me, but your argument makes certain amount of sense."

Harriet's head jerked up in alarm. "Don't do that. I don't think that talking to Lana is going to do any good, and it might make things worse. If she finds out I talked with you she might come after me with more than words."

Alex scowled at her and stopped tapping his fingers. "I can't just let a threat like that go."

"Please, Alex," Harriet pleaded. "You have to. I only told you about her threat to warn you about the stalking. Just focus on finding the killer. Lana is bound to cool down eventually. Especially if I don't see you anymore, which is probably the wisest course of action at the moment since we both have our hands full."

She ignored Alex's frown and stood. "I need a shower and food. Call me at the office tomorrow and let me know what you find out. Please?"

Alex and Payson stood as well. "You'd better let me leave first. If Lana *is* following me around then she won't like seeing us both leave here."

"Fine." Harriet watched him leave with mixed feelings. He had seemed skeptical about the stalking. Maybe she should have tried harder to make him understand the malice she'd seen in Lana's eyes. Harriet didn't need to trace the source of the gossip. She felt sure that Lana was perfectly capable of destroying her things.

"Harry."

Harriet started. She had forgotten she was standing in Payson's cottage. She must be more tired than she realized. She turned to him. "I'm so sorry I intruded on you like this."

Payson waved her apology away. "It's not a problem. What hippos?"

"What?"

"You said your clothes and hippos had been destroyed."

"Oh." Harriet gave a half-laugh. "I had a collection of hippos carved from different woods. I love real wood but it's frightfully expensive to own anything made from it, so Solly gave me a hand carved wooden hippo for my birthday one year. I loved it. He's found me one every year since, always carved from different woods."

She smiled. "I don't know how he remembers so he never duplicates the woods, but he hasn't so far. In the big picture they're nothing I suppose, but I loved those silly hippos. They made me feel loved, like someone cares about me."

"Solomon sounds like a good friend."

"He's the best. I can't imagine one better. I was fortunate he found me."

Payson gave her a long, considering look. "Something tells me that Solomon must consider himself just as blessed to have you for a friend, Harry. You're both very fortunate. Good friends are meant to be treasured as the rare gift they are."

"I definitely treasure Solly. Without his help I don't think I could have survived my teen years." She stepped toward the door. "If Lana was following Alex she should be gone by now. Thanks again for letting us meet here. I know I inconvenienced you."

"No inconvenience, Harry. You just made my day more interesting." Payson flashed a smile. "Feel free to do so anytime."

CHAPTER 25

Solly gave an appreciative whistle when Harriet modeled her new work suit for him the next morning. They had risen early and taken a run on the beach in the pale gray twilight of pre-dawn, then breakfasted on fruit and granola on the lanai.

Harriet felt it was the perfect way to start a day.

"That has to be one of the prettiest things I've seen on you," Solly said. He whirled his finger in a circle. "Turn," he ordered.

Harriet obliged by spinning a slow circle. She loved the outfit she had carried home. Made of a lightweight rose colored silk, the cap-sleeved dress skimmed over her torso, flaring slightly at the hips into a fluttery skirt that ended just above her knees. She pulled on the flowing matching jacket with three-quarter length sleeves and felt glamorous.

"Beautiful. Great color for you." Solly fingered the silk and narrowed his eyes at her. "Nice fabric. I don't recall you ever wearing silk before. Or such a strong color." He raised his eyebrows. "Care to explain the fashion change?"

"The silk makes more sense here in the tropics than it did in Portland. Do you really like the color?" She had no intention of letting Solly know she'd had help choosing her clothes.

Alex had argued with her about the dress, insisting she take it after she'd set it in the discard pile because she thought it wasn't "professional" looking. Seeing it on her body again in Solly's bedroom mirror, Harriet had to admit that Alex had been right about the dress. What constituted professional attire in the tropics was different from professional attire in New England.

She loved the way the rose color of the dress looked against her lightly tanned skin and how it made the color of her eyes pop. Alex might have the face of a street fighter but he truly had good taste in women's clothes. His sister had been wise to to bribe him to shop with her.

After a rocky start and other than the mini-meltdown in the alley, Harriet had had a great time shopping with Alex. Without him she would have shopped as quickly as possible and headed right back to the resort. She would have treated the trip as one more chore to cross off her to-do list.

Alex had turned the day into an adventure and made it extra special–exploring Miami's boutiques and out of the way shops, and finding an excellent, casual lunch spot , all the while exhibiting a degree of intelligence, patience, and wit she hadn't expected.

Alex Hayes was more than a sexy body–he was exactly the type of man she hoped to end up with one day. She felt a stab of regret that they had agreed not to see each other again but resolutely pushed it away. She had work to do and knew better than to dwell on what-ifs.

Slipping on the stylish sandals she had purchased to

replace her heels–heels made no sense on the island–Harriet headed for the door.

"I'm off to the office," she called to Solly, who was still in the kitchen. "I'll cook tonight. They'll deliver the rest of my new clothes to my office today so I'll see if Albie can give me a ride home. By the way, I'm moving back to Mermaid Cottage tonight."

She slipped out the door before Solly could start an argument about her moving back to her own cottage and hurried toward the office.

The sandals had been an excellent idea, Harriet decided as she walked briskly along the shell road. No more balancing on five-inch icepick heels that liked to sink into the road or grounds.

It was still early enough that the sun cast long shadows across the road. The birds sang, the insects hummed, and Harriet wished she could carry a tune so she could sing with them.

"You look lovely today, miss." Jeeves held the front door open for Harriet and ushered her inside her office building.

"Thank you, Jeeves. You look pretty spiffy yourself." The droid looked pleased by the compliment. He wore a blue suit with a white shirt and folded handkerchief today, the reverse of his usual uniform.

"Thank you, miss. Shall I screen all visitors again, Miss Monroe?"

"Please call me Harry, Jeeves. At least when it's only you and me. And no, I don't think screening will be necessary today, but thank you. I'm nearly done with the planning portion of my ad campaign so I'm in good shape and I won't be in my office all that long."

"Very good, Miss Harry. Ahh, Miss Montgomery, good morning."

Harriet turned and saw Cassie coming through the door, looking flustered. "Hi Cassie. You look a little rushed. Is everything all right?"

Cassie fluttered a hand, then ran it through her short brown curls. "I am a bit rushed this morning. My divorce lawyer called me last night. He's coming today with the final papers for me to sign and I have a few things on my plate to deal with before he arrives."

"If there's anything I can do to help you need only ask."

"Thanks, Harry, but I've got it. Or I will if I get to it. Ta." Cassie disappeared through the hall door.

Harriet decided to follow suit. She needed to finalize her ad campaign, then grab the motion camera Mr. Wade had provided at her request and head to the amusement park.

She hoped to run into Braxton Holliday while filming. She wanted to include him in her ad. The big bear of a man was so passionate about his park–she knew that his passion would hook viewers and add an irrestable element of human interest to her ads.

The morning passed without incident. Lana didn't show with lemonade, making Harriet wonder if she had been cut off. She could almost feel sorry for Lana–being so intensely hung up on Alex couldn't be easy when the man barely acknowledged her.

Unfortunately it looked as if Lana's feelings for Alex had crossed over into obsession–a potentially dangerous obsession. Not unlike Bradley's obsession with her, she realized.

Harriet wrapped up her script and found the motion camera in one of her lower cabinets. She pulled it out to inspect and was very pleased with what Mr. Wade had provided. The camera was a thing of beauty; small, sleek, and incredibly easy to use. Nearly foolproof.

Although Harriet hadn't done any filming since her advertising classes she felt confident. She had a clear vision of how she wanted to portray the resort and that made her job easy.

She had always loved everything about advertising—coming up with the ad concepts and working them out, physically creating the ads and editing them to get exactly the mood and message she wanted. She enjoyed every piece of the process.

But she had realized early on in her schooling that working in isolation, stuck in an advertising office working on ad campaigns was not for her. She wanted to help grow a business. A little research had introduced her to the world of public relations and she knew she had found her niche.

Harriet returned the camera to its protective case and gathered her rucksack and notes for the shots she needed to get, then locked her office and headed back to Solly's to change into clothes she could get down and dirty in.

Forty-five minutes later she was driving one of the resort's golf carts down to the amusement park with a big smile on her face. This was her first chance to really show Mr. Wade what she could do for his resort. She was ready to shine.

Alex's morning wasn't going nearly as well as Harriet's.

He'd arrived at his bare office out of sorts and grumping at the world.

First, he hadn't slept particularly well. He hated to admit it, but it bothered him that Harriet had so easily told him that it was better if they didn't see each other. All because of that busybody Lana.

He knew–*knew*, dammit–that Harriet had responded to that first kiss in her kitchen. And he had felt a slight shiver go through her body when he'd barely kissed her on the air shuttle.

She wanted him, but was too much of a coward to admit it.

He scowled down at the list of suspects in his hand. He wasn't going to let Harriet brush him off as if he was nothing more than an irritating bug. He had a few things to deal with first, but once he found Bradley Higgins' killer he intended to see a lot more of Miss Twinkle Harriet Monroe. She would just have to deal with it.

There was something about Harriet that challenged and deeply attracted him. It wasn't her physical beauty–he had dated plenty of women more beautiful than Harriet Monroe.

It was some inner quality she had, an essence of character, that made him want to get to know her better, that made him want to learn what made her tick. He already knew that she was intelligent and innocent and interesting and had a kind heart. She was even polite to the resort's droids for crying out loud.

She was a woman he could see himself with long term. A woman he could marry and have a family with.

The realization hit him like a punch to the solar plexus. It stole his breath, the same way Danny Wong had knocked the wind out of him when they'd been new recruits practicing with batons and had skipped their protective pads. Danny had connected a lucky shot with his unprotected chest that had dropped Alex to his knees and left him gasping for air.

He was having the same trouble breathing now.

Marriage was not something Alex had ever contemplated before. He thought women were wonderful–for fun and companionship and in a few cases, for friendship. But not for long term. Not for the nitty gritty of daily life year after year.

He shook his head. He didn't have time to travel down that crazy path right now. He needed to focus on the task at hand.

Looking at the short list of resort employees with criminal records, he set the names in the order he wanted for interviews. He would start with the two gang members first and eliminate them right off. He couldn't think of any reason they could have for killing Bradley Higgins so he didn't expect to get anything there. Unless it was a case of murder for hire, which he doubted.

He decided to interview the suspects in the field rather than bring them into the security office and set off to track them down.

As he suspected, he didn't get any sense from the two ex-gangers that they had anything to do with Bradley Higgins' murder, but they had had to be eliminated. He didn't consider it a waste of time. Solving murders was often a tedious process of elimination.

His interview with the employee accused of domestic violence and the one with the record for car jacking were equally fruitless.

All four employees had solid alibis for the time period in question, although Alex did warn each of them that one wrong step and they'd not only find themselves fired but also charged with any crime committed. Alex made it crystal clear that he had a zero tolerence policy for crime on the island.

That left Alex's two most likely candidates for the murder—the ex-cop forced into early retirement for employing excessive violence when making arrests, and the never-convicted-but-several-times-arrested spine cracker. He decided to start with the spine cracker. Any man who broke bones in order to force people to pay their debts was a man who could be hired to kill.

He found Raymond Mackleworth in the maintenance garage, working on a floor sweeper and polisher. While nearly spotless, the garage still smelled like a garage–of oil and grease and orange-scented cleaner.

Raymond was an older, large, pale-skinned man with broad shoulders, a tattooed bald head, and piercing, flat black eyes.

"Raymond Mackleworth? Alex Hayes, resort security. I wonder if I might have a word with you?"

Mackleworth straightened and wiped his hands on a rag before extending one to Alex. "Raymond will do. I wondered when you'd get around to me."

Alex shook the hand, noticing it's strength and rough texture. He raised his eyebrow at Raymond. "And why would you wonder that?"

"I've been arrested multiple times, and even though I've never been convicted–and I want to stress *never convicted*–I figured you'd look at me for the murder of that bloke who was hung here last week. I'll make it easy for you. No, I didn't know him. And I had no reason to kill him."

Raymond Mackleworth turned his back and knelt by the faulty piece of equipment he was trying to fix, obviously dismissing Alex.

"Maybe you didn't have to know him," Alex said mildly.

The spine cracker had a complex mandala tattooed on the top of his skull. A Buddhist spine cracker? Alex shook his head. One thing he'd learned as a cop–it took all kinds to commit crimes.

"Maybe you were hired to kill Higgins," he added. He noted with interest that a muscle jumped in Mackleworth's neck when he mentioned murder for hire. He pushed a little more.

"Could I please have your whereabouts for the twenty-four period starting the early morning of this past Wednesday through Thursday morning?"

Mackleworth stopped what he was doing and gave Alex a flat look. "I was either here or in my room. You can check the employee quarters' security disks and my log-in and log-out times here."

"I'll check the disks, I assure you. Can anyone confirm that you were here the entire time you were logged in?"

"No." Mackleworth's smile was cold. "No," he repeated. "The other guys were in and out. I could have snuck away and back again and they would've just thought I was doing my job. Sorry, I can't help you."

"I'd think you'd want to help yourself."

Mackleworth stood. He had two inches and about thirty pounds on Alex, but Alex wasn't worried. He could see that the spine cracker had let himself go soft around the middle and he knew he would be quicker on his feet than the larger, older man.

He braced himself just in case, but Mackleworth only tossed down his wrench.

"You want to know something?" he asked, his eyes fierce. "You're right. I do want to help myself. I hate this island. I hate everything about it. I miss the action of the city and I'm going back to where I belong."

"Not until I catch whoever killed Bradley Higgins. You can give your notice, but you can't leave the island until I say so."

Mackleworth's fists tightened. His mouth thinned and his face and neck flushed a deep red.

Alex braced himself again until he saw Mackleworth make a visible effort to relax. The spine cracker simply shook his head. "Yeah, sure. I'll stick. Hurry up and find the bastard, will ya? I need to get back to pavement and traffic and city lights. I'm freaking dying here on this wasteland. People are nuts to pay to come here."

"I'll let you know when you can leave." Alex left Mackleworth swearing at the floor machine and mounted his motorcycle.

One more to go—the forcibly retired cop.

He found Tarbell Fox wolfing down a huge lunch in the employee canteen. The place was about half full with mostly hotel staff. Alex studied the ex-cop for several minutes before making his approach. He saw a burly, military type with short reddish hair and a clean-shaven face, wearing a neatly pressed porter's uniform.

It was quite a come-down from cop to baggage carrier. Alex wondered how well Tarbell Fox was dealing with his current circumstances.

Seeing that the ex-cop was nearly finished with his meal Alex walked over to his table and slid into a seat opposite.

"Mr. Fox? I'm Alex Hayes, chief of security for the resort."

"Yeah? Ex-bloodhound, huh?" Tarbell Fox gave Alex a studied once-over, shrugged and went back to his meal. "So?" he asked, around a mouth full of food.

Alex had debated with himself about how to approach this particular interview. He expected Tarbell Fox to be stiff and proud, and he was. If he came right out and asked for Fox's whereabouts and alibi for the time in question he would only succeed in putting the ex-cop's back up.

Some inner sense made Alex feel reluctant to take that approach. Respect for a fellow cop?

He decided to try another tack instead. "In checking

employee backgrounds I discovered that you're an ex-cop. Where'd you serve?"

"Boston."

"Why does a cop trade his badge for a porter's uniform?"

Fox grunted. "Maybe things got a little briny." He saw the confusion on Alex's face. "I had no choice." Fox's eyes were like orbs of green ice. "But you know that already. What's it to you?"

Alex shrugged one shoulder, leaned back. "I'm investigating a murder. Bradley Higgins. Know him?"

"Nope. Never laid eyes on the dude. You thinking I wasted him?"

Alex looked Tarbell Fox in the eyes. "Did you?"

"Nope. If that's all you have I need to bring time. My boss is waiting for me back at the hotel."

"Bring time?"

"Work, man. I got to get back to work. We done here?"

Alex felt reluctant to let Fox go. "Have you heard anything? Any rumors that might help me?"

Fox pushed his plate away and folded his arms on the table. He studied Alex. "I thought you used to be a hotshot snatcher."

"Snatcher?" Alex was having a hard time following Fox.

"Big city murder cop."

"I was a homicide detective, yes. I don't know about the hotshot part. I do know that cops help each other unless they're wrong cops." He let that hang in the air between them.

Fox narrowed his eyes. "I was never a wrong cop."

"But you *were* forced out of the job."

Fox slammed his fist on the table, making the plate and flatware jump. "I was accused of using excessive force on a suspect during an arrest. The asshole came at me jacked up on dope with a pig sticker in his hand and death in his eye. I defended myself. Broke his arm. It didn't even slow him down. He was too doped up to feel pain and he wasn't going to stop. I wanted to live so I killed him.

"It was a righteous kill. Him or me. I chose me. The asshole turned out to be the mayor's wife's cousin. I was offered early retirement or a long court battle I couldn't afford. End of story and end of my career."

Alex said nothing for several minutes while he absorbed Fox's story. If true, then Fox had gotten a raw deal. If the victim had been any ordinary guy on the street Fox never would have lost his job. All aspects of the death would have been reviewed, Fox would have been tested and most likely reinstated and the case filed under Righteous Termination.

Which, if Fox was telling it straight, was how it should have been classified. Alex felt a twinge of sympathy. "You like it on the island?" he asked, trying to get a better feel for the man.

Fox shrugged. "Good vittles. Cubby's fine. It's far away from home and everyone I knew before so that's a good thing. The work is easy. Maybe too easy, but I have no complaints."

"I have a murderer on the island and no leads. Mind if I run the case by you?"

Surprise flashed in Fox's eyes followed by wariness. "Why?"

It was Alex's turn to shrug. He felt as surprised by his request as Fox, but now that he'd asked, he realized it was what he needed—another person who thought like a cop to bounce the whole case off.

"I need a sounding board. I don't have anyone on the island who understands police work to toss around ideas and theories with. It always helped me before to talk out what I had with my partner when I was working a case. You game?"

Hope flared in Fox's eyes and was quickly replaced with caution. "Maybe. I need to check with my supervisor. See if Albie can spare me."

"I'll call Albie and tell him I need your services for the rest of the day. Do you know where the security building is?"

"Yeah."

"Great. Meet me there in forty-five minutes. Change out of your uniform but into something like this." He indicated his own khakis and polo. "We'll be out in the field and you need to look as if you work with me."

As Alex rode back to his office he hoped he wasn't making a mistake taking one of his suspects on as an aide. But Fox's story rang true and would be easy enough to check out. He'd call an old friend on the Boston police force. He had time to do that before Fox arrived.

It occurred to him that if Fox worked out he could get him transferred to the security department. It would be good to have another experienced cop working resort security, even if Fox used some strange words.

He was whistling by the time he strode into the security building lobby.

A whirling red dervish launched itself at him and nearly knocked him off his feet.

"Alex!" Lana threw herself into his arms. "Oh Alex. The killer is after me!"

CHAPTER 26

Fortunately the security office lobby was empty other than Mary. Alex saw a small grimace briefly cross Mary's face when Lana threw herself at him but the droid immediately resumed her usual placid demeanor. He wondered how long Lana had been waiting. It couldn't have been too long or Mary would've called his link.

Lana wrapped her arms around Alex's waist much as a boa constrictor would seize its prey. He reached back to grab her hands and peeled her off his body. It wasn't easy. For such a little thing she was amazingly strong.

"Calm down, Lana. You're safe now," he said. "Take a seat, right here. That's a girl." After he had Lana settled on one of the cushioned chairs he asked Mary to fetch her a glass of water.

Lana grabbed onto Alex's shirt front as he knelt in front of her with the water. "Easy now," he said soothingly. "Drink this and catch your breath, then tell me what happened."

Lana took the glass with one hand, keeping the other tightly wound in his shirt. Red was the color of the day–

her hair, nails, lips, eyes all colored a bright, candy-apple red. Her red eyes seemed to glow. They reminded Alex of artwork depicting the devil.

"I needed something from my room so I ran back and–," tears spilled from her eyes, "and . . . Oh, it's just awful. All my things are cut to shreds, just like Harry's were."

Fox came in the security office door just as Alex freed his shirt from Lana's fist and stood. He took one look at the weeping woman and tried to back out.

"Oh no you don't. Get back in here, Fox. I need you." Alex turned back to Lana and indicated the ex-cop. "Lana, this is Tarbell Fox. He's assisting me. I want you to stay here with Mary while Fox and I check out your room. What's your room number?"

"Can't I wait in your office?" Lana's lips quivered.

Alex hesitated. There were things in his office that were not for prying eyes, like the background reports on resort employees.

"I'm sorry, Lana, but no. It's against regulations. Besides, I think you would be safer staying here with Mary. She'll watch over you and protect you until we return."

"Then can I come with you? I'll feel safer with you. I want to stay with you." Two tears slid down Lana's face.

"No. It'd be better if you stay with Mary. We won't be long."

"What's happening?" Fox asked as they headed toward the employee quarters on foot.

"I'm not sure. It doesn't make any sense." He filled Fox in on Bradley Higgins' murder and the destruction of Harriet's possessions. "Harriet was linked to Higgins so I can buy that the murder is connected to what happened to her things, but destroying Lana's stuff makes no sense whatsoever."

"Unless you have a whacko loose on the resort."

"Bite your tongue." Alex scowled at Fox. "If we have a whacko we'll have to close the resort until we can root him out."

They soon reached Employee Housing One–a long, two story building–and took the nearest side entrance. The employee housing was built from the same pink stone as the larger resort hotel. The four employee buildings were classy and well-designed, the way Mr. Wade did everything.

Employee Housing One was the southernmost housing unit, home to the non-droid food service workers and the gardeners who worked under Solomon Ayers. Each unit contained a furnished sitting room, one bedroom, a full bath, and a mini-kitchen. Alex had toured one of the units before taking the job and knew that the units were much nicer than what most people could afford to rent on the mainland, himself included.

The wide foyer held several lush green plants, a single elevator, a door leading to the ground floor units, and a set of concrete stairs leading up to the upper floor units. The two men ignored the elevator and headed up the flight of stairs.

The apartments were arranged on either side of a wide, well-lit corridor. Tile squares in soft taupe covered the hall floor. Bright bouquets of flowers sat on small, half-round tables set between every other door. They brightened and perfumed the space with their floral scent.

Most of the doors had been personalized with the occupant's name and in some cases artwork. The building was quiet. They heard no sound coming from any of the units. Either it was well soundproofed or most of the residents were working. Alex suspected both were true.

"Unit two-zero-five. Here we are." Alex took out his

master and let himself inside Lana's quarters. The men stood just inside the door, taking everything in. The place was in shambles.

Bright neon clothing covered the grape-colored couch and two chairs. A wineglass lay on its side on a low bamboo coffee table that had been painted bright orange. Its contents splashed the bright green rug beneath the table with dull red-purple splotches.

Bold slashes of color on canvas decorated the walls. With nowhere restful to look, the effect of all that color was almost dizzying.

It smelled of spilled wine, dirty clothes, and an overwhelming, cloying perfume that Alex recognized as the one Lana habitually wore.

"The woman sure likes color." Fox shook his head. "Not sure I like what she's done with her crib."

"Looks like a hurricane went through here," Alex muttered as he moved further into Lana's unit. Mr. Wade would not be pleased to learn that his tastefully furnished unit turned into a garish mess.

He pulled a pair of thin gloves from his pocket and handed them to Fox before pulling out a second pair and putting them on.

He went to the couch first and inspected the clothing strewn over it. "Hmmm. Check these out." He held up a pair of thin sweatpants, cut to ribbons. "Just like Harriet's. Certainly looks like the same hand."

They went through the unit carefully. The bedroom was as chaotic as the living room with clothing tossed everywhere. Every counter and flat surface in there and the bathroom was covered with tubes and bottles and jars of enhancers strictly organized by color family and precisely lined up like soldiers.

By the time they were finished Alex was seething with a cold anger. "Notice anything strange?" he asked Fox.

Fox's intelligent eyes glittered. "Other than the fact that Miss Lana is addicted to enhancers and make-up and cheese twists? Yes, I picked up on a couple things. First, not everything has been destroyed. Didn't you say nothing of– Miss Monroe was it–?"

Alex nodded.

"Right. Didn't you say that nothing of Miss Monroe's had been spared?"

"Yes. Even her shoes were destroyed."

Fox waved one hand. "Well, this doesn't appear to be the same wholesale destruction. In fact, only a small selection of the clothing has been sliced and diced."

Alex gave a nod. "I'm listening."

"Everything that *was* destroyed?" Fox picked up the thin, old sweats. "They're like these, old and worn and about ready for the rag bin. It *looks* as if someone went through here in a rage, the way everything is tossed about, but when you look closely that's not the story."

Alex nodded again, his mouth grim. "Agreed. What does that suggest to you?"

Fox's eyes narrowed. He threw the sweatpants back on the couch. "If the killer had broken in here and destroyed Miss Lana's clothing he would have swept those enhancers off their neat little counters. And he wouldn't have chosen her oldest clothes to destroy. I'd say Miss Lana cut up her own clothing in a bid for attention. The woman is a blow-top–a crazy person."

He looked around the sitting area with disgust. "And she lives like a pig."

Alex stripped off his gloves and stuffed them in his pocket. "I'll deal with Miss Lana later. Right now I want to take you to the greenhouse where the body was found and introduce you to the head gardener, Solomon Ayers. He and Harriet have been close friends since they were teens."

Alex relocked Lana's unit and they headed to the garage to grab his vehicle. On the way he placed a call on his link to Mary.

"How's Miss Lana doing?" he asked.

"I see no signs of distress, sir. Her tears dried as soon as you left. She's just sitting and waiting. I thought I heard her humming a short while ago."

Alex knew the droids possessed exceptional hearing. If Mary thought she heard Lana humming then Lana was humming. Pleased with herself. The thought disgusted him.

"Please tell Miss Lana to go back to work. I'll catch up with her later. I have–" He heard a commotion, then Lana's tearful face appeared in the link.

"Alex? When will you be back? I'm frightened. I need you."

Alex had to bite his tongue to keep from blasting Lana right then, but the conversation he intended to hold with her needed to be done in person.

"I'm sorry, Lana, but something's come up. I won't be able to get back to the office for a few hours yet. Why don't you go back to the kitchens and see if you can get some work done? There are plenty of people around there so I'm sure you'll be safe until I return."

"But-but I want *you* to keep me safe." Her lower lip quivered.

She's a good actress, observed Alex, but she's over-played her hand. "I understand, but that isn't possible at this time. I'll be back as soon as I can."

"And then you'll stay with me?"

"Then we'll figure out what the best course of action is, I promise."

"I'll wait for you, Alex."

"*No.* Go to the kitchens. You'll be safer there. I'll come find you as soon as I can."

"If you say so, Alex."

Alex cut the link call before she could say anything else. He tossed it in the console between the seats and blew out his breath.

"You have a skull-buster," Fox said mildly. He gave Alex a sympathetic look. "That girl wants you and she's a whacko. Does she have anything to do with your dead body?"

"I don't think so," Alex replied. "She's not strong enough. You'll understand when I show you where the body was found. We're here." He parked the SUV in front of greenhouse number four.

Ten minutes later, Alex reengaged the lock. Fox stood with his hands in his pockets gazing at nothing, thinking. A pair of gardeners came out of greenhouse number two laden with several pots of red flowering plants and loaded them into the back of a golf cart. They took off, chattering and laughing.

"Seems like a happy enough crew working here," he observed. "So, this Solomon Ayers is a close friend of Harriet Monroe's?"

"Yes. Since they were teens."

"Would he have any reason to want Bradley Higgins dead? Jealousy, perhaps?"

"No on the jealousy and no motive that I could find. Harriet and Solly are more like brother and sister. They look out for each other."

Fox glanced at him. "Sounds as if you like them both."

"I do. And I realize I need to keep an objective view here. The only motive I can find for killing Bradley

Higgins points at Harriet. She's his only beneficiary and he was worth a considerable amount."

"Money is a strong motive."

"Yeah, and it would be a prime motive here except that Harriet plans to set up a trust with all of it to fund a homeless shelter and a shelter for domestic abuse victims in Portland. She was honestly shocked when I told her about Higgins' will. Doesn't want the asshole's money."

Fox raised his eyebrows as they climbed back into the SUV. "Asshole? The vic was an asshole?"

Alex scowled, put the SUV in gear and peeled away from the greenhouses.

"Bradley Higgins was stalking Miss Monroe."

"Another motive to want him dead," Fox pointed out.

"Yes. One that could point to either Harriet or her friend Solomon. Except that Harriet wasn't on the island when Higgins was killed, and Solomon has a solid alibi. And more importantly, neither of them knew Higgins was stalking her."

"So we're back to no motive."

"Exactly. No motive means I have nothing to work with. If it was a random killing then I'm looking for a whacko and it could be anybody."

"That's a whole lot of whackos for one small island."

"You're telling me," Alex muttered under his breath.

CHAPTER 27

When she arrived at the amusement park to film video for her ad campaign, Harriet was pleasantly surprised to find the parking lot nearly filled with resort carts. Apparently the early guests had wasted no time finding the park. That would make Braxton Holliday a happy man.

She parked her own cart at the far end of the lot, grabbed the camera from its case and headed for the gate. The greeter, a slim young woman dressed in a sparkling blue skinsuit, also wore a fake diamond tiara in her abundant brown curls, exotic eye paint, and a bright smile on her attractive face. Images of whirling roller coaster track shimmered on her skinsuit when she moved.

"Welcome to Holliday's Park. All the rides are free, but a few are restricted to protect our guests. No one under four feet tall or with heart issues can ride the coaster, and parental supervision is required for The Drop."

She leaned close to Harriet. "I suggest if you've just eaten that you hold off on the coaster. We've already had a few "accidents" if you know what I mean." Her warm brown eyes sparkled.

Harriet grinned at the greeter. "You couldn't get me to ride the coaster if you drugged me and tied me into one of the cars. The carousel is more my speed."

She stuck out her hand. "I'm Harry Monroe, PR director. I'm here to shoot some footage for an ad campaign I'm working on."

"Raita Simms. My absolute fav ride is the coaster, but I think the carousel is our most beautiful and oldest traditional ride. If you need anything just ask. I'll be on the gate all afternoon."

"Thanks. I appreciate that." A man and a woman with two very excited young boys came up behind Harriet. The boys were urging their parents to move faster and begging to ride the coaster. Harriet winked at Raita and passed through the gate, heading straight for the carousel.

Screams rang out overhead as she heard wheels race over the metal coaster tracks. She looked up in time to catch a dozen faces–a few looking terrified, most smiling, as the cars whipped around a sharp turn and up a steep incline. Harriet pressed a hand to her belly. Even watching the coaster made her feel nauseated.

The look on the guests' faces as they came around that particular curve in the track would make great footage for her ads though. She decided to film the other rides and catch the coaster shots on her way out.

Harriet spent the next three hours filming rides and guests. She asked the guests for permission to film them and produced release forms that gave the resort permission to use their images in future ads.

Everyone cheerfully signed the forms, making her job easy. She picked the happiest faces and ended up with a nice blend of adults and children and plenty of film to edit back in her office.

Mr. Wade had thought of everything she mused, when

she found a busy food court on the far edge of the park. She remembered Raita's warning about riding the coaster on a full stomach and hoped nobody in the food court planned to follow their meal with a coaster ride.

She grabbed an icy lemonade and a crab salad roll and found an unoccupied table to sit at. The tart lemonade refreshed her waning energy. She thought she might be growing addicted to the summer drink. It tasted so much better on a warm tropical island than it ever had in Portland, Maine.

The crab roll tasted sweet and succulent, with real mayo instead of the soy mayo Harriet was used to. She moaned when she bit into it then looked around guiltily, but no one was paying any attention to her. She relaxed and turned all her attention to enjoying her meal.

When she finished she sat back in her seat and pulled her notes from her rucksack. She had the shots she needed plus a few bonus moments she hadn't planned on. She only had to catch the last coaster shot on her way out and she'd be done. Oh, and a shot of the attractive Raita greeting guests. She added the shot to her notes and put them away.

Harriet checked her watch. Time to get a move on. She needed to finish filming and return to her office. She'd lock the camera back into its cabinet with that day's film and start the edit tomorrow after a good night's sleep.

Her link rang before she made it out of the food court however, and she stepped to the side to take the call.

"Harry?" Cassie's flustered face appeared on the screen. "Where are you?"

"Hi, Cassie. I'm still at the amusement park, just finishing up. I should be on my way back to the office in about fifteen minutes. Do you need something?"

"Thank heavens I caught you. Could you possibly pick up Mr. Blattsworth—my lawyer—and bring him to my office? I've been trying to get out of here for the last forty minutes but there's been one disaster after another." She made air quotes around disaster and rolled her eyes.

"Honestly, I think my co-workers are worse than the guests. They're so worried about everything being perfect they're wound tighter than-than-I don't know what. Jeeves told me you were at the amusement park so you're halfway to the air shuttle pad. Would you mind? I'll owe you."

Harriet grinned. "I'd be happy to pick up Mr. Blattsworth and you don't owe me a thing. When does his shuttle land?"

Cassie checked her watch and grimaced. "In about ten minutes. Are you sure? I need to get this divorce finalized so I can move on with my life and I've been so busy I haven't been able to get off the island to sign the papers. I know you're working and it's a lot to ask . . ." Her voice trailed off.

"No problem, Cassie. Honest. I'll head out now. You should see us within an hour unless the shuttle is late. Call your lawyer and tell him I'm coming."

"Thanks, Harry." Someone caught Cassie's attention off-screen. "In a minute," she snarled. She turned back to Harriet. "Sorry, I have to run. Thanks again." The link connection broke.

Harriet shook her head, still smiling. Poor Cassie. The resort manager had a lot on her plate, personal and professional.

She took the few minutes she needed to get the last two shots she wanted of the coaster and Raita and headed for her car. More families had arrived over the course of the afternoon and the park was hopping. Colored lights flashed on the rides. Shouts and laughter blended with screams of delight and music. Mr. Wade would be pleased to hear that the park was a huge success.

Raita waved goodbye as Harriet slipped out the gate.

Once the carnival opened it would siphon off some of the crowd from the amusement park, but she imagined the park would remain a guest favorite. The delay in the carnival's open date had been unexpected and unavoidable, but judging from the expressions on the faces she had filmed that afternoon, no one minded the crowd at the park.

The number of resort guests was carefully regulated so they would never feel overcrowded. There were plenty of activities on offer as well as quiet things to do on the island.

Her first ad campaign featuring the amusement park would be a winner, but Harriet made a mental note to do a future campaign featuring the more solitary aspects of the resort for those that wanted to simply get away from the hustle and bustle of their daily lives.

She was smiling when she drove onto the air shuttle port. All three blue and white Resort Island shuttles were sitting side by side on the edge of the black shell pad. Thinking Cassie's lawyer must have decided to wait for her in the open lounge, she drove around the pad and parked in front of the lounge, but found only the droid barkeep inside.

"Excuse me. I'm looking for someone." Belatedly, Harriet realized she had no idea what Cassie's lawyer looked like. "His name is Mr. Blattsworth. Do you know if he arrived on the last shuttle?"

"I'll check for you, miss. One moment, please." The droid spoke quietly into the bar link, then returned to where Harriet waited.

"There was an Amos Blattsworth on the last shuttle. Does that help?"

"A little." Harriet looked around the empty lounge and frowned. "No, not really. Where is he?"

"I do not know where he is at the moment, miss, but now that I've seen his photo I can tell you that I saw him get into a cart with a man."

"What? How long ago?"

The droid's eyes blanked a second as it checked its interior data bank. "Ten minutes, miss."

"Okay, thank you." Now what? Walking to the edge of the open lounge, Harriet pulled her link from her pocket and rang Cassie. The resort manager looked even more frazzled than when she'd called Harriet less than thirty minutes earlier.

"Cassie, I'm at the air shuttle port but Mr. Blattsworth apparently grabbed a ride with someone else."

"What?" Cassie's eyes focused on Harriet. "That's impossible. I told him I had someone to meet him at the air pad."

"Do you have his link number?" Harriet asked. "Try calling him. I'll stand by." She rang off. Cassie rang back less than a minute later.

"Harry? Mr. B's link doesn't pick up. It dumps straight to message mode."

Harriet sighed. "I don't know what to tell you, Cassie. Apparently he thought whoever he caught a ride with was sent by you. Maybe he can't answer his link because he's passing through a dead zone on the island. Why don't you call Alex and ask him to keep an eye out for Mr. Blattsworth? I'm going to head back to the office since I can't do anything here."

Harriet could hear the clang of sailboat rigging on metal masts through the trees and undergrowth, reminding her that the marina wasn't far from the air shuttle port.

She was halfway back to the main road when a thought struck her. What if Big Ed had learned of Mr. Blattsworth's pending arrival? She knew the marina's assistant manager didn't want a divorce. He might have met the lawyer to try to talk him out of giving Cassie the final divorce papers.

She could easily spare ten minutes to swing by the marina and see if Mr. Blattsworth had been stranded there and needed a lift to Cassie's office.

Harriet reached the main road and turned north, driving to the marina as fast as the moderately-paced vehicle would take her. A quick check told her the marina office was empty and locked. Where was the manager and Ed?

She stepped beyond the building and scanned the docks.

A family of four were being helped into individual kayaks by a pair of droid dock workers. Beyond the docks a motorboat sped by hauling a waterskier behind it.

Seagulls called and swooped over the docks, looking for food. Further out, several pretty blue and white striped sails caught the breeze and tacked across the mouth of the marina's bay.

She spotted Big Ed beside a powerful-looking speedboat on the end of the farthest dock. A man sat in one of the boat's rear seats. The lawyer? Where were they going?

Fortunately Harriet had swapped her sandals for trainers when she had changed clothes earlier. She took off at a run, determined to catch them before they could leave.

"Ed! Ed, wait!" Harriet stopped by the boat and leaned over, gulping for air. She flapped one hand. "Give me a minute," she gasped. She took several deep breaths to calm her racing heart. "Whew. I need to get back to running."

She smiled at Ed. He stood staring at her uncertainly, with the aft mooring rope already untied and in his hand. The stern of the motor boat began to drift away from the dock.

"Is that Cassie's lawyer?" Harriet took a step closer to the dock edge. "Mr. Blattsworth? Where are you going? I'm Harriet Monroe. Cassie asked me to give you a lift to her office. She's anxious to see you."

Something was wrong. The lawyer's head lolled against the back of the seat. His eyes were closed.

Harriet frowned. "Ed? What happened to–" she never finished her question.

Ed dropped the mooring line and pulled her to him. Before she could defend herself she felt pressure on her upper arm and her knees buckled. Her thoughts jumbled into a dizzy mess. "Wha–"

The bastard had tranqed her. She lost all control of her muscles and could no longer stand. She felt big, beefy arms go around her and lift her. Then–nothing.

CHAPTER 28

Harriet fought to open her eyes, but they wouldn't obey. She felt like a sack of bruised apples lying on something hard. Pins and needles shot through her pinned arm as she shifted her body. Something sharp poked into her cheek. She tried to move away from whatever it was and pain exploded in her head.

"Ow. Holy crap." Her mouth tasted metallic, her tongue thick and dry. She took several slow, deep breaths and waited for the pain to subside.

Something wet and slimy slid against the side of her head and smelled salty. She heard the gentle lap of water and remembered.

Big Ed Whitfield, Cassie's soon-to-be-ex, had attacked her at the marina. He had hit her with a pressure syringe full of tranqs. That explained the blank in her mind and her non-responsive limbs.

"Ed?" Her voice was barely audible. She tried again. "Ed?" she croaked.

Nothing but the sound of water lapping at—at what?

Harriet forced her eyes open and closed them again in a hurry. The sun was blinding. "Ouch."

She tried to shade her eyes with one hand but it wouldn't respond. She tugged again and discovered her hands had been bound behind her. She wriggled her fingers again and felt flesh that was not her own.

Oh, what had Ed done?

"Hello?" Harriet waited but there was no response. She tried to roll to her knees but couldn't. She was tied to something. Her heart began to hammer in her chest.

"Hello?" Louder this time. She heard a groan in response. She knew suddenly who she'd been tied to.

"Mr. Blattsworth, is that you?"

Another groan.

Slowly, Harriet opened her eyes to narrow slits. Bright sunlight reflected off water and made her eyes tear. She closed them, then tried again. This time when she opened her eyes she saw dark, smooth rock.

She shifted her view to look down her body and was relieved to see that her feet were not bound. She wriggled her legs, trying to force feeling back into them.

"Mr. Blattsworth? Can you hear me?"

Another groan, then she heard a feeble "yes."

Harriet worked some saliva in her mouth. "Good. That's good. We need to sit up so I can see where we are. Apparently we're tied together so we'll have to make a coordinated effort. Are you up for that?"

"In a minute."

Relief flooded through Harriet. The lawyer was coming around. Soon they'd be able to free each other and go find Alex to tell him about Ed. She worked her legs and fingers while she waited.

"Who are you?" The lawyer's voice sounded stronger.

"Harriet Monroe. I'm the PR Director for the resort. You can call me Harry."

"Amos."

"Great. Amos, we need to sit up so we can do something about our situation. Can you pull your legs up, out in front of you? When I count to three we'll both try to sit, okay? On three. One. Two. Three."

Harriet struggled upright. Her head pounded with the shift in position. Pins and needles shot through her arms. She heard Amos panting and groaning as he tried to manage his own pain. It took them a long minute, but they made it to a sitting position.

"Don't open your eyes," she warned. "The sun is bright and it hurts. When you're ready, just slit them open." Harriet waited for the pounding in her head to subside, then carefully slit her own eyes open again.

She stared out at water. She turned her head as far to the right as she could, then to the left. Nothing but water.

"Amos?"

"What?"

"Can you open your eyes and tell me what you see? Carefully." The tension grew in her body while she waited.

"Water."

"Crap."

"What? Where are we?"

"I think we've been marooned on a small island."

Harriet scanned the ground in front of her. Smooth rock covered with seaweed.

"It gets worse."

Amos groaned. "How? How could it get any worse?"

"The rock we're sitting on is covered with seaweed."

"So?

Harriet took a deep breath. "So that means that at high tide this rock will be covered with water."

Amos sat silent for a minute. "When is high tide?"

"I have no idea. I haven't been here long enough yet to track the tides."

"How deep will it get?" Harriet heard the panic in the lawyer's voice.

"Sorry. I can't answer that either. Do you think we can try to stand up? I want to see if Ed left my link in my pocket but I can't reach it sitting."

Standing proved to be far more difficult than sitting had. It took several tries before Harriet hit on the plan to push against each other's backs while they tried to push up with their legs. She was drenched in sweat by the time they stood.

Amos Blattsworth was not a tall man, Harriet soon discovered. His shorter build dragged down on her when she tried to stand to her full height. She had to bend her knees in a half-stoop to reduce the pressure of the rope on her wrists.

"Sorry I'm so short," Amos apologized. "It's one reason I became a lawyer. Sitting behind a desk disguises my height, or should I say, my lack of height."

"No apology needed. It's not your fault. If anything, I'm too tall for a woman," Harriet replied.

Off in the distance she could see the faint, blue-gray shoreline of the resort island. There were no boats anywhere near them.

"Do you know where we are?"

"I think that's the resort island over there." Harriet turned slightly so Amos could see. "For all the good it does us. It's too far to swim. And even if we could swim I don't know if there are sharks in the water here."

"So we're stuck until someone comes to rescue us."

"Yes, I'm afraid so."

"In that case let's sit again so you don't have to crouch.

It will be more comfortable."

They struggled back to the ground and sat in silence. Harriet had no idea how much Amos Blattsworth understood about tides and she wasn't about to ask. There would be plenty of time for them both to panic later.

That didn't stop her from thinking about what was going to happen, however. The tide would rise. The rock they sat on would be covered with water. How deep it would get, she didn't know.

What if the waves from the incoming tide washed them off the rock? Already they were lapping closer than she liked.

"Do you think we could try untying the rope? My arms hurt."

Amos's question shook Harriet from her unpleasant thoughts. "We can try. We need to stretch the rope some to make some wriggle room. Spread your hands as far apart as you can."

Harriet pressed against the rope until her wrists were rubbed raw. "Now press your hands together, see if you can slide one hand out. I'll hold my hands together to create as much slack as I can."

The rope burned against her raw wrists when Amos tugged against them. He grunted and panted as he tried to pull a hand free. "No good. You try."

Harriet waited until the burning sensation lessened a little, them tried to pull her left hand free. It stuck at the joint where palm meets wrist. "Nope. Start from the beginning. We'll pull as hard as we can on the rope, then relax and we'll try pulling our hands free again."

They repeated the process, again and again, until Harriet's wrists were slick with blood. The tide continued to rise until the rock disappeared and they were sitting in several inches of water.

"How deep will the water get?"

Harriet fought to keep the impatience from her voice. "You asked me that once already and I still don't know, Amos. Keep working on the ropes." She didn't want to tell the lawyer that at full tide the water could be well over their heads.

By the time they had freed their hands the water was up to their chests. They scrambled to their feet and leaned against each other for extra stability against the waves pushing at them. At least when standing the water only lapped at Harriet's knees.

Harriet checked her pockets. No link. Amos turned out his, also empty.

"It doesn't look very good for the home team, does it?"

Harriet looked down at the slightly chubby lawyer. Until now, he had offered no opinion about their situation and quietly followed her suggestions and orders without complaint. His shirt and jacket cuffs were stained with blood from his wrists. His face was sunburned. His mild brown eyes held only regret.

"Can you swim?" Harriet asked.

"Reasonably well. I'm no Olympian, but I can float."

"If we stay here we'll probably die. I want to try for the island. We can tread water, side stroke, and float on our backs to rest. Those are the most restful strokes I know. If we do that we should be able to keep afloat for hours, long enough to reach the island or for someone to find us. I'm hoping the tide will help by pushing us toward it. What do you think?"

"I think it sounds like insanity." He smiled. He had a surprisingly sweet smile. "Let's try. It's better than standing here until the water's over my head."

Harriet smiled back. "I like you, Amos. Take off your jacket and let's go."

CHAPTER 29

After leaving the greenhouse, Alex and Tarbell Fox checked Harriet's cottage before driving back to the security office. Alex liked the way Fox listened with his full attention and waited to speak until he was sure Alex had finished what he wanted to say. He also had sharp eyes that missed very little.

Fox had the right makeup to be a good cop.

Alex parked the SUV in front of his office and jumped out. "I'm going to deal with Lana first," he told Fox, "then I'm going to put in a formal request to have you reassigned to security. I'm sure the transfer will go through, no problem, and it shouldn't take longer than a day. In the meantime you should probably report to Albie until you get word the transfer has gone through. Take the SUV, I don't need it."

Fox climbed over the console into the driver seat. "Thanks, I appreciate that you're giving me a chance. Private security isn't quite the same as being a paddy, but it's better than carrying luggage."

Before Alex could reply, Cassie came running down the

alley that ran between the business and security offices. "Alex! Something's happened to Harry. I can't get her on her link. It keeps going to voice mail."

Alex frowned. "Maybe she's busy and doesn't want to be disturbed."

"No." Cassie wrung her hands. "She was doing me a favor. She finished filming at the amusement park and she drove down to the air pad to pick up my lawyer and give him a lift back here."

"Your lawyer flew to the island today?"

"He was supposed to come last week but he couldn't make it so we rescheduled for today. I called the air pad—Amos flew in okay and Harry showed up, but now they're both missing. You need to find them."

Alex's blood ran cold. He hadn't known Harriet long but he felt sure that she would never worry Cassie by going incommunicado. Something had happened.

"We'll find them." Fortunately Fox had waited. Alex climbed into the passenger seat. "Head for the air pad. I'll fill you in on the way."

When they reached the air pad they had to wait for a newly arrived shuttle to unload its passengers before they could track down the droid who had checked Amos Blattsworth onto the island.

"Yes, sir," answered the droid, a pretty redhead dressed in a smart, well-fitted uniform. "I recorded Mr. Blattsworth's arrival at fourteen hundred hours, twelve minutes. He went into the lounge to wait for his ride rather than take the scheduled shuttle bus to the hotel."

"Did you see his ride?"

"No, sir. Once the passengers are checked in I wait in deactivation mode until the next shuttle either arrives or prepares for loading to leave."

"Okay, thank you. Fox, stand by." Alex strode into the

packed lounge. Couples, young and old, held hands or sat talking quietly. Parents herded their young children and teenagers dressed in baggy clothes and glittery trainers tried to act as if they visited fancy resorts every day. Everyone wore smiles and looked vacation-mode happy while they waited for their luggage to be loaded onto the shuttle buses.

Alex wound his way through the crowd toward the refreshment bar where a droid was busy mixing fruit smoothies and pouring lemonade. Slapping his security badge on the bar, he leaned forward. "I need a quick moment," he said.

"I am able to multitask, Mr. Hayes. What do you need?" The droid continued to mix and pour, handing over drinks and taking fresh orders with a smile.

"I'm looking for Amos Blattsworth and Harriet Monroe."

"A young woman was looking for Mr. Blattsworth earlier. I told her he was here, then he wasn't."

Alex grabbed the droid's wrist. The hell with multi-tasking—he wanted the droid's full attention.

"What time did the young woman come looking for Mr. Blattsworth?"

He watched the droid's eyes go blank as he checked his data bank. "That would have been at precisely fourteen hundred twenty-three minutes."

"And Mr. Blattsworth wasn't here?"

"No, sir. His ride had already picked him up."

Alex didn't relax his grip. "Then what?"

"Then what?" repeated the droid.

"Then what happened? Where did the young woman go?"

"I understand now, sir. The young woman in question drove off in a resort cart."

"Which way did she go?"

"I believe she headed west, sir. Towards the marina."

Alex freed the droid's wrist. He ran out the back, figuring it would be faster than working his way through the crowd again. He threw himself into the SUV.

"Harriet headed toward the marina over an hour ago."

Tarbell put the SUV in gear and raced across the air pad. He didn't have to ask where they were going. "Doesn't Leonard Dixon manage the marina? Do you think he's involved in the first lawyer's murder?"

Alex looked at Fox. "The first lawyer," he repeated. "Oh, crap. Bradley Higgins wasn't killed because of *who* he was, he was killed because of *what* he was. That's why I couldn't find a motive." His eyes went flat. "He's had too much time. I hope we aren't too late."

"Who's had too much time?" Fox asked as he pressed down on the accelerator.

"Cassie's soon-to-be-ex, Ed Whitfield. He's been fighting the divorce. If I'm right, he killed Higgins thinking he was Cassie's divorce lawyer."

It took them less than five minutes to get to the marina. They found Leonard Dixon in the marina office, cheerfully selling sunscreen to a mother of three teens who were nagging her to hurry, they needed to get out on the water *now*.

"Dix, where's Big Ed?" Alex demanded, interrupting the sale.

The marina manager frowned at him. He could see that Alex was upset about something. Still, one of the resort's cardinal rules was to treat every guest with courtesy and respect.

"I'm not sure, Alex. Have you tried the docks?" He smiled at the woman as he put the sunscreen into a bag and handed it to her. "Thank you, ma'am. You have a nice day now and come back if there's anything else you need."

As soon as the woman left the shop he glowered at Alex. "What's wrong with you, man? You don't interrupt a guest like that."

"I need to find Ed. Now. It's important, Dix, or I wouldn't have interrupted you."

"Last I saw him he'd just come in from taking a guest waterskiing and was tying up at the end of the far right dock."

Alex whirled around and headed for the door.

"Alex, no upsetting the guests."

But Alex was already out the door. "Far right dock," he called as he ran past the SUV where Fox stood waiting. Fox fell in behind and they both raced for the dock, dodging guests as they ran.

Alex stopped at the head of the dock. "He's not here." His gaze skimmed over the motorboats. One was just heading out, driven by a father with a young boy and a girl, all grinning madly.

Kayakers and paddle boarders were practicing their strokes just beyond the two far left docks. Alex checked their faces carefully. Droids stood on the dock encouraging the paddlers while more stood in the water helping those who needed more hands on instruction. There was no sign of Big Ed.

"Check the sailboats," he instructed Fox. "I'll check the speed boats in case he's hiding aboard one. Be careful, if he's kidnapped Harriet and the lawyer he could be feeling desperate."

He didn't say "kidnapped or killed" because that was something he couldn't bear to contemplate.

They split up and Alex quietly headed down the dock. The tide was coming in. Waves slapped against the dock pilings and splashed up against the underside of the dock. The sun felt hot on his head. He smelled the brine of the sea and the tar used to waterproof the docks.

The guests' laughter floated across the marina. The resort's first group of guests sounded happy. If it wasn't for a dead man, a missing lawyer, and his worry about Harriet, he would call the resort's grand opening a success.

Halfway down the long dock, a large black and white gull left its perch on top of a piling with an angry squawk.

Alex stopped. He wasn't close enough to the bird to have caused its sudden flight. He glanced over to the next dock where Fox was slowly checking each boat. He was too far away to have caused the gull any concern.

His gut tightened. Ed was here, hiding on one of the speed boats, he felt sure of it. He moved forward slowly, his eyes and ears on full alert. A cabin cruiser, three boats up and opposite the gull's perch, caught his eye.

He crept closer and saw that the cabin's padlock was lying on the deck. It should have been locked–unless a guest was aboard.

It could be a guest. But after unlocking the cabin a guest would have fully opened the hatch to let in the sunshine and air.

Alex stopped. As soon as he stepped aboard Ed would feel the boat rock and know he was there. He turned to look at the sail dock and saw that Fox had stopped and was watching him. The man's instincts were good.

Alex raised a hand, then pointed at the cabin cruiser. Fox nodded, turned, and hurried back up the dock. Alex contemplated how to best capture Ed while he waited for Fox to join him. Apprehending Ed would be easier and less disruptive for the guests with two of them.

Before Fox could reach Alex, the hatch slid open and Big Ed burst out of the cabin. He leaped on the dock and barreled into Alex, leading with his shoulder. Alex pivoted and stuck his foot out.

Big Ed went sprawling face first onto the dock and Alex and Fox both pinned him down. He bucked and cursed and nearly threw them off until Fox pulled the restraints he'd grabbed from his back pocket and locked Ed's wrists together behind his back.

Alex gave him a nod. "Good thinking." He leaned down close to the big man's ear. "Where are they, Ed? What did you do with Cassie's lawyer and Miss Monroe?"

"Nothing. I don't know who you're talking about."

"Come on, Ed. I know you killed that lawyer last week. You thought he was Cassie's lawyer, didn't you?"

Big Ed jerked. "She's got no right divorcing me. Makes me look like a fool."

"Killing her lawyer won't stop the divorce, Ed. There are always more lawyers. It's a fact of life. Where is Miss Monroe?"

Big Ed remained silent.

"Fine. If you won't help us then we don't need you anymore. Fox, give me a hand rolling this guy off the dock, please."

"My pleasure."

They rolled Ed to the edge of the dock.

"I'll just push this boat away enough for you to slide him in, Alex. You ready?"

Alex looked at Big Ed. "Last chance. What did you do with Cassie's lawyer and Miss Monroe?"

Ed sneered at Alex. "You won't do it. You can't. You're a cop."

"Wrong, Ed. I'm not a cop any longer. And while I'm not fond of lawyers, I care about Miss Monroe." He stood, placed his foot on Ed's broad back and pushed him off the edge of the dock.

The big man sank like a stone. The two men watched him struggle in the clear water.

"How long you figure?" Fox asked.

"I'll give him a solid minute. Not long enough to drown him but long enough to make him think I will. Hold the boat off while I jump in, will you?"

Alex went in after Ed and brought him gasping to the surface. He held him there, one hand on the dock, the other fisted in Ed's shirt. "I'm giving you one last chance, Ed, then I'm dropping you. Where are they?"

Ed spluttered, coughed, gasped. "Halfway Rock. I dumped them on Halfway Rock."

"Fox, help me haul this piece of slime onto the dock, please."

It took them ten minutes to get Ed out of the water and into the marina office. Alex fumed with impatience the whole while. He quickly explained the situation to Dix, locked Ed into the marina storeroom, and took the keys for the marina's fastest boat.

Five minutes later they were speeding out of the harbor into open water.

"What's Halfway Rock?" Fox gripped the edge of the windshield with both hands and spread his legs in an effort to stay on his feet as the boat bucked over the waves.

"It's a barren rock halfway between the resort island and a small, uninhabited island ten miles west of us."

"So they'll be okay until we get there."

Alex shook his head. His hair whipped in the wind and his eyes watered, but he didn't dare cut the boat's speed.

"You can only find Halfway Rock at low tide," he answered. "The rest of the time it's buried under ten feet of water."

"Well, shit," Fox said.

Alex spared him a look. "Exactly."

CHAPTER 30

Conserving her energy, Harriet tread the warm water while she waited for Amos to catch up to her. The lawyer was game, but his shorter arms and legs couldn't move his pudgy body through the water as fast or as easily as she could swim.

At least the water was a comfortable temperature and hypothermia wouldn't be an issue. If the light breeze held the waves would stay manageable.

"You're doing great, Amos. Take a break and tread water." She couldn't tell if her companion's face was red from the sunburn or exertion. The thought that the lawyer might suffer a heart attack by pushing too hard filled her with panic. "Relax. You're using too much energy."

"When I get back to the mainland I'm buying a membership to the local Y's pool. I'm too fat to swim."

Harriet shook her head. The guy had spunk and hadn't lost his composure or sense of humor even once, despite their difficult situation. "Think of seals, Amos. They're big sacks of blubber and are as graceful as can be in the water."

"Seals. I need to think like a seal." He dove under and came up closer to Harriet. "How was that?"

She grinned at him. "Marvelous. I think you've got it. Shall we move forward again?" She turned onto her side and began a slow sidestroke, keeping a close watch on her companion.

He did the same, although his strokes were short and jerky. "So, do you think your lawyer friend–what was his name?"

"Bradley Higgins."

"Right. Do you think your friend Brad was in the wrong place at the wrong time and Cassie's husband killed him?"

"It makes sense." Harriet stroked and thought about it. She had told Amos about the murder to take his mind off their predicament.

"Bradley arrived the same day you were supposed to bring the final papers for Cassie to sign. I think Ed Whitfield found out that he was a lawyer and snapped. He thought Bradley was you–not that he knew your name–only that you were coming to the island to deliver the divorce papers. He choked Bradley to death, then hung him in the greenhouse to throw suspicion on my friend Solly. That's my current hypothesis, anyway."

"Ed was dead set against Cassandra divorcing him," Amos said. "I know I shouldn't tell you that, but since we're both going to die anyway I'm not feeling quite such a stickler about the rules."

"We aren't going to die." Harriet scowled at Amos. "At least not if I can do anything to prevent it. I just landed my dream job," she added in a softer tone. "I'd like the chance to enjoy it."

They stroked in silence for several more minutes.

"Why did you leave the air pad with Cassie's husband? You were supposed to wait for me."

"Cassie only said she was sending someone to meet me, she didn't specify who. By the time I realized Ed wasn't taking me to her office it was too late–he popped me with a pressure syringe and that's all I remember until I woke up in the middle of the ocean with you."

"At least he didn't kill us. As long as we're breathing we still have a chance." Harriet lifted her head to make sure they hadn't veered off course. The resort island looked no closer. She stifled a sigh and concentrated on moving her limbs smoothly through the water.

Water water everywhere, and not a drop to drink. The tranquilizer Ed had used left her with a dry mouth and a dull, pounding headache. She let a little water dribble through her lips to wet her tongue and spit it out. She knew if she swallowed the salt water her body would become even more dehydrated.

"Harry?"

"Amos?"

"I'm not sure how much longer I can go on. My arms feel like lead weights."

"Okay. Flip over and just float on your back and let the salt water hold you up. Rest. I'll be here, right beside you."

Amos did as he was told. "You're a nice girl, you know that, Harry? And beautiful too. I'm surprised you're still single."

Harriet felt ridiculously flattered. Nobody had ever called her beautiful before. Even Solly would only admit to her being attractive. Since he never lied to her he'd never call her beautiful.

"Yeah, well. I guess Mr. Right just hasn't come along yet." She thought of Alex, how safe she had felt in his arms, how his kiss had ignited something inside her that she didn't know lived there. Would she ever see him again? Would she see her best friend Solly?

Poor Solly. He'd be devastated to lose her this way. He's the one who had taught her to swim, who insisted that she learn how because, as he said, anyone who lived on the ocean needed to know how to survive in the water.

Solly was big on surviving, no matter what the circumstances you found yourself thrown into.

She missed her friend. If he was was with them he'd be cracking jokes, making them laugh and helping them forget that they were close to drowning.

She twirled a small circle while she tread water and stopped cold. There was something sticking up from the water's surface, something that looked suspiciously like a shark fin.

Harriet watched the fin for several long moments but it didn't move. She frowned. That wasn't right.

"Amos."

"Yeah."

"There's something over there."

Amos sank and came up spluttering. "What? Where?"

"I'm not sure. I thought it was a shark at first–"

"Shark?" Amos'a face paled beneath his sunburn and he sunk again.

Harriet waited for him to surface. "–but it hasn't moved so I don't think it is," she finished. "I want to swim over to it. You stay here, okay? Either tread water or float on your back. I won't be long."

She didn't wait for a reply. She struck out toward the object at a steady overhand crawl and soon reached it.

"It's a tree trunk," she called back to Amos. "We can use it as a float. Swim to me." She dove under the tree, came up on the other side, and began to push it toward Amos.

"This could save our lives, Amos," she said, when they met up and Amos grabbed wearily onto the tree.

"Works for me. What's the new plan?"

"Support the upper part of your body on the tree and kick. It will take longer because the water will resist it, but eventually we'll end up at the resort."

Amos pulled himself over the tree and set himself beside Harriet. The tree sunk into the water.

Harriet quickly pushed herself off the trunk and it bobbed to the surface again. "It will only support one of us," she told Amos. 'You ride first and I'll just hang on. I'll kick until I'm tired. Then we'll switch off."

Amos wrapped his arm around the base of the broken branch that Harriet had thought was a shark fin, propped his head against it, and promptly fell asleep.

"That works too," she said. It didn't matter. Amos was nearly spent. Once Harriet had to support his body as well as her own she would have quickly fatigued and they both would have drowned. Finding the tree vastly improved their chances of survival. They were lucky it wasn't a branchless palm or she never would have seen it.

She looked at the branch jutting three feet into the air. They needed a flag, something to flutter in the wind and attract attention.

Fortunately the bra she had put on that morning was a decent one. Actually it was the only bra she had until the purchases she'd made the day before were delivered.

She slipped out of Solly's borrowed white shirt and worked the sleeves over the end of the branch, careful not to disturb her sleeping companion. It hung limp and dragged in the water.

"Dammit." She pulled the shirt off the branch and wrung as much water as she could from the fabric, then stuck it on the branch again. This time she didn't pull the shirt as far down on the branch. The breeze caught it, and while it didn't flutter as wildly as Harriet had hoped, it did move. It was the best she could do.

She kicked slowly, steadily, always keeping the cloud covered image of the resort in front of her. The sun felt hot on her bare shoulders and exposed back. She began to count her kicks, stopping every one hundred to just drift and rest. Amos slept on.

Her headache grew worse, a steady throb at the base of her skull. Her tongue felt fat and thick in her mouth. She tried to work up some spit but failed. She placed her face in the water and opened her mouth, letting it flow around her tongue.

When she picked her head up she saw Amos's warm brown eyes watching her. "You okay?" he asked.

"Thirsty. How about you?"

"Thirsty. And an awesome headache."

"Yeah, that's from whatever Ed gave us to knock us out."

"Another reason to hate the bastard." Amos slid off the log. "Your turn to rest. I'll kick for a while. I think we're getting closer."

"We're definitely getting closer." She pulled her torso onto the log and let her legs hang in the water, then began to kick.

"What are you doing?"

"We'll move faster if we both kick. I'm not that tired," she lied.

"I just want you to know that if we live through this I'm never leaving the mainland again."

"And if we live through this I'm never doing another favor for a friend."

They grinned at each other and kicked.

The tide seemed to be racing toward the island. Alex knew the water wasn't moving any faster than usual, but because he needed the tide to slow–in fact needed it to stop doing what it had been doing ever since the moon started spinning around the Earth–it seemed to be coming in faster than usual.

The offshore breeze blew against the incoming tide, kicking up waves. Waves that Harriet and her companion would have to navigate. The fiberglass hull of the boat slapped hard against those waves, making for a rough ride, but Alex refused to slow their speed.

"I see something white." Fox handed the binoculars to Alex. "About two o'clock off the bow."

Alex eased back on the throttle and looked. He didn't see anything. Then the boat rose on a wave and he saw the small flutter of white.

"Let's go check it out." He handed the glasses back to Fox and pushed the throttle forward. The bow rose, then settled as they gained speed.

Fox kept the binocs trained on the white flutter. "It's

them!" he cried. "I can see them now. A man and a woman. The woman just raised her arm. She's trying to signal us."

Alex wished he could get more speed from the boat but the engine was maxed. He willed it forward as it slammed and bounced across the crests of the waves. Spray kicked up from both sides and a long rooster tail shot from the stern.

Finally the boat drew close enough that Alex could see Harriet without the glasses. They were hanging onto a broken tree trunk waiting for the boat to reach them. Even from this distance, he could plainly see the relief and exhaustion on Harriet's face.

He cut the engine and floated gently to the tree. "Want a lift?" he asked as he reached over the side and grabbed Harriet's hands.

"I don't know," the man answered. "I thought we were doing pretty well on our own, thanks to Harry."

Alex felt a tiny twinge of jealousy that the lawyer called Harriet by her nickname. "He gets to call you Harry?" he said quietly as he lifted her into the boat. She stood trembling—her knees knocking together, her back, face, and shoulders sunburnt—and he let it go, ashamed of being so petty. What mattered was that she was alive.

Harriet's wet bra hid nothing and her thin, borrowed shorts clung to her hips. She realized that the man with Alex was looking at her with a great deal of interest. Suddenly embarrassed, she crossed her arms over her chest.

Alex scowled at Fox, then whipped off his shirt and pulled it over Harriet's head. She gave him a grateful smile. "Water?" she croaked.

"Here." Fox shoved a container in her hands, then lowered a ladder over the stern of the boat. "Can you climb?" he asked Amos.

Amos pulled himself up the ladder with Fox's help and collapsed on the deck. "I honestly didn't believe we were going to make it," he whispered. "If it wasn't for Harry I'd be dead right now."

He rolled onto his back and grinned foolishly at his rescuers. "I can't tell you how happy I am that I was wrong. It's not often you'll hear a lawyer say that."

Introductions were made all around. Harriet rescued Solly's shirt and spread it on the console to dry. Alex pulled her onto the seat next to him and turned the boat back toward the island. Fox settled with Amos in the aft seats.

"Ed killed Bradley." After downing the tube of water Harriet found her voice and broke the silence.

"We figured that out. He's being held until the mainland police can pick him up. Are you sure you aren't hurt?"

"He didn't hurt me. I'm exhausted and my head aches and the sunburn hurts like crazy, but I'll recover." Fox offered another tube of water and she gave him a grateful smile. It tasted so good. It didn't taste like salt, just cold and smooth. Refreshing. It helped soothe her raw throat.

"Ed told me that he wasn't the one who destroyed my stuff."

Alex took her hand and linked his fingers with hers. "I know. It was Lana. I'll deal with her after we have the medics check you out and get you settled with Solly. I called him to let him know I was bringing you home."

"Lana?" She saw Alex flush and look uncomfortable. Was he remembering her warning about Lana and realizing he should have taken it more seriously? She waited for him to continue, curious to know if he'd admit that she had been right about the kitchen manager.

"I guess she became fixated on me or something and considered you a threat. I'm sorry. It's all my fault."

"How is it your fault? Did you lead her on?"

Alex shook his head. "No, of course not. Until you came along I'd been keeping to myself. No flirting, no dates. Celibate."

Harriet fought to keep her voice even. "Until I came along? We haven't exactly had a date, just pizza while you interrogated me. Oh, and the shopping trip to the mainland, but that wasn't a date."

"I intend to rectify that as soon as possible."

Was Alex telling her that he cared about her?

He brought Harriet's waterlogged hand to his lips and kissed her scraped wrist. Heat shot through Harriet's body and she shivered.

"Cold?"

"No. I'm fine."

Alex tightened his grip and leaned close enough to brush his lips on her ear. "I was afraid I'd lost you, Twinkle," he murmured.

"Twinkle? Why–" Sharp pain speared behind Harriet's eyes. She groaned and pressed her free hand to her forehead and rubbed.

"What's wrong?"

The pain subsided and she dropped her hand. "Nothing. Residual after-effect from the tranq Ed shot into me, I suspect. Or too much sun. What are we going to do about Lana, Alex? She scares me a little."

Alex watched Harriet worriedly for a minute but she seemed okay. He felt an overwhelming desire to smack Big Ed a time or two for the pain he'd caused her.

"Alex?"

"What?"

"What are we going to do about Lana?"

"I'm going to speak with Mr. Wade first, but I think the resort will be looking for a new kitchen manager. Lana is good at her job but she has issues that can't be overlooked.

If you want, you have every right to bring criminal charges against her. She broke into your home and destroyed your property."

Harriet shook her head. "I don't think she's going to miraculously get over her fixation on you, but I don't see how pressing charges will help. But you could use that threat to get her to leave the island. Tell her I'll press charges if she doesn't leave."

"I'll see what Wade says. I have a feeling he'll want to see her punished for the way she treated you. At the very least he'll make it difficult for Lana to get another job in the food and hospitality industry."

Fox jumped out to tie up the boat as soon as they pulled into the marina dock. Harriet gave him back his shirt and put Solly's back on.

Fortunately Alex had called ahead and the island medics were waiting to greet them as Amos was severely dehydrated and running a fever from sun exposure. He was too weak to argue against being wheeled off the dock on a stretcher. Harriet insisted on walking, despite the fact that her leg muscles felt like pudding.

She was relieved to find her camera and rucksack still in her vehicle. Since Alex had to transport Ed to the security office, Fox drove Harriet back to her own office in her own vehicle .

The ride back to the main resort seemed to take forever. She was shivering despite the heat, and ached everywhere. Her head ached with a dull throbbing beat and her eyes felt swollen and scratchy.

She found Solly anxiously waiting for her when they pulled up in front of the office building. He helped her out of the cart and pulled her into his arms, then let her go so he could check her over, his eyes filled with concern.

"What happened, Harry? Dammit, I've been beside

myself with worry." He ran a hand through his thick brown hair, leaving it in tufts. "No one could tell me anything. Cassie called me to see if I knew where you were. She said you went to pick up her lawyer and then you disappeared. What happened?" he repeated.

Harriet grabbed her friend and held on tight. Hot tears pricked her eyes. "I was afraid I'd never see you again. I'm fine, now. Ed Whitfield kidnapped me and Amos and left us on Halfway Rock. I didn't know it was Halfway Rock at the time, Alex told me after, when he and Tarbell rescued us. Have you met Tarbell Fox yet?" she asked, her face still buried in her friend's chest.

Solly reached out a hand to the ex-cop. "I'm Solomon Ayers. Thank you for rescuing Harry."

Tarbell took the offered hand and shook it. "Tarbell Fox. Most people call me Fox. And you should thank Alex. I was just along for the ride."

"I will." Solly pushed Harriet away from him again. "And just who is Amos?"

"He's Cassie's divorce lawyer."

"All right. Apparently this will take more than a minute or two to catch me up. Let's go home. Your new clothes arrived. I'll draw you a bath, we'll put some lotion on that sunburn and get you into some soft clothes, then you can tell me the whole story over a bottle of wine."

Harriet realized that her saltwater-soaked clothes had dried stiff and felt like rough boards rubbing over her sore, sensitive skin.

"That'd be great." She turned her head toward the cart. "Thank you for the lift, Tarbell. Oh, Solly, could you grab the camera and my bag, please?"

"There's no need." Tarbell climbed out of the cart. "Why don't you two take the wheels? I'll walk over to the security office to see if Alex needs anything more from me."

"We couldn't–" Harriet was interrupted by Solly.

"We certainly can. Anyone can see you're ready to fall down. Thank you, Fox. That's considerate of you. Back in the cart, Harry. You don't have the strength to walk home and I can't carry you." He practically lifted her into the passenger seat and patted her arm. "We'll be home in no time."

Fox watched them drive off. Did Alex know how close Solomon Ayers was to Harriet, he wondered? A little competition there maybe?

He had seen the look on Alex's face when they found the foxy lady alive. The man was definitely in love. Whether Alex knew it or not–well, Fox had only met the security director that day. He didn't know him well enough yet to know what went on inside the man's head, let alone his heart, but any fool could see that Harriet Monroe was important to him.

Fox set off toward the security office whistling. It had been a good day. They'd rescued the damsel in distress and a pudgy, funny lawyer. Best of all, he was getting back into work that suited him.

He would never be a cop again, but working resort security with a fly guy like Alex was damn close, and far, far better than humping overpacked luggage.

CHAPTER 32

Harriet woke in Solly's bed. Soft night air fluttered the bed curtains. Outside the lanai doors the moon cut a wide, ivory path across the water. She lay, relaxed and safe, and tried to figure out what had awakened her.

Her sunburned skin tingled and felt hot but she didn't think that was what had woken her.

She turned her head slightly to check the time on Solly's antique Big Ben clock. Harriet had bought it for him as a joke gift one Christmas–a gaudy lime green, wind-up alarm clock with analog numbers, moving glow in the dark hands, and two big bells on top that made enough racket to wake the dead. Solly loved it.

Eleven o'clock. She'd slept three hours. She had fallen asleep over the dinner Solly prepared, she remembered. The bath, soothing sunburn lotion, and soft pajamas had done her in. Solly had carried her in here, despite her protests that she could sleep on the couch.

She heard muted voices coming from the living room. Either Solly had the screen on or he had company. She listened harder and recognized Alex's deep rumble. A part of her wanted to get up and join them, but her body argued against that.

She closed her eyes, more than willing to fall back asleep. Solly would tell her anything she needed to know about Alex's visit tomorrow. She breathed in the sweet scent of night jasmine that grew in pots on Solly's lanai. She'd have to ask him to pot some for Mermaid Cottage. It was such a lovely scent.

Drifting on the softly perfumed night air, she was nearly asleep when she caught a sour smell and sensed someone moving in the room.

"Who's there?" she asked softly.

The bedside lamp snapped on revealing Lana in its muted light. Her red curls looked disheveled, her lipstick smeared toward one cheek. She curled her upper lip into a snarl.

"I told you to stay away from him. But you won't, will you? You just can't leave him alone. So I'm going to have to make sure that you do."

Harriet's blood ran cold at the venom in Lana's voice.

"Alex rescued me today, Lana. That's the only reason we were together. He saved my life."

Lana didn't seem to hear Harriet's words.

"Alex told me I have to leave the resort tomorrow." Lana's eyes glowed with a malevolent light. "Because of you. But I'm not the one who's going to leave, Harry. You are. If you're gone I'll get to keep my job and Alex."

She stepped closer and put a knee on the bed. "You just can't leave him alone, can you?"

They were back to that. This was all about Alex. Harriet wondered how she should handle the situation. Lana must have followed Alex to Solly's cottage and slipped inside through the bedroom's open lanai doors.

"Listen to me, Lana, *I am not* chasing Alex."

"He's here now, isn't he? He's here for you and I won't have it." She raised her hand. A long, slim blade gleamed in the lamplight.

Harriet gasped. "Lana, please, think about what you're doing. You don't want to go to prison. Put the knife down."

"No." Lana lunged at Harriet, slashing through the insect netting with the knife.

Harriet rolled away from the blade and screamed for Solly. She heard Lana swear and felt her climb after her on the bed.

"Man-stealing bitch. You won't get away with it. I saw him first. He's mine!"

Harriet tried to scramble off the bed and found herself tangled in the gauzy bed curtains. She felt Lana behind her and shouted for Solly again.

The door crashed opened and Solly came rushing in. "Harry? Bad dreams, honey? Lights on full."

The room was suddenly bathed in bright light.

Lana paid no attention to the lights or to Solly. She grabbed Harriet by her hair and slashed at her again. This time she caught Harriet on the upper arm and laughed.

"Alex!" Solly threw himself at Lana before she could slash at Harriet again, trapping her in the bed curtains. He pressed his knee on Lana's wrist and she dropped the blade.

"Bastard! Let me go." Lana rolled free of the curtains and scratched at Solly with her free hand, catching him in the neck, raking his skin with her long red nails.

"I have her." Alex grabbed Lana's hand and slapped a restraint on it, then grabbed the second hand and did the same.

"Lana Tso, consider yourself under arrest. I'm handing you over to the mainland authorities in the morning, along with Ed Whitfield." He eyed the filet knife lying on the mattress and was filled with a cold fury.

"You'll be charged with attempted murder." Harriet had fallen down beside the bed where he couldn't see her.

"Harriet, are you all right?" He spotted the blood on the mattress and his fury turned to frantic worry.

"Harriet?"

"She'll be okay," Solly answered from the floor where he was pressing a corner of the sheet to Harriet's arm wound. "It's shallow. Call the medics on your way out, will you?"

Harriet didn't look at Lana as Alex led her, alternately swearing at him and begging for his love, out of the bedroom. She shuddered at how close she'd come to dying. Twice in one day. If she hadn't woken up tonight . . . she didn't want to think about it.

She curled into Solly's chest and fought back her tears while waiting for the medics to stitch up her arm.

CHAPTER 33

"The medics did a neat job on your arm," Cassie said as she settled her bulk onto a chair in Harriet's office. "I can't even see the scar."

Harriet reflexively felt her arm where Lana had sliced her. The wound had healed, the only evidence of Lana's attack a thin red scar that the medics had assured her would disappear completely.

"They did do a good job, didn't they?" She didn't want to talk about that night and changed the subject. "How was your date with Amos last night?"

A week had passed since Ed and Lana's arrests. One of the head chefs was filling in as kitchen manager until a replacement for Lana could be found. Leonard Dixon had already filled the assistant manager vacancy at the marina caused by Ed's arrest. All handled with little fanfare and without any inconvenience to the guests.

Amos Blattsworth had recovered from his ordeal and asked Harriet to dinner. She had declined until he confessed to her that he was sweet on Cassie and needed someone to talk to. After the life-threatening ordeal they had endured together the young lawyer felt like a good friend, so she had gone to dinner and enjoyed herself immensely. It had taken Amos another week to find the courage to ask Cassie out.

Cassie wagged her hand in answer to Harriet's question, jangling the brightly colored bangles she wore. "I like Amos a lot, but only as a friend, you know? Besides, it could never work. I'm committed to my job here on the island, and Amos's life is on the mainland. I think I'll just enjoy being a single divorcée for a while. Play the field." Her brown eyes sparkled. "What about you?" she asked with a smirk.

"What about me, what? You know how busy I am."

Harriet's life was finally beginning to settle into a routine. She had moved back into Mermaid Cottage the day after Lana's arrest. She and Solly ran on the beach together every morning before work and usually shared dinner at the end of the day.

It was almost like the old days when they shared an apartment, only they each had their own place. It was the best of both worlds as far as Harriet was concerned and she suspected Solly felt the same.

Alex had stopped by her cottage the previous evening and taken her for a ride on his motorcycle. It had been the most romantic experience of Harriet's life. The stars blanketing the sky, the warm, soft breeze in her face, her arms wrapped tight around Alex's strong body and the power of the machine between her legs. Alex had even kissed her when he dropped her back at the cottage. Her lips tingled again thinking about it.

She didn't share any of that with Cassie, however.

They talked instead about Harriet's first ad campaign featuring the amusement park. It had begun running four days earlier and the results were more than she had dared hope for. The resort was once again fully booked. She was already sketching out her next campaign.

"You should make some time for romance, honey," Cassie advised as she finished her drink and stood, her colorful, loose robes flowing around her. "Trust me. Especially living on the islands. It doesn't get much more romantic than a tropical island."

The resort manager stretched up to give Harriet a peck on the cheek. "Don't push yourself too hard," she warned, patting Harriet's arm. "I'd better get back to my office. I have two interviews this afternoon with candidates hoping to fill the kitchen manager position. I must have had at least a thousand applicants. It seems that *everyone* wants to work for the Island Resort. I just wanted to give you my gift and tell you again how sorry I am that I got you tangled up with Ed."

"The scarf is beautiful, Cassie. I love it, thank you. I'll think of you whenever I wear it. And you don't have to apologize for Ed. None of what happened was your fault." She walked Cassie to the door and hugged her friend.

She had just stepped back to her desk when there was a knock.

"What is this, Grand Central Station today?"

She walked back to the door and disengaged the locks. Since the night Lana had attacked her in Solly's bedroom Harriet had been locking her cottage and office doors and windows and compulsively double checking them. She knew it was a reaction to the attack and hoped that soon she wouldn't feel the need to lock herself in.

When she opened the door she found Payson Douglas standing in the hallway with a broad smile on his handsome, lean face. He leaned down and kissed Harriet's cheek. "How are you, my dear?" he asked as she moved back to let him enter.

Harriet had kept her Thursday lunch date with Payson the day before. She found that she truly enjoyed spending time with the older man. They talked about a variety of topics and laughed often, and she loved listening to his stories. He was like a favorite uncle, not that she knew what having a favorite uncle was like. But *if* she'd had one, she imagined he'd be like Payson.

So when she saw him at her door she greeted him with a wide and welcoming smile even though they had made another lunch date for the following week and she hadn't expected to see him again this soon.

"What can I do for you, Payson? How about some lemonade? One of the under chefs has begun bringing me a fresh pitcher every day. I have to admit, it's making me feel spoiled. I've become addicted to the stuff."

"No, thank you, Harry. This will only take a minute. I just wanted to drop off a package."

Harriet noticed the box wrapped in brown paper under Payson's arm and frowned.

"Package? I haven't ordered anything."

"It's from Douglas." He handed her the box and turned to go. "I'll see you next Thursday then?"

Harriet looked at the package in her hands. "Yes, I'll see you Thursday. Wait, what is this, Payson? Why is Mr. Wade sending me a package?"

"You'll have to open it and see for yourself, Harry. I have to run." And he was gone.

Harriet locked the door behind him and set the box on her desk. She looked at it for a long moment, trying to figure out what Mr. Wade could possibly have sent her.

"Only one way to find out, Harriet. Don't be a dope. Open it." She took a small art knife from the container of pencils and markers she preferred to sketch with and sliced open the paper. It fell away, revealing a plain wooden box with a fitted lid. She ran her hand over the smooth, glossy wood, admiring the pattern of the grain. Oak, she was pretty sure, with its blend of honey color and darker brown lines.

She tipped it to watch the light on the lid and heard something rustle inside the box. Curious now, she lifted the lid and set it aside. Tissue paper protected and hid whatever lay inside. She gently pushed the tissue paper away from the contents. Her hands trembled as she pulled a perfectly carved, three-inch, red wooden hippo from its folds.

"Rosewood," she whispered, her voice thick with tears.

She pulled hippos from the box one by one, identifying the type of wood for each one until eighteen of them stood on her desk, all carved from different woods, all sanded smooth until they gleamed.

Some had open mouths complete with teeth. A couple sat on their fat hind ends, two looked like they were swimming. Each one was executed in exquisite detail. It was a magnificent gift, one Harriet would cherish forever.

For the first time since the loss of her parents, she felt hopeful and excited about the future.

For the the first word about releases, sales, news, and special notices, sign up for my newsletter. https://charleymarshbooks.com/mystery-newsletter/

You can find the next book in the series, *Masked in Paradise,* at your favorite retailer: **https:// books2read.com/MaskedinParadise**

Turn the page for a preview of the next book in the Destination Death series, *Masked in Paradise.*

MASKED IN PARADISE

Harriet Monroe, known to most as simply Harry, stood on her lanai and looked out over the turquoise waters lapping the white sand beach at the rear of her cottage. She'd only been working at the Island Resort for six weeks but the place already felt like home. This was where she was meant to be.

A soft breeze freshened off the ocean and ruffled her honey blonde hair. The breeze smelled of salt and dried seaweed left on the beach by the receding tide.

She'd landed her dream job–public relations director for the most exclusive resort on the planet. Who'd have thought that a high school dropout could do so well for herself? Not that she'd dropped out of school by choice. It had been forced on her when she had run away from her unloving aunt and warped uncle at the tender age of fifteen.

Harriet grinned. Warm, salt-scented air, exotic flowers, turquoise waters, an incredibly beautiful cottage all to herself–she'd come a long way from the cold New England winters of the last twenty years.

The days when she'd sought shelter in doorways and stairwells because she had nowhere else to sleep seemed to belong to another person.

Dream job, dream location. What else could she ask for from life?

"You ready to do this, Harry?"

Her best friend Solomon Ayers called to her as he stepped out onto the lanai of the cottage next to hers. Tall, slim and well built with the chiseled features sculptors worked hard to recreate, all finished off with thick sable brown hair and warm brown eyes–Solly was a package that made many a girl's heart stutter.

Unfortunately for those girls, Solly's interests lay elsewhere, a fact his father hadn't been able to accept. The senior Ayers had tried beating the "sickness" out of his son until Solly decided he'd had enough and run away.

The two young teenagers had met up on the streets of Portland and had immediately connected, helping each other avoid those who preyed on young runaways.

Harriet grinned over at her friend. "I'll meet you out front. I just need to lock up." She turned away from the view and hurried back inside the cottage, locking the double glass doors that led from her bedroom to the lanai.

A massive king-size bed surrounded by filmy white insect curtains dominated the large, mahogany-paneled room. The room felt cool and soothing after the brightness of the sun's rays bouncing off sand and water, a deliberate effect created by the resort's interior designer.

Harriet had yet to meet Jan Rhymes, but when she did she intended to give the designer a big hug. Jan had done an outstanding job putting together not only Mermaid Cottage where Harriet lived, but also Harriet's new office. Both places were luxurious beyond Harriet's wildest expectations.

She hurried through the cottage and double checked the remaining two sets of doors that opened onto the wrap-around lanai. It had only been two short weeks since she'd been attacked in her cottage, and while her brain understood that the threat no longer existed, her emotions insisted that she still take precautions.

Grabbing the small canvas knapsack that served as her handbag, Harriet let herself out the front door and locked that as well. Solly watched her but said nothing about her paranoia. Solly always understood, and for that she loved her closest friend more than she could ever express.

Harriet tucked her hand inside Solly's arm and they headed up the crushed pink shell road toward the main resort. She preferred walking to her office over driving one of the resort's open carts, probably because she had the choice. Walking to work on the coast of Maine during the winter had never been an option.

"Have you tried the spa yet, Sol?" she asked.

"Nope. It wasn't finished when I first arrived, and then I got too busy with the greenhouses and grounds crews to take the time. I've heard good things about it, though."

Harriet knew that her friend loved his work. She wasn't the only one who had landed their dream job. Solly was in charge of the seven greenhouses that grew the flowers for the guest cottages and the arrangements for the public areas like the dining rooms, various lobbies, and anywhere else flowers were needed—which was pretty much every-where a guest might roam.

The greenhouses also provided the kitchen with some of the more exotic greens, fruits, and vegetables that they served to the guests. And if that wasn't enough, Solly also managed the groundskeepers who kept the resort looking pristine and other-worldly beautiful.

He did the work of three men and seemed to thrive on

it, but in the last few days Harriet had noticed a slight tightening around her friend's eyes that told her he needed a break. He had confirmed her suspicion when he readily agreed to take a day off to visit the spa with her.

They walked along in a companionable silence, the road's crushed shells crunching softly under Harriet's sandaled feet. The waves lapped at the shore on their left in a steady rhythm and brightly plumed birds darted among the trees and shrubs to her right.

Harriet took a deep breath of scented flowers and fresh sea breezes and wondered if she'd ever felt this happy. Maybe when her parents had been alive, but she had so few memories of that time. A dull throb started at the back of her head and she sent up a prayer that she wouldn't get one of her migraines.

She shook off the thoughts of her parents. This was not the time to think of sad things.

"Thank you for doing this with me, Sol. I need to experience the spa so I'll know how to best showcase it, but I want to be sure I can represent what will appeal to men as well as women."

Solly grinned at her, his brown eyes sparkling. He had the longest, thickest eyelashes she had ever seen on a man or woman. It was really quite unfair. Women paid good money to have eyelashes like Solly's implanted.

"No need to thank me, Harry. I've been looking forward to this ever since you asked. I'm just glad you asked me instead of McDreamy."

"Don't call him that. His name is Alex." She tried to sound stern but couldn't help the grin that stole across her face.

"I stand corrected. *Alex* McDreamy. I admit that I'm curious—just a bit you understand—as to why you asked me and not him."

A blush crept up Harriet's neck. An ex-New York City murder cop, Alex Hayes headed the resort's security department. Secretly she agreed with Solly's assessment—when Alex was close by the man made her pulse pound—and that's exactly why she hadn't asked him to join her at the spa. He was too . . . distracting.

"I didn't ask Alex because I wanted to do this with you," she told Solly firmly. "I'm more comfortable with you than anyone else I know and I trust that you'll tell me the truth without trying to be polite about it."

"What time is our appointment?"

"Ten." Harriet checked her wrist unit. "We'd better get moving or we'll be late. Let's grab a cart."

The resort provided stylish, chrome trimmed, turquoise blue golf carts for the guests and staff to get around the island. The hydrogen powered carts ran silent and emitted nothing to pollute the island's pristine atmosphere.

Several carts sat outside the stone building that housed Harriet's office. She resisted the urge to stop in and check for messages and slid into the driver's seat of the nearest cart instead. Solly climbed in beside her and they took off.

The spa had been built on a secluded cove on the west side of the island, nestled between the resort proper—which consisted of several office buildings, the two story main hotel, the kitchens, and several dining spots—and the four coves which held the more private guest cottages. Another group of cottages which Harriet had yet to see lay on the island's remote northeast shore.

The amusement park, marina, air pad, and the recently opened circus were located on the northwest portion of the island. The resort truly had something for everyone.

"There's the turnoff." Solly pointed to a narrow, almost hidden lane leading off to the left. A four foot tall, pale yellow obelisk with the word "SPA" carved into it marked the narrow lane.

Harriet turned the cart down the side road. Two minutes later they parked at the entrance to the spa.

"Five minutes to spare," she announced, pleased. She hated to be late and usually made sure she arrived at least a few minutes early no matter what the occasion.

They exited the cart and stood looking at the long, windowless pale stone building in front of them. Harriet frowned.

"It doesn't look very luxurious from out here," she said. "I expected the place to be over the top, you know? The rest of the resort meets that 'best in the world' expectation. I would think Mr. Wade would want the spa to be even better."

She turned a slow circle, taking in the pink shell parking pad dotted with palm trees and tall, furry-leaved plants she didn't recognize. Large showy clusters of hanging trumpet shaped flowers in pastel tones of pink, peach, white, and yellow covered the plants.

Harriet took a couple steps closer to one of the flowers and sniffed. The heavy scent made her step hastily back. "What are those flowers? They must be a foot long."

Solly walked over to stand next to Harriet and grinned. "Brugmansia. Also known as Angel's Trumpets. You should smell them at night. They're pollinated by bats so the scent intensifies after sundown. The spa is only open during daylight hours because of them."

"Huh." Harriet headed for the building. "Why did you plant them if they're so offensive?"

Solly held open the heavy, carved wooden door and ushered her inside. "I didn't. They're native to the island and Mr. Wade wanted me to leave them. He decided to limit the spa's hours rather than destroy native fauna."

Harriet's already high opinion of the resort's reclusive owner soared. Someday she hoped to meet the mysterious Mr. Wade so she could thank him for all he'd done for her.

The nondescript outside of the building gave no hint of what waited within. Stepping into the spa was like stepping into another world. Harriet looked about her with wonder. Here was the best in the world spa that she had expected to find.

The lobby wall facing the door was entirely missing. Lush green jungle plants took its place. Small prisms hanging from the roof edge caught the sunlight glinting off the private cove's waters and tossed subtle rainbows into the lobby. Water cascaded quietly down the pale yellow stone wall to Harriet's right, landing in a wide trough filled with white water lilies and brightly colored koi.

The soft tinkle of outside wind chimes blended with the soothing sound of the water wall. Two receptionists dressed in resort-blue skinsuits, one male and one female, stood behind a black granite counter in the center of the lobby waiting to greet them. Genuine smiles were plastered on both of their faces.

Harriet crossed the honey colored wood floor with Solly at her side. "Good morning," she said.

She had expected the couple to be droids, as Mr. Wade used droids to fill most of the receptionist positions in the resort, but apparently he had opted to use humans in the spa as these two were definitely human. Human and beautiful.

The woman's hair fell in a silky black curtain down her back to her narrow waist. The hair, combined with her smooth mocha skin and bright blue eyes, dainty nose, and bow-shaped lips proclaimed her mixed ancestry. The male possessed the same mocha coloring and black hair but with mossy green eyes. Their skinsuits revealed every curve and line of their bodies. Both were in incredible physical condition.

Harriet resisted the urge to rub the bump on the bridge of her own rather prominent nose and suppressed an inward sigh. Since she stood five feet eleven inches in her stocking feet, petite women with perfect faces always made her feel like a giant ogress.

It wasn't the receptionist's fault she had great genes, Harriet reminded herself while she forced a smile. "I'm Harriet Monroe, the resort PR director. I have a ten o'clock appointment."

The woman tapped a few keys on her PC. "Yes, Miss Monroe, we have you down for the works." Her blue eyes sparkled at Harriet. "You are really going to enjoy this, I promise you. I just need a little information and then the doctor will ask you a few questions before we begin. Have you ever used a spa before?"

Before Harriet could answer, she heard a commotion behind her and turned. A woman clasping the neck of a thick white robe entered the lobby from an opening next to the water wall. It was difficult to tell the woman's age as her face was covered in cracked, green clay.

The woman stumbled closer to Harriet. Something was off about her face. It took Harriet a moment to realize that it was horribly swollen.

"Mrs. Haggedorn." The female receptionist started around the counter.

"Help. You must . . . help me." The woman reached out a green hand toward Harriet. "Miss . . . take–"

The woman grabbed at Harriet's arm, letting her robe fall open. She wore nothing but a layer of green mud underneath.

"Mrs. Haggedorn, what happened?" The receptionist sounded truly alarmed.

Unfortunately Mrs. Haggedorn was beyond answering. Her knees buckled and she gurgled something Harriet couldn't make out. Her hand slipped from Harriet's arm as Solly caught her and eased her carefully to the floor.

"Do you have a doctor on site?" he asked the hovering receptionist.

"Yes."

"I already called. She'll be here in a few moments." The male receptionist hurried out from behind the counter.

Solly closed the robe to preserve the woman's modesty. He checked the woman's wrist for her pulse, frowned and tried her neck.

A woman in the familiar white coat that doctors wore everywhere hurried in from the hall opposite the water wall.

"What's wrong, Aaron? I was with a client–" she stopped talking as soon as she spied Mrs. Haggedorn on the floor.

Harriet had to admire the doctor's calm efficiency. She wasted no time kneeling next to the unconscious woman and checking her pulse and pupils. She looked at Solly, who knelt on the other side of Mrs. Haggedorn.

"Are you a friend of Mrs. Haggedorn?" she asked.

Solly shook his head. "No. We just got here. She's dead, isn't she?"

https://books2read.com/MaskedinParadise

ABOUT THE AUTHOR

In her younger days Charley Marsh's curiosity drove her to climb mountains, canoe rivers, and explore caves and wilderness areas from Maine to California. She's been shot at, caught in a desert flash flood, and almost drowned off the Maine coast. Once she tobogganed down a 5,000+ foot mountain.

Life is always an adventure if you have the right attitude.

Charley never set out to be a storyteller, but looking back on the elaborate lies she made up as a troubled teen she can see that she always had the makings. Now, in the words of Lawrence Block, she happily "makes up lies for fun and profit."